THE DRY
WOOD

CATHOLIC WOMEN
WRITERS

SERIES EDITORS

Bonnie Lander Johnson, *University of Cambridge*
Julia Meszaros, *St. Patrick's Pontifical University, Maynooth*

ADVISORY COMMITTEE

Alana Harris, *King's College, University of London*
Andrew Meszaros, *St. Patrick's Pontifical University, Maynooth*
Kenneth Parker, *Duquesne University*
Michael Hurley, *University of Cambridge*
David Deavel, *University of St. Thomas*

THE DRY WOOD

Caryll Houselander

WITH AN INTRODUCTION BY
BONNIE LANDER JOHNSON AND
JULIA MESZAROS

The Catholic University of America Press
WASHINGTON, D.C.

First published in 1947 by
Sheed and Ward, Ltd.
Reprinted with permission

Introductions Copyright © 2022
The Catholic University of America Press
All rights reserved

The paper used in this publication meets
the requirements of American National
Standards for Information Science—
Permanence of Paper for Printed Library
Materials, ANSI Z39.48-1992.

∞

Cataloging-in-Publication Data available
from the Library of Congress
ISBN 978-0-8132-3461-8

CONTENTS

THE DRY WOOD

THE DRY
WOOD

The Catholic Literary Revival was concentrated primarily in Britain, France, and America. Spanning the hundred years between the late nineteenth century and the late twentieth century, the movement saw an unprecedented quantity of writing by and about Catholics emerging after a protracted absence of Catholic faith and culture from the public sphere. In Britain the catalysts for this flourishing of poetry, prose fiction, and nonfiction were the beginning of the Oxford Movement, John Henry Newman's conversion to Rome, and the re-establishment of the Catholic hierarchy after three hundred years of persecution. In France, amid continuing anti-clericalism following the revolution, Catholic literature flourished alongside new religious orders and lay spiritual communities. And in America, European immigrants arriving in the nineteenth century were entering a society marked by a long history of anti-Catholicism. They utilized literature to explore a dimension of human thought and experience that was still largely absent from the American imagination.

The Catholic Literary Revival is exemplified by the work of Hilaire Belloc, Robert Hugh Benson, Georges Bernanos,

Léon Bloy, G. K. Chesterton, Graham Greene, Gerard Manley Hopkins, Jacques Maritain, Thomas Merton, Charles Péguy, Walker Percy, J. R. R. Tolkien, and Evelyn Waugh. The works of all of these writers have been consistently in print, in modern editions, throughout the last century and up to the present day. The Revival's most numerous members, however, were women, and although some of these women remain well known—Muriel Spark, Antonia White, Kate O'Brien, Flannery O'Connor, Dorothy Day—many have been almost entirely forgotten. These include Mary Beckett, Kathleen Coyle, Enid Dinnis, Anna Hanson Dorsey, Alice Thomas Ellis, Eleanor Farjeon, Rumer Godden, Caroline Gordon, Clotilde Graves, Caryll Houselander, Sheila Kaye-Smith, Jane Lane, Marie Belloc Lowndes, Alice Meynell, Kathleen Raine, Pearl Mary Teresa Richards, Edith Sitwell, Gladys Bronwyn Stern, Josephine Ward, and Maisie Ward.

There are various reasons why each of these writers fell out of print. Broadly, we can point to changes in the commercial publishing world after World War II as well as changes within the Church itself and in the English-speaking universities that redefined the literary canon in the last decades of the twentieth century. Yet it remains puzzling that a body of writing so creative, so attuned to its historical moment, and so unique in its perspective on the human condition should have fallen into obscurity for so long.

This series brings together the English-language prose work of Catholic women from the nineteenth and twentieth centuries, work that retains its literary excellence and its accessibility to a broad range of readers. Although the series includes some short stories and nonfiction, it concentrates primarily on the novel. The novel was modernity's chief literary innovation. It grew out of several prose traditions, especially the spiritual autobiography, and yet it has been called both a Protestant and a secular form. The novel usually concentrates on the personal lives of a small cast of characters drawn from a range of social demographics; its demand for psychological realism and the nuances of lives lived in the material world mean its vision is usually more earthly than spiritual. The novel is able to contain and explore religious concerns, especially the roles of providence and personal conscience, and many great novels depict elements of religious experience. Yet these novels nonetheless tend to remain worldly, secular or materialist in structure and vision. This is no surprise, for the novel is ultimately resistant to "the pressures put upon it by many writers to transcend the limits" of the secular world.[1]

However, many of the writers in this series used the novel as an opportunity to rethink the form and its capacity to express a uniquely Catholic perspective. In doing so, they not only developed and advanced the form itself but also brought an ancient faith to bear on life in the modern world. There is a certain paradox here: Catholic writers effectively helped to push the novel into newer, and therefore more "modern" forms, even though they did so in pursuit of a truth that sometimes required a rejection or questioning of modernity's broader cultural movements.

The novel has often been characterized, especially in its

---

1. George Levine, *Realism, Ethics and Secularism: Essays on Victorian Literature and Science* (Cambridge: Cambridge University Press, 2011), 210. See also Deirdre Shauna Lynch, "Gothic Fiction and 'Belief in Every Kind of Prodigy,'" in *The Routledge Companion to Literature and Religion*, ed. Mark Knight (Oxfordshire: Routledge, 2016), 252–62, 252.

early-eighteenth-century form, as primarily concerned with female experience and the domestic sphere. Although prominent counter-examples to this thesis exist, such as in the work of Fielding and Dickens, the genre nonetheless frequently explores the internal lives of female characters and their negotiation of personal relationships within the more limited geographical settings of a single house, village, or city. But the novel is also a genre well suited to the exploration of social and political change. Unlike drama or epic, it can provide a voice for those who do not possess great social power, who must navigate moral challenges, often on their own and in direct conflict with the culture around them, and who, in doing so, offer criticisms of the society in which they find themselves. In this respect, the novel offered a perfect vehicle for exploring the challenges faced by a Catholic in modern society.

The historical period in which the Catholic Literary Revival emerged witnessed a complex renegotiation of almost all European social institutions, from the aristocracy and the family to party politics and the role of the state. There were Catholic writers among the many voices calling for change as well as among the many questioning its validity. Many of the novels in this series are concerned with distinguishing between stale social conventions that confine, suppress, or limit human capacities and timeless spiritual traditions that are morally and doctrinally true and authentic. Indeed, Catholic writers of the period drew on their faith to interrogate their society while also exploring how modern Catholics could live faithfully in a rapidly changing world.

The nineteenth and twentieth centuries were religiously tumultuous; they were often defined, even at the time, as an age of both faith and doubt. Writers and artists of every stripe examined the role of institutional religion in public life and the personal consequences of lives lived with faith or without it. The period has been described as the beginning of a modern secular society, but it also witnessed powerful resistance to secularization; writers from Austen to Eliot, Wilde to Waugh identified religious belief as newly urgent and necessary. A nonreligious or strictly materialist worldview was for many an increasingly dangerous proposition. In 1935, T. S. Eliot criticized writers who failed to resist the drift toward secularism: "the whole of modern literature is corrupted by what I call Secularism.... [I]t is simply unaware of, simply cannot understand the meaning of, the primacy of the supernatural over the natural life ... something which I assume to be our primary concern."[2] Indeed, the period saw many conversions to Catholicism, notably among writers and artists, all of whom helped to shape in new and dynamic ways the "Catholic imagination."

This term can be broadly defined as a vision of the world in which the drama of salvation is played out in the mundane experiences of the everyday, in which the visible and created things of the world, the development of individual character and community identity, and the adventure of human relationships—all these are phenomena through which readers can touch spiritual realities. The Catholic imagination is that state of awareness through which the seemingly abstract doctrines of Church teaching are played out in a person's day-to-day experiences and moral actions, to the point

2. T. S. Eliot, "Religion and Literature," in *Selected Prose*, ed. Frank Kermode (New York: Harcourt Brace Jovanovich, 1975), 97–106, 104–5.

that some of the smallest human endeavors become nothing less than matters of life and death. From a technical point of view, the novel was uniquely suited to exploring these varied levels of human experience. Its innovations in voice and point of view, in narrative time and the role of description and world-making in constructing human interiority, predispose it to the dramatization of both earthly and cosmic dimensions and moral or spiritual battles both social and personal.

The neglected female representatives of the Catholic literary revival cast a distinct and important light on the Catholic imagination. Typically writing from within more introspective, domestic and romantic contexts, they often root Catholic experience in the everyday, revealing its relevance in and to the lives of ordinary men and women. This less socio-political touch may be one reason for their fall from the public eye, but it is also what makes them so uniquely relevant to contemporary life. As politico-cultural and religious institutions continue to drift into separate spheres of public influence, Christians today often struggle to grasp how faith should or does inform their day-to-day lives. Through fiction, the authors in this series provide a bridge over the divide between religious belief and everyday experience.

If the women writers involved in the Catholic literary revival often wrote from a more domestic or interpersonal angle, they were by no means unaware or uncritical of the social, cultural, political, and ecclesial developments of their time. Indeed, their more marginal role in Anglo-American society often allowed them to adopt a uniquely perceptive outsider's view. For many of the women in this series it was precisely their Catholic faith that empowered them to adopt a prominent voice. Inspired by the rich intellectual tradition of the

Church and the prominent female saints throughout history, these writers made important contributions to Catholic thought on human dignity and the sacramental potential of the ordinary.

A large number of writers in this series were converts from Anglicanism or from no religion at all. Their imaginations were therefore shaped by a radical change in perspective. Becoming Catholic meant accepting a place outside of the British and American establishment, but it also meant they could often see their society with clear eyes for the first time. Many of the writers in this series also experienced personal suffering to an inordinate degree. Catholic teaching on the salvific nature of suffering provided them with means by which to understand the role that their loss played in the small drama of their own life as much as the bigger cosmic drama in which we are all players. Caryll Houselander, for example, understood personal suffering to be a means by which Christians could "give birth to Christ" in the lives of others. Like many writers, she understood that the novel is itself a vehicle for understanding suffering. Houselander turned to the novel after decades of writing spiritual prose. She did so because she no longer wanted to "preach" to her fellows; she wanted instead to "take sinners by the hand" and walk in their lives for a time. The wounds experienced by our writers, when combined with the existential awakening of a conversion to faith, shaped their particular view of human experience and divine truth. Faced with the emotional and spiritual reality of deep suffering, convert novelists often saw in Catholicism what they saw in the novel itself: a space able to contain all the mysteries of human experience.

Benedict XVI said that "the only really effective apologia for Christianity comes down to two arguments, namely, the *saints* the Church has produced and the *art* which has grown in her womb."[3] We should not, therefore, underestimate the importance of artists for defending the credibility of the Christian faith. This pertains also to the Catholic women writers of this series. Few of these writers will go on to be canonized; indeed some of them may not have been particularly saintly, but through their interventions in literary tradition, these women powerfully reshaped the literary and religious landscape.

For the Catholic reader, the writing in this series provides a fictional exploration of the moral and spiritual adventure offered by Catholic life. It also offers a way of holding together themes that have become increasingly partisan in the Church today. Most of the women in this series were writing at a time when the Church was grappling to define its relationship to an increasingly secular world. They were innovators who raised questions that would eventually be posed at the Second Vatican Council, but they were also loyal to many of the traditions and doctrines that disappeared after the Council. Their vision incorporates both a rigorous personal morality and a concern for social justice; an awareness of God's grandeur and an appreciation of his presence in the ordinary; and the importance of both piety and charitable works.

For the non-Catholic reader, the writing in this series offers a crucial but overlooked vision of modernity. It provides

3. Joseph Cardinal Ratzinger (with Vittorio Messori), *The Ratzinger Report: An Exclusive Interview on the State of the Church*, trans. Salvator Attanasio and Graham Harrison (San Francisco, Calif.: Ignatius Press, 1985), 129.

insight into a unique form of female experience but also a unique means of understanding how the Catholic faith is played out in the everyday. For those interested in the history of the novel, these writers demonstrate some of the ways in which the genre is able to explore and express the highest and most timeless spiritual realities, often through the application of the most avant-garde novelistic techniques.

Bonnie Lander Johnson and Julia Meszaros

FURTHER READING

Tom Woodman. *Faithful Fictions*. Washington, D.C.: The Catholic University of America Press, 2022.

James Emmett Ryan. *Faithful Passages*. Madison: University of Wisconsin Press, 2013.

INTRODUCTION TO *The Dry Wood*

THE AUTHOR

Caryll Houselander (1901–1954) was a mystic, visionary, writer, and artist. She drew, painted, and worked with wood, producing statues and crucifixes for many English Catholic churches in the first half of the twentieth century. She also wrote numerous volumes of spiritual literature, both prose and verse, and was for many years Sheed and Ward's highest selling author. Near the end of her life she wrote one novel, *The Dry Wood* (1947). Maisie Ward's brilliant biography of Houselander, *That Divine Eccentric* (1962), is itself one of the books in this series; for a full introduction to Houselander's remarkable life, we refer you to it.

As a young woman, Houselander was beset with crippling neurosis. Because of this early experience and her mystical sensitivity she became a consummate healer of the psychologically distressed and was known after the wars for her ability to heal both adults and children for whom the medical establishment had lost all hope. Her unique contribution to the Catholic understanding of psychological distress has mostly been overlooked: she wrote a spiritual meditation during the Blitz, *This War Is the Passion* (1941). It reminds readers that even at the most frightening moments of war all Christians, indeed all humans, are called to see Christ in the enemy, to comfort others in their suffering, and to overcome hatred and fear even when disaster strikes and loved ones die.

Houselander developed a sophisticated understanding of the psychological traumas of war. But one of her final works, *Guilt* (1952), addressed a more subtle form of distress. It diagnosed modern man's spiritual boredom as a sickness, the healing of which, she argues, can be found in Christ. *Guilt* is a synthesis of Catholic spirituality and psychoanalysis that presents Christ and the sacraments as the central pillars of human reality and human health. Houselander's psychological sensitivity, developed through countless personal and professional relationships and informed by wide spiritual and psychological reading, shapes her approach to her characters in *The Dry Wood*.

Houselander never married and her one romantic attachment ended abruptly before the war. But she lived most of her life with a female companion, Iris Wyndham, with whom she raised Wyndham's granddaughter. She was a devoted friend to the many people with whom she shared her life. Fully and passionately a lay woman, she felt no vocation for the consecrated religious life but also resisted joining in any official capacity the various lay Catholic movements emerging around her (although she always offered her help to them when it was needed). A sharp-tongued bohemian, she drank, smoked, and was notorious for her odd appearance: bright red bangs, round spectacles and pure white face-powder.

And yet, she ordered her working life with all the rigor of a religious sister, dedicating every waking moment to the needs of others, through her copious correspondence, her spiritual writings, her care of the vulnerable, or conversation with friends. By the last decades of her life she was living very austerely: barely eating or sleeping, owning few possessions, and spending every waking hour writing, working, or in conversation. In this way, her life offers a unique model of sanctity for lay men and women, especially artists. Houselander viewed artistic production as a divine activity through which the artist realizes his or her fullest self and brings Christ into the world:

The great tragedy that has resulted from modern methods of industry is that the creativeness of Advent has been left out of work. Production no longer means a man making something that he has conceived in his own heart.... No man should ever make anything except in the spirit in which a woman bears a child, in the spirit in which Christ was formed in Mary's womb, in the love with which God created the world. The integral goodness and fittingness of the work of a man's hands or mind is sacred.[1]

For Houselander, the making of true art is the work by which Christ is conceived in the heart of the maker.

THE NOVEL

Piers Paul Read has said that Catholic writers see a drama of good and evil that other authors do not see.[2] From its earliest developments, the novel form was structured around patterns of virtue and vice, temptation and redemption. But usually this is not done in an explicitly theological manner, and some-

---

1. Caryll Houselander, *The Reed of God* (Notre Dame, Ind.: Ave Maria Press, 2006), 35.
2. Interview with Michael Barber, *Book Choice* (January 1982), no. 13:18.

times—especially in the modern novel—such themes are used in subversive ways. When Catholics have turned to the novel, they have frequently explored the deeper spiritual or moral potential of the form's technical innovations: the subtleties of narrative voice, the plot development of a single moral consciousness through linear time, the group dynamics of a community of sub-characters, and the potential for depicting providential or extra-human forces as agents of change that operate upon human characters but do so from beyond the human narrative.

Among the writers in this series, Houselander is perhaps the most innovative in her use of novelistic techniques to depict Catholic experience. This may in itself be one reason why her novel has been out of print for so many years; that is, her novel may have been perceived in the late twentieth century as both too Catholic and too experimental. But *The Dry Wood* deserves a prominent place not only in the canons of Catholic writing but in the Anglo-American Modernist literary movement. Houselander's uses of Modernist literary innovation enables her to produce a vivid Catholic experience, but in doing so she also breaks new ground in the technical advances of literary Modernism; a contribution that has yet to be acknowledged by literary scholars.

It was only near the end of her life that Houselander ceased her spiritual writing to instead write a novel. She claimed that she could no longer "preach" to her fellows. "I prefer writing fiction: it's more like a big gesture of sympathy—like taking hold of another sinner's hand and pressing it lovingly as we walk together." Perhaps because of the lateness of this decision, Houselander's novel is a little less than perfect. *The Dry Wood* approaches greatness in its structure and design and in the brilliance of its author's powers of description—of place, event, atmosphere. But it is also impaired by Houselander's tendency (developed through decades of spiritual writing) to become homiletic or didactic in a manner not unlike that of John Henry Newman in his novels *Callista* and *Loss and Gain*.

In *The Dry Wood* Houselander uses each chapter to focus on a different member of the community—an approach enabling her to interleave the prayers of the community through each character's individual personal suffering. Each of these separate struggles is then drawn, together with all the others, into the book's final Mass, where we see the great prayer of the Church depicted in both its earthly and its heavenly dimensions. In this way, Houselander draws upon some of the technical innovations developed by her early-twentieth- century literary peers, who were shaping the *nouveau roman* through narrative experimentation with time, place, multi-vocalism, and metonymic characterization, even a kind of quasi-spiritualism. English Catholics of Houselander's generation were often highly critical of modernity, but Houselander was open to new artistic movements. She felt that "the modernist writers are not the contemptible egoists which they are too often supposed to be." However, not unlike Waugh, she used modernist techniques to specifically Catholic ends. Through its development of modernist methods, particularly in its structure and voice, *The Dry Wood* is able to show the movement of suffering and redemption within a whole community. The reader is invited to see with the intimate eyes of each individual consciousness but also with the eyes of God.

In one sense each chapter, with its single-character perspective, suggests a fractured community. But it is a community that is ultimately brought together by the action of communal prayer. Readers are drawn into this experience, thereby feeling for themselves the reality of Catholic fellowship and communion. However, by giving each chapter to a single character, Houselander also emphasizes the individual subjectivity of each person; she adopts in narrative voice the Catholic reality that each person is unique and deserving of dignity. The structure might seem disjointed but in fact Houselander is showing the variety of human beings and their lives, the way in which each person is caught up in his or her petty projects and concerns, living ordinary, flawed, and in many ways banal lives, but that they do so alongside one another, and that these lives are gathered up and united in and through Christ. The narrative of *The Dry Wood* is expressly Catholic in this regard. From a worldly perspective the characters of *The Dry Wood* are all disconnected and different or even at odds with one another, but at those moments in which each of them is open to Christ they become one without losing their distinctiveness.

Other writers of the modernist novel used similar techniques to demonstrate both loneliness and community, but they did so in secular ways. Henry James's descriptions of character through metonymic object-depiction produced an experience of isolation, while Woolf's experimental use of stream of consciousness in *The Waves* sought to depict a conversation between friends in which individual voices are drawn together into one world or one mind. Instead, Houselander utilized modernist techniques to create the reality of the Catholic life of faith as something that occurs at different levels of reality simultaneously; the solitary and collective, the earthly and divine, the pedestrian and the liturgical. It is also important that *The Dry Wood* exploits the potential of an omniscient voice to enable readers to see the world as it might appear from the heavenly sphere, if only in the novel's final Mass. In this way, we come to understand that all of the book's characters are in fact united in their faith even when they do not experience themselves to be so. Even when they are not participating in the Mass, even when their thoughts are turned away from him, Christ's arms are seen to stretch around them.

CHRIST IN CREATION

Shortly after Houselander's death, one of her priest friends wrote that her "entire spiritual life consisted in, first, a determination to see Christ in everyone, though chiefly in the most apparently degraded; and secondly, a determination to sacrifice self to the uttermost in the service of Christ in those others." For Houselander, to be Christian is to be "in love" and become "another Christ." *The Dry Wood* is her attempt to bring these views to life through fiction. In doing so, Houselander has in fact achieved a novel whose themes address the full range of Christian theological concerns: the ideas of Christ and the Church, of sin and conversion, of holiness and redemption. Equally daring and persuasive is her attempt at showing the mysterious, redemptive power of the suffering of the innocent.

The novel's title reflects Houselander's consistent interest in depicting the life of faith through the botanical imagery with which Scripture is so replete. In other parts of her writing, Houselander speaks of Mary as the "reed" of God. And in *Wood of the Cradle, Wood of the Cross*, she describes the ways in which God has hidden in the earth remedies for pain and sin. These healing plants, "called by names as melodious as the names of angels," are all lowly wildflowers: camomile, hellebore, heartsease, thyme, verbena, lavender, dwale. And, most wonderful of all, God sowed wheat for bread:

In His field He had one little plot apart, lying under the snow where no foot had ever trodden, silent with the silence of snow that no voice had ever broken. In it He sowed the Living Bread. This little plot was our Lady. In her was sown the seed of Christ. The good seed which God had sown was the seed of His Son's life.[3]

Houselander frequently returned to the idea that "a germ" or "a seed of Christ" is present in the soul of every baptized person (including those baptized by desire) and that "this seed of Christ grows and flowers in them as they correspond to grace."[4] In the Christian theological tradition, the life of grace is that "higher" life by which the Christian participates in God's divine nature by mystically uniting him- or herself to Christ. This process—which is a core theme in Houselander's work—is called *theosis* or *divinization* and is described in the Scriptures (Gal 2:20; 2 Pt 1:4). Houselander's organic imagery highlights how, just as the bodily life develops, so also does the spiritual life develop, and flourish, and ultimately bear fruit.

3. Caryll Houselander, *The Wood of the Cradle, The Wood of the Cross* (Manchester, N.H.: Sophia Institute Press, 1995), 7. Originally published by Sheed and Ward in 1949 under the title *The Passion of the Infant Christ*.
4. Maisie Ward, ed., *The Letters of Caryll Houselander: Her Spiritual Legacy* (London: Sheed and Ward, 1973), 9.

The Dry Wood itself is full of references to the world of plants. These botanical metaphors illustrate the quietness of Houselander's spirituality and her conviction that the growth of Christ's presence in the human soul is akin to the growth of a plant: it occurs slowly and, until its ultimate bloom, almost invisibly. For instance, the fact that after his conversion Timothy Green does not feel as different as he might have expected or hoped points to the changing "spiritual seasons" that each of the novel's characters undergoes: seasons of growth and stagnation or even decay.

For Houselander a saint is as simple, as beautiful, and as easily overlooked as a wildflower by the wayside. At certain points in the novel, she appears to be using this imagery to compare a quiet spirituality with the zeal of, for instance, the novel's ecclesial youth movement "The Flames." In *The Dry Wood*, the forceful efficacy of fire is possibly found wanting in its capacity to overpower the lowly. However, in depicting the life of faith through botanical images, Houselander is by no means proposing an easy or idyllic spirituality. On the contrary, she is fully aware that nature is as harsh as it is gentle. Echoing Jesus' words in John 12:24—"unless a grain of wheat falls into the earth and dies, it remains alone; but if it dies, it bears much fruit"—Houselander frequently acknowledges that a seed must be buried in the cold dark of the earth and patiently await its season. In an inadequate environment, plants wither and wood turns brittle.

As a metaphor, the "dry wood" reflects this same fragility in nature. It is a reference to Luke 23:31—a passage as sobering as it is mysterious: "Do not weep for me, but weep for yourselves and for your children.... For if they do this when the wood is green, what will happen when it is dry?" These words of Christ can bring no consolation unless the hearer deciphers in them a loving exhortation to repentance and a merciful warning about what is at stake in human existence. When a perfectly good green tree is burned up (that is, when Christ sacrifices himself on the cross), what can the dry wood of fallen and broken humanity expect to find when it meets with fire? Fallen humanity can follow Christ to new life, but only at a price. If even Christ, in his innocence, underwent great suffering, then there is little doubt that we too must suffer in order to blossom and bear fruit like the green tree.

Houselander's novel is, among other things, a meditation on the challenges—but also the possibility—of living out the Christian faith in a personal and social environment that is dry or thirsty for grace. If, as Houselander was so firmly convinced, the seed of the Christ-life is still present in each of us, then *The Dry Wood* is a novel about how that seed might once again bring forth new life, how the dry wood might once more become green. It is a novel about the hidden and unassuming path to holiness, toward what Houselander calls becoming "other Christs" by nurturing the Christ-life within ourselves and one another.

THE CHRISTIAN DRAMA TODAY

The novel's Riverside characters represent the key figures of the life of Christ. It puts forward two, if not three, Christ-figures: Fr. Malone, the parish's much-loved priest of 50 years, now dead; Fr. O'Grady, his successor; and, most unambiguously, Willie Jewel. All three figures are entirely inconspicuous, externally unattractive characters, by worldly standards even failures. And yet, their Christ-likeness allows them to nurture the Christ-life in others, thereby unifying the wayward Riverside residents into one community.

This is especially true of Willie, the innocent suffering child entirely at the mercy of others. Truly and most completely another Christ, "a living crucifix," Willie has an irresistible power of love: he is silently joyful, inspiring love and devotion in the many simple sinners who come into contact with him, from hopeful factory girls to worn-out seafaring men, from the glamorous drunk, Rose O'Shane, and the questing communist youth, to the secular Jew. Not despite but through his weakness, Willie unites this disparate group of people into one body and has the power to convert their hearts. If the Riversiders can unite in a novena to save Willie's life, it is because, consciously or unconsciously, they see Christ in him. This makes the suffering child a stumbling block to the self-righteous (the Monsignor) and the scientific rationalist (Dr. Moncrieff). It also makes Willie the throbbing heart of Christ's mystical body.

Willie's parents, Art and Martha Jewel, are analogues of Jesus' parents. Martha possesses Mary's formidable faith and devotion. Like Mary, she considers herself blessed even in her trials, and she has the grace to experience a profound joy that emerges out of her suffering. Martha embodies every Christian's Marian calling: knowing where to find her own salvation, she "gives birth to Christ" within her life, she loves him through suffering in and for him, and she offers him up to the world as an object of love and devotion. In some ways at least, Willie's father Art resembles St. Joseph. Like Jesus' foster father, Art finds his life interrupted, for the better, by a

child who "should not be." And like Joseph, he finds his vocation through this very interruption and steps up to the task
with a great sense of responsibility, dedication, and sacrifice.

The book's many other characters are drawn to this little
holy family and, like Jesus' parents, Martha and Art increasingly come to learn that their son "belongs to all of Riverside."
Their home becomes little less than a pilgrimage site where
people mysteriously come for small, almost unconscious acts
of devotion and love. Willie's visitors are like the shepherds
in Bethlehem, and various women who are especially close to
the family resemble the women of Jerusalem. The child's detractors also have loose biblical counterparts: the Monsignor
is something of a Pharisee, Dr. Moncrieff is a combination of
Pontius Pilate and Saul on his journey toward Paul.

THE PATH TO HOLINESS

The theme of sanctity, or Christ's life in the soul, runs throughout not only this novel but so much of Houselander's writing.
Significantly, the pursuit of holiness is not limited to the priest,
the monk, or the nun, but is incumbent upon all Christians.
This central aspect of Houselander's thought, both in her fiction and in her nonfiction, places her squarely within that
twentieth-century theological and pastoral effort that prepared
the Second Vatican Council's teaching on the universal call to
holiness and the priesthood of the laity.

Despite this universal call to holiness, *The Dry Wood* leaves
no doubt that in this struggle against sin Houselander assigns
a particular responsibility to the priest. The priest's is classically considered the higher vocation—not because of a greater level of sanctity (on the contrary lay people certainly can,

and often do, exceed priests in holiness)—but because it directly serves the highest good: the sanctification of souls and eternal happiness. In addition to his sacramental ministry, the priest models and teaches his flock the ability to suffer and makes sacrifices on behalf of his flock. Among other things, the celibate Catholic priest's lack of familial ties is intended to provide the freedom to take on such suffering. As we all know, this same freedom can tempt the priest in the opposite direction, toward heightened comfort, self-indulgence, or even grave sin.

Houselander's understanding of the priesthood is robustly Christocentric and cruciform. For this reason, the novel's Monsignor is found wanting: he does not state basic Christian truths as they are but qualifies and hedges to the point of denuding Christian teaching of its content. This makes him incapable of the "contemplation and visible, voluntary poverty" embodied by Fathers Malone and O'Grady, which Houselander considers essential prerequisites for keeping one's spirit alert to Christ.[5] By contrast, Fr. O'Grady is conscious that, as a priest, he must keep up his routine of self-renunciation and mortification even when, amidst great grief and disappointment, he considers the laity deserve a little gentleness and rest.

In portraying the priesthood in this way, Houselander is offering neither an idealized nor an exclusive picture. Fathers Malone and O'Grady bear uncanny resemblances to real-life priests of Houselander's time, men famous for giving their boots away as soon as they acquired them (such as Blessed

---

5. Ward, *The Letters of Caryll Houselander*, 6.

John Sullivan SJ, 1861–1933). At the same time, Houselander would not deny that the Catholic priesthood can manifest
itself in many different ways and that asceticism is not the
only priestly virtue. Contemplative prayer, charitable works,
intellectual study, judicious guidance: these are all important priestly virtues and will be lived out differently from one
priest to another. Nonetheless, Houselander would insist that
every Christian, and the priest especially, is called to a life of
self-denial. For self-denial is the prerequisite of service: what
is forgone can be given to others. According to the logic of
the Gospel, it is also regained eventually: "he who finds his
life will lose it, and he who loses his life for my sake will find
it" (Mt 10:39).

Houselander's conviction of Christ's presence in all people
amounts to a spirituality of the ordinary, even the humdrum.
Christ's work of redemption and our path to holiness are not,
for Houselander, ethereal abstractions. They unfold in the
concrete and seemingly banal realities of our everyday lives.
Houselander's thought here is in keeping with a wider theological turn toward the world in the first half of the twentieth
century, which culminated in *Gaudium et Spes* (the Second
Vatican Council's Pastoral Constitution on the Church in the
Modern World). Among other things, this turn involved an
effort to re-anchor Christianity in the everyday lives of those
for whom a set of apparently bourgeois devotions and ethics
seemed out of touch with their struggles for peace and justice. In Houselander's spirituality we find resonance with a
range of movements within the twentieth-century Church,
such as the French worker-priests, who sought to evangelize
the working classes, the farming communities set up by Dor-

othy Day, and the ideas of Josemaria Escriva, for whom mundane work was a privileged locus for working out one's sanctification. Houselander's spirituality also shares important similarities with that of Catherine Doherty of the Madonna House Apostolate: Houselander's simplicity and asceticism resembles Doherty's idea of the little mandate. All of these newly simplified spiritual practices were influenced by one of modernity's most significant contributions to the spiritual life of the Church—Thérèse of Lisieux and her "little way."

Houselander's novel, like her life, illustrates that she too is deeply conscious of the spiritual significance of our mundane, working lives. The distinctiveness of her spirituality, however, lies in the fact that she couples this commitment with a mysticism centered on Christ's presence in every human being, and with a profound awareness of the reality of sin and our consequent need for redemption. It is this combination which informs Houselander's insistence on the redemptive power of human suffering.

SANCTITY AND SUFFERING

One of the most challenging aspects of Houselander's spirituality is the centrality of both suffering and asceticism as essential means toward sanctification. The necessity of suffering becomes intelligible only through what theologians call the "law of the Incarnation" or that pattern which God himself has set for us by taking on flesh and assuming the toils and weaknesses of human existence. Houselander's mysticism explains this: we must suffer because Christ lives within us. Sanctity involves an ability to suffer well. If Christ is present in us and is to grow in each of us, then the call to become "another Christ" can surely not be followed without suffering. Elsewhere, Houselander writes that the life of faith is about lovingly uniting ourselves with Christ and learning how to suffer with him. Our sufferings and tribulations are "His Passion going on now."[6]

This explains why for Houselander the life of faith does not tend to imply worldly success but—often—suffering and (seeming) failure. It is through such means that God chose to redeem us. By allowing Christ to undergo and share our troubles with us, we in turn are enabled to participate in His eternal life and thus to taste the divine joy. This is precisely what the people of Riverside and those who come into contact with them experience: their sufferings are, if only for a moment, transformed into joyful ecstasy because they united themselves with "their Christs," Fr. Malone and Willie Jewel. In the process, their disparate and often lonely lives merge in a deep communion that involves both insiders and outsiders, both men and angels.

The Dry Wood affirms the redemptive power of suffering. This is in many ways a traditional Christian claim but one that is deeply at odds with the modern quest for comfort and pleasure. It also sits uneasily with our increased awareness of the oppressive and exploitative risks associated with an idealization of innocent suffering. Ivan Karamazov's claim that he wants no stake in a heavenly kingdom based on the suffering of children resonates as deeply today as the perception that Christianity has used the Passion to justify the injustices of patriarchy. If theologians of the twentieth and twenty-first

6. Ward, *The Letters of Caryll Houselander*, 4.

centuries have had an aversion to proposing theodicies, or
have de-emphasized the salvific role of suffering, they can
hardly be blamed. And yet, this tendency has created a new
problem: suffering remains a part of human life and we now
often find ourselves incapable of making sense of it, or even
of responding to it at all.

The Dry Wood might take us some way toward untangling
this problem. In it, Houselander attempts the seemingly impossible: she celebrates the redemptive potential of innocent
suffering without denying the fact that it is an evil that should
not be, and without minimizing the hardship, pain, and grief
it causes. She can do this because of her strong sense of our
need for redemption from sin and by holding on to the dis-
tinctively Catholic idea of an economy of salvation.

Sin pulls at human beings and deadens the seed of Christ
within us. The characters in *The Dry Wood* struggle to rise
above their pride, their fear, their desire to be liked and respected. And yet, just as the seed must be buried in the earth,
left to germinate and then die in order to bring forth a flower, so our worldly selves and desires must be sacrificed if the
Christ-life is to take root in us. Fathers Malone and O'Grady
make regular acts of self-renunciation, such as watering down
their beer or denying themselves sleep. For Houselander
the acquired virtues—or those habits built through repeated efforts and perseverance—can be elevated and perfect-
ed by grace. They are ordered to the good of one's self and
others. Self-denial is thus to be pursued not for its own sake
but for the sake of serving others: asceticism cultivates an
other-centered disposition. As the novel illustrates, practices
of self-denial, for example those by the parish priests, are

aimed at building the inner strength and spirit needed for making subsequent charitable sacrifices for their parishioners—anything from the sacrifice of time to the sacrifice of one's boots.

Although the contemporary mindset is not entirely at home in asceticism as a preparation for charity, such a practice is still intelligible enough, for we can see the ultimate tangible benefits of one selflessly helping another. What moves beyond this earthly understanding of self-gift, however, are Houselander's examples of sacrifices whose benefits are expected to be spiritual more than temporal. In this respect, *The Dry Wood* is saturated with examples of the Catholic doctrine of merit—again, following the law of the Incarnation—according to which our prayers, sacrifices, or acts of charity, when united with Christ and moved by the Holy Spirit, merit for ourselves and for others spiritual goods or graces and even at times temporal goods, such as health, according to God's wisdom. When Fr. O'Grady "offers up" a tedious conversation with a parishioner, or when Sister Anne turns her indigestion into a prayer, Christ is meriting spiritual and temporal goods for others through them and their willingness to suffer discomfort.

This affirmation of the economy of salvation is taken even further in the figure of Willie Jewel. Where Fathers Malone and O'Grady also have their own sins to atone for (as well as having a psychological need to unlearn the patterns of sin), Willie's suffering, like Christ's, is entirely innocent suffering. This means that it is most purely for others and thus has the greatest redemptive value for others. His own perfect innocence means that his suffering need not serve his own redemption. Instead, and like that of Mary the Mother of God or of St. Paul, his suffering, when joined with Christ's, completes "what is lacking in Christ's afflictions for the sake of his body, that is, the church" (Col 1:24).

The question remains, however, why suffering would have redemptive power in the first place. Ultimately, the Christian answer is that we do not know, except to say that one's faith in its redemptive power is rooted in the wisdom of the cross (cf. 1 Cor 1:18–31). It remains a mystery why God uses suffering to redeem the world. However, in keeping with the Christian tradition, Houselander's novel suggests that there is a difference between believing in the redemptive power of suffering (that God has transformed suffering or created something good out of it) and believing that suffering's salvific value is a license for moral complacency. This becomes most clear in Fr. O'Grady's sermon toward the end of the book, in which he plainly states that we don't know why the innocent suffer and die: it is certainly not God's will. But "God in His Mercy uses these things for love." Houselander's own efforts throughout her life underline her commitment to alleviating suffering and injustice where possible and, especially, where they are purely destructive.

The Dry Wood indicates, however, that Houselander equally endorsed the need to accept suffering as life-giving. Indeed, herein lies the difference between the saint and what Houselander calls the ego-neurotic. In her book *Guilt*, she writes:

The real cause of frustration, of the lack of fulfilment and the failure of human beings as human beings, is the will not to suffer. In proportion to our willingness to suffer we succeed as human beings; we fail in proportion to our will not to suffer. This, because it is the will to accept suffering which liberates the capacity to love, and on the capacity to love, and on that alone, our fulfilment as human beings depends.[7]

The willing acceptance of suffering liberates our capacity for love because it is an integral part of letting Christ live in us. Christ cannot fully live in us if we do not allow him into our suffering such that we recapitulate his Passion. For, as House-lander writes, "it is actually in what *we* do that He wants to act and to suffer.... And we shall come to realise that when we resent our circumstances or try to spare ourselves what we should undergo, we are being like Peter when he tried to dissuade Our Lord from the Passion."[8] In all of this, House-lander does not, to be sure, advocate a masochistic pursuit of suffering. The saint "does not choose suffering at all, but he accepts it without conditions, because he surrenders himself to life and his personal destiny and makes no conditions."[9]

If we are still troubled by the idea of innocent suffering, it might help to call to mind Jesus' words to the weeping wom-en of Jerusalem whilst carrying his cross: "Do not weep for me but weep for yourselves and for your children." Jesus is here challenging us precisely not to get stuck (in the fashion, say, of Ivan Karamazov) in sorrow or outrage over the suffer-ing of the innocent. Instead, he invites us to focus on our own sinfulness and the suffering this causes. In an ingenious way, *The Dry Wood* mirrors even this nuance, as the novel's culmi-nation in chapter 21 brings forth in the reader intense (and rightful) emotions of outrage but then takes us beyond these

7. Caryll Houselander, *Guilt* (London: Sheed and Ward, 1952), 124.
8. Houselander, *The Reed of God*, 77.
9. Houselander, *Guilt*, 131.

feelings, toward higher and more lasting truths. These truths include the uneasy fact that, when given over to Christ, great suffering can also lead to great joy; and that, precisely in order to counter suffering, we must keep going in the difficult struggle against sin.

A HOLISTIC SPIRITUALITY

What is particularly refreshing in Houselander's spirituality and theological perspective is its balance between feasting and fasting, between mercy and rigor. On the one hand she upholds a traditionalist emphasis on the need for individual struggle against concupiscence and external temptations. But on the other hand she recognizes the more contemporary view that society itself promotes sin and that this often relativizes individual sin, making it especially deserving of mercy.

While she is sympathetic toward the worker-priests and suspicious of all forms of bourgeois Christianity (in the novel, the ecclesial movement of "The Flames" as well as "pious ladies"), she is unwavering in upholding Christianity's traditional moral precepts. And while she maintains a high bar for Catholic belief and practice, she equally endorses the importance of mercy, especially via those priests in the novel who, due to their asceticism and virtue, are benign, gentle, and forgiving. She is honest about ecclesial kitsch that leaves much to be desired aesthetically, but recognizes the indispensability of traditional piety and devotion in its accessibility, materiality, and imaginative potential. Where contemporary ecclesiastical debates have become increasingly polarized in post-conciliar Catholicism, Houselander offers a balanced view of the faith that renounces false and unnecessary dichotomies.

For all its austerity, Houselander's spirituality is deeply

human. Holiness is not a sanitized ideal but an unassuming, almost unattractive reality that emerges from allowing Christ into the regular failures, feelings of inadequacy, minor frustrations, and major sufferings of ordinary life. Houselander's depiction of holiness is as challenging as it is realistic. Suffering—whether involuntary or voluntary in the form of asceticism—is the path toward holiness. Given her emphasis on suffering, Houselander's is not a picturesque or glamorous Christianity. On the contrary, *The Dry Wood* illustrates this Christian inversion of values on every level, from its characters to its places. The novel does not shy away from even the most difficult and uncomfortable aspects of the Christian faith, and it embraces their concrete relevance for our everyday lives. It invites us to leave ecclesial politics behind and, instead, simply to focus on becoming "other Christs" for one another: this alone will build the true Body of Christ.

Bonnie Lander Johnson and Julia Meszaros

THE DRY WOOD

*For if in the green wood
they do these things, what
shall be done in the dry?*

CHAPTER 1

A PRIEST LIES DEAD

... The Good Shepherd giveth
his life for his sheep.

The Riverside Dock Road stirred with mysterious life. The doorsteps swarmed, the people thronged the streets, silent grey flocks moving in one direction like birds migrating. Silence accentuated the sense of exaltation, silence and the eagerness that sharpened the lifted white faces.

Timothy Green stepped down from the crude red bus into a supernatural world. He had not expected anything like this. He could not make out what had happened, or what was happening. It was not a royal visit for there was no chatter, no flutter of paper streamers, no bunting. It was not the return of a charabanc party for there were no groups at street corners, no waiting, no gossip. These people moved together, as people impelled by one purpose. They were one.

It could be no common event, but something new and unearthly that possessed them and united them in the integrity of a secret and solemn joy.

Timothy began to move along with the crowd, watching the faces, looking for one less concentrated, less intense than the others, one whom he might question without feeling himself an intruder. He found himself beside a young man wearing no shirt under his buttoned coat, the shape of his spine and his shoulders showed through it. Timothy touched his arm. "What is it all about?" he asked.

The young man swung round to him as if he were startled. He answered in a husky, rushing whisper, "Don't you know? Father Malone is dead."

Timothy made no answer, he could not understand why their priest's death should move these people to exultation.

The harsh, rushing voice went on, "I'm not a Catholic myself—I'm nothing. But it didn't make any difference to Father Malone, he'd have given the shirt off his back to the devil himself, if he'd thought Satan might be cold in hell. He gave me his boots."

"Gave you his boots?"

"Yes, that's what he did. Happened this way. We were under this very arch that we are under now, it was raining cats and dogs and we were taking shelter. I remember my boots were stiff with mud and with blood too—"

"With blood?"

"Yes, you see I'd been on the roads—tramping—and my feet were bleeding. All of a sudden Father Malone said to me, 'Let's see the soles of your boots.' And when he saw them and the holes in them letting the water in, down he went on his knees on the wet pavement and before I properly knew what was happening, I'd got his boots on and he'd got mine."

"Shame on you, then!" a woman's voice broke in.

The young man went on, "He was a very little man, was Father Malone, but he always had his boots a size or two too big, so as he could give them away more often. They were fine for me, but mine were three sizes too big for him. I'll never forget him shuffling off in them with his umbrella up and the rain dripping off the brim of his hat."

The woman who had interrupted turned sharply and said, "You should never have taken his boots, Sam Martin—and you a wastrel that never did an honest week's work! You shouldn't have taken his boots!"

"No, I shouldn't have, but somehow or other I couldn't help it."

Another voice joined in, "That's true, the priest was for ever giving away what he should have kept for himself and somehow or other you couldn't help but take what he gave."

"Sure," it was the soft voice of Rose O'Shane, "no one can say 'no' to the charity of Jesus Christ."

Others began to join in the conversation now, their voices gathering and fading, sweeping close and sweeping away as they moved along, so that all round Timothy, washing like waves of the sea, the story of Father Malone was told. And it might have been not the poor Riverside people speaking to a strange young journalist, but the angels bearing witness in whispering choirs to God at the private judgment of the old priest who had just died.

"It was cancer he died of."

"No it wasn't, it was just that he'd worn himself out."

"No, nothing would have worn him out; it was just that his work was done."

"That's it, he had finished his work and God took him home."

"Anyhow, it was for two years that he was in pain."

"Two years or more—pain like a knife twisting, Dr. Moncrieff said; he never said a word himself."

"No, he never said anything, but I've seen his face like mustard at the Altar."

"He never took a holiday, not once in fifty years."

"Fifty years!"

"That's right—fifty years; he was here in this parish for fifty years and he never took a holiday."

"He said he would go for a holiday when nobody needed him."

"But somebody always did need him."

"He baptized my children."

"He gave me food to eat."

"When my man was on the dole he gave my children food."

"He gave me my First Communion."

"He gave my children theirs."

"And mine—and mine—and mine."

"He gave my father the last Sacraments."

I was hungry and you gave me food.

"When I docked at Riverside, I was a foreigner, he took me to his home to sleep."

"When I came out of gaol he took me home and gave me a glass of beer."

I was a stranger, you brought me home.
I was thirsty, you gave me to drink.

"He gave me the coat on my back."

"When I was down and out he gave me a coat."

I was naked and you clothed me.

"He anointed my old mother."

"He used to visit mine and make her a cup of tea."

When I was sick you cared for me.

When I was thirsty you gave me to drink.

"When I was doing time he came to see me."

"I'd have gone off my rocker only for him when I was in gaol."

I was in prison and you came to me.

"He married Jim and me."

"And Mary and me."

"And my girl Sally and Jack."

"He buried my father and mother."

"And now he has gone himself."

"May he rest in Peace!"

"Amen—Amen—Amen."

"Somebody *always* needed him."

"People used to laugh at him."

"Ones who didn't know him."

"Silly fools they were—but they didn't know him."

"They laughed at his long hair."

"They laughed at his old coat."

"They laughed at his turned-up shoes."

"They laughed at him because he talked to himself."

"But we knew he was talking to the angels."

"Yes, and the angels talked to him."

Timothy had by this time a vision of an old man with long white hair, a broad hat ringed with raindrops, shuffling along in the vagrant's bloodstained boots beside the Angelic hosts.

As they came near to the priest's house, the voices faded back into the silence from which they had come, a silence that breathed like the breathing of sea water in the twilight.

The priest's house was no different to any of the others in the row—all flat grey houses with blank, blind faces behind drawn blinds; little houses standing very close together as if they leaned on one another for comfort in the face of unresisted adversity. Behind their crooked chimney pots the masts of ships rose up from the docks, giving the illusion of dream ships, moored lightly at street corners.

From aloft, in one of them, came the plaintive twang of a one-stringed Chinese fiddle. Somewhere nearby a little Chinaman on a journey was homesick, and here an old priest's journey had ended and he had gone home.

A shadow moved across the yellow blind of the upstairs room, a black silhouette with bowing shoulders there for a minute and then gone, leaving only the square of dim gold that was the only light in the street. Someone whispered to Timothy, "That will be Father O'Grady and it's heartbroken he will be."

A woman began to weep, and now it seemed strange to all of them that upstairs Father Malone was lying dead. That death could be so final, that the warm heart that everyone had taken for granted was actually there, a frozen thing that would fit into a man's hand, and would never beat again. They could not help imagining that small body lying there on the pallet behind the yellow blind. It would be in vestments, the white hair in a long stiff curl behind the flat waxen ear, the feet pointing stiffly up like those of a puppet, pushed into the buckled shoes that he wore at the Altar, the only respectable shoes that he had left. The nose would be pinched, the mouth slightly open, the hands set like little blocks of wax upon the crucifix.

He would look very small, and perhaps he who had been so compassionate would for the first time inspire compassion, for the body where the changeless but infinitely adaptable Holy Ghost had for so long been at home was now only a handful of dust.

A woman was sobbing, a stifled sobbing, but in the hush upon the world it was noisy.

"Now give over, Magdalena Hogg, dear," a soft Irish voice said. "Give over, for we have not lost him, he is our own saint in Heaven now!"

Again the soft wash of the people's voices rose like waves creaming the shore on a summer evening.

"Our own saint—our own saint in Heaven." They took it up and breathed it to and fro—"Our saint—our own saint in Heaven...."

Come, you that have received a blessing from my Father, take possession of the kingdom which has been prepared for you since the foundation of the world. For I was hungry, and you gave me food; thirsty, and you gave me drink; I was a stranger, and you brought me home; naked and you clothed me; sick and you cared for me; a prisoner and you came to me—

"Our own saint, our own saint in Heaven...."

Every face was lifted up towards that one patch of light, every face was lifted up and lit with the secret of proud and inexpressible joy. Timothy Green understood their exultation.

CHAPTER 2

IN MY FATHER'S HOUSE

There are many dwelling places in
my Father's house: otherwise, should I
have said to you, I am going away to
prepare a home for you?

The Archbishop of Southminster leaned back, put the tips of his fingers together and sighed. It was an almost inaudible sigh that seemed to come from far away and to be related, not to the room but to the world outside, to the muffled sound of traffic, and of people passing up and down the street. Inside the room the melodious voice of Monsignor Frayne flowed on and on.

By the Monsignor's side sat his secretary, Father Perivale. Never before had this golden-haired young priest been so near to a live Archbishop, or even to a dead one. He looked at him all the time with that awe which trembles between ecstasy and fear, he felt as he had once felt as a small boy when he was taken to see Father Christmas at the toy bazaar of a big store, and experienced the same nervous temptation to put out an adoring finger to touch and see if this was really a man of flesh and blood.

It was difficult to believe that the Archbishop could not see through his closed eyes, so thin were the lids, like crumpled tissue paper; his face was a face of silver, etched with fine lines of light. It was impossible to judge whether the mind behind that remote and gentle face was shut off from the world outside it, or whether it was merely withdrawn from the distractions of the eyes in order to listen more attentively.

It was well known to his clergy that the Archbishop was a prudent man, slow in coming to decisions, his mind like a delicately-adjusted weighing-scale. It had been said of him that he weighed every grain of thought, sifted every particle of evidence, like a dispenser weighing out medicines which though curative in precise measure, could be changed by the least discrepancy to deadly poison. This caution, about which many little ecclesiastical jokes were current, was a source of secret exasperation to Mgr. Frayne. He himself was dogged by a sense of urgency, haunted by a fear that the Catholic Church in England was going to let slip through her fingers—or through the Archbishop's fingers—the biggest chance that she had ever had of showing forth her glory upon earth.

It was an age of new movements, of reforms, of the striking off of old fetters, of emerging from ignorance, overcoming sickness and pain, of putting off the old rags of misery, weakness, and dirt, and of putting on beauty, knowledge, strength and joy. It was an age of giant co-operation, of the massing of human power, of solidarity.

Surely, thought Mgr. Frayne, the Church should come forward now as the greatest of the great blocs of power? Surely her children in England had been persecuted and humiliated enough. Now they should know her strength, should feel her glory surging through their blood. Surely this strength should be manifested in outstanding personalities—lawyers, politicians, statesmen, Harley Street specialists, film stars, writers of best-sellers, portrait painters, company directors and so on. People, moreover, not only gifted by nature, but with some worldly substance at their disposal, which would enable them to compete with Satan on his own terms. They would be able so to reform the economic and cultural conditions of the Faithful that no Catholic should ever feel the need—which the Monsignor had sometimes felt himself—of apologizing for some of the embarrassing manifestations of piety. There was nothing he hated more than this occasional dilemma, for the Church was his mother and after all it takes a cad to apologize for his mother.

The Church was indeed his most dear mother, but there were moments when his attitude to her was like that of a small boy at boarding-school, torn between anxiety and longing for his mother's first visit, knowing and loving her as the source of all good things, yet secretly apprehensive that at any moment she might humiliate him by some preposterous breach of taste or school convention; she might, for example, arrive at the school eccentrically dressed, call him by a family pet name, admonish him loudly to say his prayers, or clean his teeth, or air his undervests.

For a long time the disconcerting aspects of Mother Church had even been a stumbling block in the path of the

Monsignor's conversion. Wherever he went in pursuit of truth, he had been met by simpering plaster statues, by indescribably painful attempts at hymn singing, by books of piety written by sufferers from spiritual diabetes, and by short, rotund priests wearing long albs hitched up round their waists into bunches and flounces, and surmounted by ugly over-ornamented Roman chasubles, stiff with vulgar embroidery and shaped like fiddles.

It was to his eternal credit that Monsignor Frayne, a highly successful clergyman of the Church of England, had acknowledged his mother in the true Church, for he was in the position of a young man adopted at birth by an immensely satisfactory aunt and raised by her in an environment as gracious and beautiful as he could desire, and moreover one exactly suited to his temperament, the atmosphere of what is loveliest in an old English village—if one lives in the manor house. His aunt (if we follow this image) was the lady of the manor, in her company life was serene, she dispensed soup and woollens to the poor, she distilled peace in the home, she sang hymns at the piano and her singing endowed even the most banal of them with a quality of sweetness and wonder. She made no demands on him, but her actual presence quite naturally evoked his inborn qualities of chivalry and tact. In her house he enjoyed quiet libraries, and long galleries of family portraits; he associated her with bells, and grey spires, and deep green lawns; in her company the even tenor of his life was never disturbed by thought. Her clothes were always beautiful, and—what mattered more to him—always right; her hands were cool, her kiss discreet, and above all she could be relied upon to say and do the right thing, to have all the correct inhibitions and reserve, in all and every circumstance, at the prep. school and the public school, at home, when he brought Smith minor back to stay, at Lord's, in fact anywhere and everywhere. Such an aunt, to the Monsignor, was the Church of England, when he suddenly found himself in the position of a boy who, having been raised by her and accepted all her standards and values, believing her to be his true mother, suddenly discovers that she is not, and that his real mother is living, and is a disconcerting, unknown quantity, who apparently violates every one of the conventions that he has learned to love, and is likely to make constant and probably unreasonable demands on him.

Appearing at times like a rowdy pearly Queen in sequins and feathers, ready to dance to a barrel organ in the Old Kent Road, at other times in the habit of a nun, or as a merry washerwoman, or a beggar in rags. Such was the Catholic Church in the eyes of Monsignor Frayne when he first knew her to be his mother, and with the realization that she *was* that, came the other realization of the essential Aunthood of the Church of England, not only was she an aunt, but a maiden aunt, despite her married clergy, her country houses, and her deep-green lawns. Whereas the Catholic Church, with her celibate clergy, her virgin heart, her disconcerting vulgarity, and the riff-raff of the whole world clinging to her flamboyant skirts, was unquestionably the Universal Mother.

While still loving the gracious Aunt, and for ever aware of a debt to her that he could never discharge, while still shining with the graces received at her hands, the Monsignor acknowledged his true Mother and submitted to her devastating love.

Having submitted, he did all that he could to reform his mother's dress. But it went deeper than that, and for him it was an act of love to attempt to clothe her for the eyes of the world in her splendour, that the world might see her beauty and love her. He worked for the promotion of Art and Culture in the Church, for the reform of Liturgical worship, for an educated laity. With the rise of the great blocs of power, he conceived a vision of Catholic youth as fervent as Communist Youth, as disciplined as Nazi Youth. For this end he mobilized Catholic ladies to stitch their wasting libido into banners and flags and jolly uniforms, to teach singing and country dancing, to drill adolescents and to give lessons in Arts and Crafts. He scoured the Universities for the most intelligent, the homes of the rich for the most leisured, and the working class clubs for the most gullible youth.

In that section of the community known as "influential" he was worshipped; ladies in black mantillas were round him like bees round a pot of honey, and within his circle he had the satisfaction of seeing youth become visibly rounder and rosier and happier, and more self-assured daily; priests became more and more interested in plain chant and Gothic chasubles, and more and more Society girls taught basket-making to the poor. Though he knew perfectly well how little any of these things were in themselves, they seemed to the Monsignor at least to be signs of the stirring of the waters, even if only of himself stirring them with a stick.

One thing, however, disconcerted him, namely the curious decisions, presumably made in Heaven, concerning the canonization of saints. There are, of course, millions of saints in Heaven who are not canonized and not known on earth.

When a particular saint is chosen and set before the eyes of the world, there is a reason for it. They show some special kind of holiness urgently needed by the generation to which they are given.

This being so, it seemed to Mgr. Frayne a most disconcerting thing that no saint has yet appeared in our times who has all the characteristics desirable in a Catholic youth leader in the modern world. So far Almighty God had pointed to no saint of this type; it seemed that all the more attractive, vivacious, practical and charming saints of our day remained hidden in the dazzling light of glory, while those who exhibited the very opposite characteristics to Mgr. Frayne's ideal were being canonized one after the other.

What a motley crowd they were, these saints of our times! An Italian vagrant who stank, a dull-witted Pyrenean peasant girl, an ignorant old French priest who kept the devil in his bedroom, a little consumptive nun who immortalized the crudest sentimentalities of the bourgeoisie—and they were talking about a Dublin labourer who before he started to be a saint was sodden with drink. Now, to crown the Monsignor's vexation, the people of a big London slum were demanding a saint of their own, and the saint they demanded was one who had lived but yesterday and united in his one person all the most unfortunate characteristics of which sanctity is capable. That was why he and Father Perivale had come to Archbishop's House this afternoon.

At last the Archbishop opened his eyes and looked attentively at the Monsignor.

"And so," he said, "they want to make poor old Father Malone a saint! He always did give his bishops a lot of trouble, God rest his soul! And it seems that death has not stopped him! Well, if he *is* a saint, no doubt he will prove it; is not that so, Father?"

Monsignor Frayne wondered if Archbishop Crecy really had been asleep, as he seemed to be unaware of one single word that he had been saying to him.

"The object of my visit, was to bring to the notice of your Grace, the fact that this—er—cult, yes definitely *cult*, of Father Malone is causing scandal."

"Ah! Scandal!" The Archbishop began to look meditatively at his own finger tips, and paused before going on. "Scandal. Yes, we can hardly be too careful in avoiding that—that is, of course, when it is possible. It is not always possible, alas! But we need not—nay should not—be overdisquieted on that account, as Our Divine Lord has warned us Himself that scandals *must* come."

"This scandal, however, *could* be avoided; and I have no doubt that your Grace recalls the fact that Our Lord completed His prophecy with a most terrible warning to those *through whom* they should come."

"Terrible indeed, Monsignor, but it seems to me—at first sight only of course—and subject to further consideration, that the very natural devotion of a poor flock to its old shepherd will give scant cause for scandal."

He turned to Father Perivale. "You, Father," he said, "may never have met Father Malone. Monsignor Frayne and I both knew him well, of course. He was parish priest in Riverside, where he lived, first of all as curate and afterwards as vicar, for fifty years. Think of it, my dear Father; he had the astonishing record of having remained in that slum, without even taking a holiday, for fifty years. Not a thing to emulate of course, it could hardly be imitated without imprudence, grave imprudence; but it seems to me a natural thing, nay more, inevitable, that his memory should be venerated."

"No, I never had the pleasure of knowing him," said Father Perivale. "But," he added out of loyalty to Monsignor Frayne, "I have heard a lot of things about him, your Grace—rather exaggerated things."

The Archbishop smiled. "In human nature there is always a tendency to exaggerate," he said.

Monsignor Frayne controlled his impatience and his voice with an effort. "May I," he said, "go over my few points once more?"

"By all means."

"No inquiry has yet been instituted into the virtue of Father Malone, and such is the fervour of the people of Riverside, that one is forced to the conclusion that they are presuming to anticipate the possible future decision of the Church."

"On the other hand," said the Archbishop softly, "the popular verdict is the beginning of the process of every canonization."

"My second point is that Father Malone's successor is encouraging the abuse. His encouragement is, in the eyes of these ignorant people, an official sanction, and should it become necessary to quash the whole thing, the people would be left bewildered."

"I will talk the matter over with Father O'Grady, who, I presume, does not organize anything in the nature of public prayers to the servant of God?"

Monsignor Frayne winced at the term "servant of God."
"My third point," he said, and now he spoke slowly with the
relish of one about to produce a trump card, "is Solly Lee."

"Solly Lee?"

So, thought the Monsignor, so you *have* been dozing, old
man. "Solly Lee," he said, "is a very unsavoury person, who
has started, purely as a commercial stunt, to manufacture holy
cards representing Father Malone, and the people are buying
them like hot cakes. Solly Lee is not a Catholic, of course;
he knows exactly how to turn people's emotions to profit. As
to these cards, they are shocking—believe me, Your Grace,
shocking. They represent Father Malone with upturned eyes,
folded hands, and a halo!"

"Dear me, Monsignor! Folded hands and even upturned
eyes are, of course, harmless, more especially so in the case
of the dead; but a halo! A halo can hardly be said to be altogether and certainly harmless in any circumstances, and the
fact that the wearer is dead is distinctly an aggravating circumstance. However, since the gentleman responsible is not
of the true Fold, therefore not in my jurisdiction, I see no way
by which I can restrain him, though I might perhaps suggest
to Father O'Grady that he appeal to his better nature to remove the offending halo as a matter of courtesy."

"Or forbid the Faithful to buy the cards."

"That is a matter for consideration. I might be doing an
injustice to this Mr. Lee, who may have expended large sums
on the cards, and should he prove willing to remove the haloes what remains might be no more debatable than a simple memorial card to which any person is entitled merely by
being dead." He laughed gently. "I was wondering," he said,

"what dear old Father Malone would have to say to all this himself."

The Archbishop's face was suddenly tender. Across the mental image of the holy cards passed his own memory of the dead priest—an old man with a battered hat, a ragged coat, and broken shoes, with large gnarled hands and exhausted eyes, with a worn face, sharp and sallow, and etched deeply with lines of pity and laughter and love.

"One more point, Your Grace, before I ask permission to take my leave. I do not doubt that in his way ... er ... his very *individual* way, Father Malone was a holy—an exceptionally holy priest, but I question whether it is advisable to throw the limelight on this particular type of holiness at the present moment, at this moment when it is surely vital to set before the public an ideal of Catholic living and holiness, which is—well, shall I say healthy—radiant, in keeping with the spirit of modern youth, and moreover a wholly *English* kind of holiness. Is it not possible that the piety of this old Irish priest, with its rather fusty atmosphere, and the stress all upon poverty and austerity—and, who knows, a touch of Jansenism—might prove damping, discouraging? Might not the non-Catholic majority be led into the mistaken view that the personal idiosyncrasies of the dear old man, and the exaggeration of certain elements which were peculiar to him, are in fact the things which we Catholics set up as the essentials of sanctity? Do we not, Your Grace, require a young, flaming saint, one who would take the imagination of modern youth, who by his—or her—example, would encourage them, not to seek out eccentric ways of mortification, but to offer their health, their merriment, their talents, their money, and, yes, their good looks, their taste in dress, their charm, in the service of God?"

The Archbishop was silent for what seemed an insufferably long time. Then he said, "In my Father's house there are many mansions. There is room for everyone in Heaven, and there is room for everyone in the Church on earth, Monsignor. We have every possible type of saint on the calendar, and I doubt if any of them have really done very much harm, troublesome though they undoubtedly were to their contemporaries. Kings and Queens, aged folk and children, simpletons and geniuses, they are all there, and I am bound to say that in my opinion the imagination of a boy or girl is as likely, nay more likely to be caught by a Curé d'Ars or a Joseph Labre than by a school prefect or a blue-blooded Girl-Guide captain!

"As to eccentricity, I have been told that this is sometimes an expression of vanity and sometimes of love. I think that in the saints it is always an expression of love for, when all is said and done, what is a saint? Simply someone who is in love with God. Perhaps everyone who is in love seems a little absurd to everyone who is not.... But be that as it may, the decision concerning the sanctity of Father Malone rests not with me, or the poor people of Riverside, but with Almighty God. If He chooses to manifest His glory in the humble old man He will; there is nothing at all that we can do about it. But as you know, there is no process so long, and exacting, and searching, as that of canonization. If he passes it, we can be sure that there will have been no mistake. For one thing, there is the first-class miracle to be obtained through his intercession—"

He was silent again, and then softly, as if he were talking aloud to himself—"and, suppose that Father Malone *does* work the miracle?"

Monsignor Frayne was momentarily stunned. Of course he had no doubt at all in his own mind that Father Malone was in Heaven, no doubt of the daily heroic virtue that an inquiry would endorse. But there was always the hope, faint though it was, which he cherished secretly, that happy though he was in Heaven now, he had nevertheless come there by way of a swift, not uncomfortable journey through Purgatory—Oh, a superbly easy journey of course, like a first-class sleeper on the Blue Train, carrying one swiftly through the darkness to awake in the light of the sun, a wonderful journey, but one which nevertheless would have made the old man ineligible for canonization!

Now the Archbishop was repeating his question and seemed at last to want an answer. "Suppose Father Malone *does* work a first-class miracle?"

"That," said Monsignor Frayne, "is another point that I wish to bring to Your Grace's notice. The people are openly praying for a miracle of their own choosing, which, in itself, is a cause of scandal. There is a little child, a boy of six, afflicted by some rare disease from birth. He is helpless, unable even to sit up alone, and he is dumb. Many doctors are interested in his case for its rarity, and all are agreed that he cannot now live for more than a matter of months. It is for this child's life to go on that the people are praying."

"It would seem difficult to find a more fitting subject."

"Yes, if a complete cure were asked, but that this child shall live as he is—?"

"Has it been stated that they are not asking for a complete cure?"

"Not in so many words, but if you question them you find that they simply cannot think of him as other than he is."

The Archbishop nodded. "It is often so with simple people," he said. "A child who is weak or crippled is more dear to them for that, it somehow makes him belong to them all. It is an instinct like that which makes a mother love the weakest child the best, and God the naughtiest!"

"True, but the problem of a little child suffering is one that causes more loss of Faith than anything else, and it is no time to focus the whole attention of the Protestant community in England on so unfortunate an instance of it."

"We cannot foresee the design of Almighty God, Monsignor. He may grant a complete cure and show forth His Glory, or He may wish to draw attention to the very problem that scandalizes. At the same time, the whole matter may fizzle out within a few months, and truth to tell, I am inclined to think it will, if we do not take it too seriously."

He turned suddenly to Father Perivale with a smile which seemed to dismiss the whole subject. "I am sure, Father," he said, "that you are ready for a glass of wine."

Father Perivale glowed. He had the sense of a child being "grown up," the idea that the Archbishop of Southminster should take it for granted that he was expecting a glass of wine exalted him, though actually it was the last thing that would have ever entered his head. Now that the Archbishop was actually handing him a glass, he recalled that Monsignor Frayne had said to him, "His wine is execrable, and he always insists upon one swallowing it."

To Father Perivale, however, it was nectar. Never had he savoured wine so fruity, heady, and, as he thought, mediaeval; never had wine flowed through his blood with such sweetness and exhilaration, or so emboldened him. Yet he was surprised at his own presumption when he heard his voice putting a suggestion to the Archbishop: "I have an idea—I do hope I am not just being presumptuous"—actually he was now so crimson in the face that his golden hair looked platinum.

"Pray go on, Father, tell me your idea."

"I wondered, Your Grace, if you, being Father Malone's bishop, could just forbid him to work the miracle; then there couldn't be any scandal."

There was not a shadow of a smile on the Archbishop's face, he seemed to be turning the suggestion over in his mind. At length he said, "The question which arises is this; is he still subject to my authority in Heaven—always supposing but never presuming that he *is* in Heaven. Saint Peter would very likely be his Bishop now, although it is true that he died a priest in my diocese. The whole position is, I am sure you will admit, Father, somewhat ambiguous, and I am not at present in a position to discover what view St. Peter would take of the matter."

He rose as he finished speaking and Monsignor Frayne knew that the interview was at an end and had achieved precisely nothing.

He spoke once only on the drive home. "Execrable!" he said. "Execrable!" Father Perivale said nothing. He presumed that this was another reference to the wine, since it could not possibly be a reference to the Archbishop.

CHAPTER 3

THE MULTITUDE

'But now Jesus called
his disciples, and said, "I
am moved with pity for
the multitude."

Upstairs in Archbishop's House silence returned to the room, falling flake by flake on the Archbishop's soul, as snow falls flake by flake on the world. Silence settled and became peace, as snow becomes stillness when the sky is emptied.

Archbishop Crecy crossed to the window and looked down. The people were passing in an endless grey procession below. The shops and offices had poured out their hosts of workers. They moved in great blocks and automatically, as if they were obeying orders from some invisible controller, and yet they seemed isolated from one another. Every face in that multitude of faces was a separate, blank loneliness.

In the office they must have worked, talked and giggled together; they must have shared syrupy black tea, and known a kind of communion in its warm sickliness. They must have been bound together by the loyalties and affections, by the pettiness and even the quarrels of the office. In the littleness of the office world, they must have ceased to be insignificant even to have sometimes become part of something small enough for smallness to taste omnipotence. In that pigmy world they must have found an escape from even a hint of awareness of the immensity of which they were really a part, and which they could not face.

Now they disintegrated as if, when the clock struck six, with six sharp little blows, it struck off the chains that bound them together, and they fell apart—each from the pigmy unity that they had achieved, back into the vastness of the Universe in which each was an individual and alone.

They appeared intent on getting somewhere quickly, yet there was no eagerness in their faces, only a certain tenseness as if they were driven and could not stop hurrying if they would. The very idea of one of them sauntering home slowly, enjoying the twilight, his hands pushed into his pockets, whistling as he strolled along, was unthinkable.

"Where?" Archbishop Crecy asked himself. "Where were they all going to?"

To the cheap boarding-houses of Hampstead, Belsize Park, Bayswater and Maida Vale, tawdry and drab, with the stucco flaking off from the damp walls, like heavy make-up, flaking off from the raddled faces of old women who weep. To the lodging-houses beyond Vauxhall and Pimlico, with texts that have hung unread upon their walls for fifty years, to be mocked by the dreary sins of the drifting population of lodgers, and with washstands of varnished yellow wood and awful china jugs and basins that have mocked the dreams of generations of young men. To the Students' Hostels where the least adventurous young men and women live in cubicles as wide as coffins, and feed in common dining-rooms on a diet of cold mutton, beetroot, stewed pears and tepid water. To the tawdry hotels round Bloomsbury where the dark rooms smell of dust, cheap scent and mice. To the attics of small hotels in Notting Hill and Kensington, where for a good address and hotel note-paper poor, frustrated little snobs can sleep under the roof with no fire in the winter and vermin all the year round.

And these slightly more prosperous, more respectable, City men? Where are they hurrying to, these pale small men in bowler hats, with shy moustaches on their upper lips, and the beginning of little paunches and a pathetic, sprouting pomposity in their bearing? Where are they going to?

Out to the little egg-shell houses in the suburbs, the houses designed and built for one-child, and childless marriages, more terrible than those in London that are visibly rotting and falling into decay, more terrible because of their very neatness and whiteness and sweetness, because of the roses in the prim gardens that the master of the house shows off so proudly on Sundays to the privileged junior clerks invited for the day; more terrible because of the neat rows of cultivated flowers standing against the new white wall that are the pretty sepulchres of the murdered unborn children.

More tragic than all the rest, because here, having attained to that which they put their faith in, having attained it at the cost of all the adventure, all the risk, all the romance, all the poetry in life, and by years of monotony, years of boredom, years of drudgery, they are afraid of life still, afraid even in security, even in the cage.

The goal is achieved, the regular salary, the assured pension, the Life Insurance, the detached residence, the garden, the wireless, the car, the wife with the permanent wave, the heavy lunch on Sundays, and the after-lunch discomfort and somnolence that is the symbol of success—all that achieved, and in that achievement all the natural capacities of the little man developed and stretched to their limit, and yet he confesses in his heart, and by his deeds, that this life, that has cost him everything and is the sum of his happiness, is not worth having, for he refuses it to his children and murders them in the moment of conception.

Like his Divine Master, the Archbishop was moved with pity for the multitude. It seemed small wonder to him that those who had Faith wanted a saint of their own. One who was one of themselves, who was close to them, living their life in their day. Not one of the great but one of the least, not one of the élite but one of the multitude, one who knew the same nagging cares, the same haunting fears, the same incessant temptations as they did, and yet believed in the Fatherhood of God. One who was subjected to the same exploitation and greed as they were, to the same disillusionment and betrayal, and who yet believed in the Communion of men. One whose clothes smelt as theirs smelt and were worn to the same grotesque shapes that theirs were worn to, the sad, sagging shapes of original sin, and who yet believed that this life is a putting on of Christ, like a garment. One who shared the dullness of their thoughts, the weariness of their minds, the feebleness of their loves, and yet believed that the Holy Spirit is at home in man's soul. One who shared their need for the comfort of sensuality, the drag downwards into the warm darkness at the root of their being, and who yet kissed, in the dust of the common street, the print of the feet that shone like snow upon Tabor. One who shared the wearing monotony of their poverty, and yet would crack the walls of materialism that they had built around themselves and let in the Light of Glory.

"That is what they need," said the Archbishop and he spoke aloud to the darkening room. "A saint. I would like to give the people a saint."

He saw a newspaper boy hurrying down the street, the people snatching his papers as they passed, and he remembered yet again that war threatened England, that all the squalor and mediocrity might at any moment be uprooted and that the drifting multitude might hear the echo of that mysterious warning in their own lives. "Thou fool, this night do they require thy soul of thee." He thought of Poland, of Czechoslovakia, of Russia, of the Martyrs who had already answered the demand for their country's soul. How would England answer? Whom would she yield up if her soul were challenged, were demanded of her this very night? Would it be found that among her multitudes there were a few who would come, not driven, not compelled, but with the will of Jesus Christ to be sacrificed, to be given for the people?

Or might it be that even now there were some who were immolated in secret, given already for the multitude, if so would they save the people? Would Willie Jewel—? The Archbishop suddenly caught his breath. What was this absurdity that he was thinking? But was it absurd? Might not a suffering child be the greatest power in the world, the only force stronger than the power of evil? Crucified innocence; could God withstand *that*, and could God allow *that* for any reason less than the redemption of the world? He wondered what kind of child Willie was, whether he had made his first Communion, how he expressed himself, being dumb, how he had made the love of the whole of Riverside his own. And he thought, "The life of a little child like that, silent and helpless, is like the life of the Host."

He turned and looked at the Cathedral, the shrine of the silent Host, and for him the symbol of the Church. He, like Monsignor Frayne, thought of the Church as his mother, and as the mother of the whole world. But for him there was no cause of anxiety in her illimitable variety, she was both peasant and queen, a queen crowned with stars, who wore her jewelled cope over her peasant's frock and her wide apron, a mother who must wash her children with her own hands in the shining waters of Baptism and absolution, who must feed them at her table on the living Bread and the water of Life, who must close their eyes with her own firm, pitiful fingers, for the little sleep between death and Resurrection.

It was part of her wisdom that the glory of the saints is secret, that we on earth see their tears, their struggle, their wounds, the old clothes they have left off, and their bones; that she cherishes their bones as a mother cherishes her children's milk teeth, when the children have grown to manhood, because they remind her that once they were little and weak, and were fed at her breast. Part of her illimitable wisdom that we must ask a miracle of every new saint, that to prove that they are at God's side they must reach a hand through the cloud to alleviate our sorrow. The sign of their glory, a touch of love in the darkness.

The people had all gone and the streets were empty, twilight drained out of the sky, and the Cathedral became a vast silhouette, dark against silver emptiness.

The Archbishop remained standing still by the window, his shoulders bowed as if he actually felt the weight of the world's sorrow heavy upon them. The ring on his finger glowed like a drop of blood.

Above the tower the beauty of the world gathered to a single star that shone over London like the Star of Bethlehem.

CHAPTER 4

A DOOR IS OPEN

Then a vision came to me;
I saw a door in Heaven
standing open.

Father Malone had been dead for nearly a year, but his presence in the parish did not diminish. It grew, it was almost tangible. Every day joy increased like a warm and lasting spring after a long winter. At first, sunlight pale as primrose, in whose constancy no one dared to trust; and then miraculously, the world flowering in light, day after day. His people had always known that their Father Malone would never leave them, he would never really go away as if they had no need of him. He would never take a holiday from them, even though now, thank God, he was at rest. They knew this because he was proving it, showing it to them, he was answering their prayers.

At every house on his round of parish visits Father O'Grady was told of answered prayers. Father Malone had cured styes in eyes, headaches and bad colds, he had found rooms and jobs, he had averted operations, cured scruples, he had brought home lost kittens and sailors whose ships were overdue. He had eased rheumatics, made the sun to shine on the mothers' outing, had grown flowers in window boxes. But all these things were nothing at all compared to the wonder of the simple awareness of his presence, the sense of Heaven in the marrow of their bones, of miracle beating in their hearts.

The streets had a new and lyrical air. Scarlet geraniums flamed from green window boxes. Canaries were more yellow and sang more shrilly, front door steps were whitened. The skies above the crooked chimney pots were bluer, with the soft liquid blue of a child's eyes smiling through tears. Washing hung across the houses like a flutter of pennons. Snatches of laughter and of singing came through open doors and windows.

Fr. O'Grady found himself quoting from the Apocalypse. "And God shall wipe away all tears from their eyes and there shall be no more death, neither sorrow, nor crying, neither shall there be any more pain, for the former things are passed away."

"All the same," he added, "that's not quite applicable. There certainly will be sorrow and weeping and pain and death, for we haven't done with sin by a long way yet, or with its consequences, and as long as there is sin there will be sorrow, and there will be the Passion of Our Lord Jesus Christ going on in men."

But Father Malone had sent a blessing on his people's sorrows, as if he had poured a bucket of light over them.

From house to house went Fr. O'Grady, listening to the

same litany of troubles, the aches and pains of rheumatism, the damp seeping into the walls, the swarms of rats, the way the landlord wouldn't repair the roof (God have mercy on the black hearted devil), the long wait at the Labour Exchange, the hardness of the Means Test, the children who had to be hidden when the inspectors came, the new flats with hot water laid on where you mayn't have children or dogs or cats, so no one can live in them. There were the mothers who were always hard at it, who hadn't sat down all day, and the mothers who had been taken off suddenly to hospital for an operation, there were the daughters who stayed out all hours, and the daughters who were not allowed to bring their young men home. There were the sons who couldn't get work, and the sons who wouldn't get up in the morning, and the sons who were morose and sulky at home, though as charming as you like everywhere else. There were the fathers who were on strike, the fathers who were worn out, the fathers who spent their money in the public house instead of bringing it home on Saturday night. There were ankles that swelled, hands that chapped, backs that ached, and so it went on and on and on. The same interminable litany of unholy poverty that had been poured into Fr. O'Grady's ears day after day, week after week, for years. But now, though the same hardships prevailed, a change had come about. Everything shone in a new light, as if the sun had come out on a heap of rubble and where before there had only been rusty tin cans, dry bones, and broken glass, now there was silver, ivory and crystal and, forcing its way up through the dust and the rubbish, triumphant in loveliness, a flowering weed lifted a pure and shadowless face to the sun.

Everyone hoped, every workless boy knew that there was a job for him just round the corner, every boy and girl in love waited breathlessly for the miracle that would enable them to marry, every old woman felt sure that her aches and pains were a little better to-day and would be a lot better tomorrow, everyone expected a softening in the hearts of landlords and employers. Everyone's senses were wakened to wonder at the loveliness they looked at, listened to, touched and breathed. People saw one another and heard one another's voices for the first time.

Everyone was made new. Every mind quickened. Every heart broke into splendour like a spray of red blossoms breaking from the wood of an old black thorn.

In spite of so much joy there was a flaw, one infection that seemed to spread from tongue to tongue. The scandal about Carmel Fernandez. Not that she was the only one who had brought shame to her people. Far from it, there was young Lizzie Jones for example, who was expecting a child and would not marry the father of it, because she said that if she did, she would be like a cat with a rattling tin can tied on to its tail for the rest of her life. But Lizzie was plain and downcast, whilst Carmel was beautiful and proud. Lizzie wept noisily and confided her troubles to everyone, while Carmel was aloof and apart and would not have accepted sympathy. She moved like an Indian, delicately, like grass swaying lightly. Lizzie had been betrayed by a sailor in port, while Carmel had it in her power to betray—Solly Lee!

"Have you heard about Carmel Fernandez, Father?"

"I have heard idle talk and I do not encourage it."

"It is no idle talk that she is gone away as brazen as a

brass gong with Solly Lee. She has broken her father's heart."

"Maybe there wasn't enough love in her home."

"Her father brought her up well and hoped she would be a nun. And she a Child of Mary too!"

"We cannot know the extenuating circumstances."

"The what?"

"The things that provide excuses."

"Excuses indeed! There are no excuses, she is a proper little hussy."

"Now child, remember what Our Lord said, the harlots and sinners—"

"That's what she is all right, a harlot and sinner—"

And so it went on and on and it seemed to the priest who had baptized Carmel Fernandez and given her her first Communion, that she was like a wild bird lost in a storm, who was thrown back on to his heart as on to a rock for shelter.

To sweeten the bitter gossip he wove it through with prayer: "Have you heard about Carmel?"

"Carmel Fernandez?"

Have mercy on her, O Lord, according to your great mercy.

"She is a harlot and sinner."

"She has broken her father's heart."

If Thou, O Lord, wilt observe iniquities, Lord who shall endure it? Who shall endure it?

"She has pearls round her neck. Pearls are for tears."

The kingdom of Heaven is like unto a merchant seeking good pearls.

"She's lost to perdition, that's what she is."

Who when he had found one pearl of great price—

"She is a worthless hussy, that's what she is."

—went his way and sold all that he had and bought it.

"Pearls are for tears, she has pearls round her neck. She is painting the town red, so people say."

Tears of Christ wash her, tears of Christ, wept over Lazarus, lave her in the water of everlasting life, tears of Christ shed for Jerusalem, restore her to grace, wash her in your tears, and she shall be white, whiter than snow, though her sins are as red as scarlet, she shall be white, whiter than snow.

"Have you heard about Carmel, Carmel Fernandez, she is dressed up like a film star straight out of Hollywood."

By your seamless garment that the soldiers cast lots for, have mercy on her, on Carmel Fernandez.

"They say she smells of scent that Solly bought in Paris."

By the right spikenard, shed for your burial, have pity on Carmel, Carmel Fernandez.

There was one other subject of which everyone spoke even more willingly to-day than of the scandal of Carmel— the Novena for Willie Jewel. This too embarrassed Father O'Grady, but for quite other reasons.

There was nothing, absolutely nothing closer to his heart than the cause of Father Malone. In fact, if the plain truth must be told, he had almost anticipated the judgment of Holy Church and already beatified his old friend in his own mind.

He experienced not a little uneasiness of conscience, because he secretly gave the reverence due to a relic to Father Malone's stinking old black pipe, and he had put his disgraceful mossy hat, and his boots with the turned-up toes, and holes in the soles, away into a locked cupboard for the veneration of posterity.

But it so happened that he had a letter in his pocket from the Archbishop's secretary warning him, though in the most courteous terms imaginable, to go easy with his saint, to observe every possible caution, constantly reminding himself that "Prudence is the Queen of virtues." To allow nothing which could possibly be interpreted as public prayer, to watch for the least symptom of hysteria, and, in general, to remember that the longer a saint is allowed to settle in the grave the less troublesome he is likely to be. He was also advised that owing to somewhat disquieting reports that had reached the ears of His Grace, it would be wise to approach Mr. Solomon Lee tactfully, on the subject of haloes. Fr. O'Grady had already considered tackling Solly on this subject, partly because of the increasing annoyance of his mass production of nimbuses, and partly because his lamb that was lost, Carmel Fernandez, was lost in Solly's lush and heady pastures, to which therefore, he wanted, in his role of shepherd, to find a way in.

Every mantelpiece exhibited one of Solly's holy cards and each was less like the original than the last. That in Magdalena Hogg's living room was, or at least he hoped it was, as far as even Solly could go.

In this one, although the hair which curled repulsively on the shoulders was white, the face was smooth and girlish, a uniformly salmon pink, like the face of a pale City clerk in the first phase of sea-side sunburn on a bank holiday. The hands which were the heart-shaped, tapering hands of an old lady of the Victorian convention, clasped a sheaf of wax-like lilies. The background was a foaming heap of white meringue framed by sugar-pink garlands of roses, and, most offensive of all to Father O'Grady's troubled eyes, was the enormous halo, which had now developed from a tentative, hair-like ring, to a solid plate of glory, shaded from deep orange vermilion to saffron, and resembling an illuminated poached egg.

He felt that with the letter from the Archbishop's house metaphorically biting him in his pocket he ought to start protesting. But Magdalena drowned his first hesitating words in a flood of hospitality. "Now, Father, a cup of tea. I know you are dying for it. The Irishman never lived that was not, and Hogg always said to me, 'Meg', he said, 'no one can make a cup of tea like the cup you can make, yours is *tea*.'" And with a proud flourish she poured out a bitter black brew that was stewing on the hob.

It was the priest's sixth call and so his twelfth cup of tea, his stomach revolted, in violent conflict with his charity. He fixed his eyes on the portrait of the late Hogg, a huge enlargement of a small indistinct snapshot so vague in the enlargement that it looked like a spirit picture of an ectoplasm. "Accept, O Lord," he said inwardly, "this horrible cup of tea, for the holy souls in Purgatory and in particular for Hogg."

"You will surely be joining in the Novena with us, Father—the Novena for Fr. Malone's first-class miracle."

"I hope you all understand, Magdalena, that the Novena is only a private affair. I couldn't allow it at all, were it not that Holy Church allows us to pray both to saints in Heaven and souls in Purgatory, so that we are not really presuming anything about *where* Father Malone is."

"I don't know so much about that, Father. Now Hogg's in Purgatory and you might as well pray to the leg of the table as to him. God rest his soul. Not that he was much good on this earth, come to that, but he never could answer a prayer, not even for one of his own orphans. But no sooner did I ask Fr. Malone to create a new heart in young Clem, than the lad changed so much for the better that I thought he was sickening for something, and I got that worried about him that I had to ask Fr. Malone to make him himself again."

"And did he?"

"He did indeed, and a nice trouble he has been to me ever since—and do you know, Father, Mrs. Murphy thought her son was lost at sea, and hardly was the prayer to Father Malone out of her mouth, when he came round the corner whistling, with a parrot in a cage as a present for her. And then there is old Mrs. Greenthorn in the workhouse, she didn't ask for anything, for she is too old to enjoy anything if she got it, and all those she loved are dead and gone long ago, she has outlived her children, every one of them; but she just told Father Malone it was mighty lonely sitting on a bench in a row of other old women, waiting for death to come, and ever since, she says, he comes to visit her, and he is sitting there beside her, comforting her, and telling her it's just the easiest thing in the world to die when your time comes, and as sweet as the morning of First Communion."

And so it went on, as he went from house to house, everyone had a story of blessedness to tell. The more he heard of them all, the more did Fr. O'Grady caution and warn as he conceived it his duty to do, but the more, too, did his own heart glow within him.

It was as if when Father Malone went to Heaven he forgot to shut the door behind him, or perhaps deliberately did not shut it, so that now between Heaven and Riverside a door stood wide open letting the light of glory stream through it, showing a patch of the celestial blue to whoever chose to lift his eyes and look.

⁀

For fifty years on earth Father Malone had worked to open that door, and now at last he had done it by going through it.

CHAPTER 5

A SON IS BORN

*Their angels always see the
face of their Father.*

The last call of the afternoon was to the Jewels. It was after five when Fr. O'Grady reached them and Art Jewel was home from work, sitting on the steps with Willie in his arms and Martha beside him. They were sitting very still, and for a moment they reminded the priest of a Christmas card that he had received that year, a woodcut by a contemporary artist, showing the Holy Family in modern clothes. Fr. O'Grady had been very suspicious of it, as indeed he was of all contemporary art, but now he reflected that after all perhaps it was not so absurd as he had thought at the time, since undoubtedly the Jewels were like it.

Art was a great big man, with broad shoulders and muscles like thongs of leather. His hair was dark and thick, and fell over his forehead in broad locks, his skin hard and brown. He had a strong flavour of the gipsy about him; indeed, many people said that there was gipsy blood somewhere in the Jewel family. But the same thing could have been said about Martha if looks were an indication. She too was dark and large and handsome. Her face, carved out in magnificent planes, might have grown hard had not Willie compelled her by his helplessness to be for ever the mother of a little baby.

All her life Martha had been a fighter. First of all she had had to fight for her own survival, and then, during the early years of her married life, for Art's. He was a man without roots, he could hold no job, he could keep no home. With a wife so much stronger than himself, his sense of responsibility was undeveloped. There was no objective in his life strong enough to drive his will. He was like a beautiful ship lying idly in harbour, its crowding sails empty, with no wind to fill them, and to carry the vessel out to sea.

He was sympathetic to a fault, and being very lazy, and a good listener, he was loved to his undoing. He would sit in the doorways for hours, listening to old women's complaints, or on the docks, happy as a cat in the sunlight, listening to the yarns of sailors from foreign parts.

Everyone with a trouble to lament, or a story to tell could rely upon Art to be at hand to listen. It was only when it came to settling down to a trade, that he became elusive. Indeed, he had never learned a trade. His people put him as apprentice to one after another, but when he found out the huge demand a man must answer if he is to acquire skill, Art was missing. Later, when, one after another, he had forsaken every possible occupation, he took himself to the docks, simply as a labourer loading and unloading freight. He managed to be dismissed by one company after another. Everyone wanted to employ him for he was immensely strong and immensely popular, but no one *could* employ him, for when he was most wanted he was not there.

Martha married him with her eyes wide open to his faults, and their life became one of wandering from one poor room to another. No sooner did they settle, than Art defaulted with the rent. He was always open about it and often enough landladies asked them to stay on another week and see if the tide turned. But Martha knew how swiftly the tides ran on to yet more bitter poverty when Art was in his idle moods, and they moved on.

Any woman but Martha would have left him, or, to save her own humiliation, would have gone to work and kept them both. In the first event Art would either have become one of those who drift from doss-house to doss-house, in the other event he would have become an abject hen-pecked husband, for before Willie was born, Martha's nerves were beginning to wear thin, and the very persistency of her character might have made her a nagger.

But Martha loved Art and she loved him more than herself—more (which is much, indeed, for a woman) than her own vanity. Every time he lost a job she urged him to go out after another. When they were without a meal and without a penny in their pockets, she would not borrow, or let him borrow, she went hungry and made him go hungry. When they could not pay the rent she pawned their clothes—if they had any that would pawn. If it was winter and she had to pawn their coats, she pawned them and they went cold. Moreover, Martha prayed. She made Art pray and she prayed herself, she prayed literally without ceasing: She was like the man in the parable who woke his neighbour in the night to ask for bread, and would not cease clamouring until she had it. She prayed for their necessities, necessities of body and heart and mind and soul. She prayed bravely and regally with a dauntless faith, reminding God that He promises to give, not merely a pittance, a crust, and a drab coat, but whatever He, the maker and searcher and lover of the heart, knows to be the real need of every individual, whether it be a cottage or a castle or a whitewashed cell, whether it be wealth or poverty, pleasure or pain, a crown of gold or a crown of thorns, whether it be the habit of a monk or a garment iridescent as the lilies of the field.

She prayed the prayer of importunity, she prayed the prayer of desperation and exasperation, she prayed the prayer of obsession, never knowing how it could possibly be answered, and when the answer came, she did not at first recognize it. Who would have? For the answer was a little child, born when she was past thirty, when Art was out of work, and born with a rare and obscure disease of the bones, which made him a helpless and incurable cripple.

The effect on Art was a miracle, and it happened with the suddenness of miracle, in the hospital on the night of Willie's birth.

For the first time in his life he realized himself to be a man. It amazed him that *he* had brought life into the world, he who had never achieved anything, whose psychological discouragement had been so complete that he had accepted himself as a poor thing, unworthy of Martha, unworthy of the air that he breathed.

He had brought *life* into the world. Suddenly he realized that an immense reverence for life had always been dormant in him, that is why he had sometimes stood gazing like a girl at barrows of flowers, why he had nursed lost kittens under his coat and taken them home to Martha on cold nights, why the flight of a bird made him catch his breath, and why he had stood sometimes for half an hour at a time just looking at the first pricking of green on the stunted black tree in the children's play park.

To others the most apparent thing about Willie Jewel was his weakness, he had no power in his back or limbs, as he grew he had to be propped up to sit, he never learnt to talk coherently and he had tragic little helpless hands.

Art saw in him the astonishing power, the tenacity of life itself.

He was born at what is perhaps the most depressing hour for onlookers in any hospital, half past six on a winter evening, a time when the perpetually hungry nurses were all thinking with emotion of the beetroot and cold sausages for supper, and the sweet, sickly cocoa after it.

The white shiny walls, the faint smell of anaesthetic, the hard uniform light of the electric lighting, all took away from any feeling of romance in this stupendous thing, a new life coming into the world.

Art was aware of his complete unimportance when, as the father, he was told to sit on a bench in a passage and wait. The nurses passing up and down, thinking of cold sausages, beetroot and cocoa, did not even glance at him, excepting for one who several times brought him a different form to fill up. He had no idea what was on these forms, and he was too nervous to read them, but he put whatever the nurse told him to and signed them. On some of these visits the nurse said,

"We won't be long now, Mr. Jewel," as if she was talking to herself, and Art was surprised that she knew his name. Then suddenly he became the centre of attention, and tragically important.

The nurse hurried towards him and he stood up, feeling sure it was over, that he was a father, though he had felt none of the things which other fathers had warned him about. Some had declared that they themselves suffered the pains of childbirth, or at the very least, a mystical toothache. All went through agonies of suspense, but so far Art had only felt foolish. He held out his hand expecting a form. Surely he would have to fill in a form saying that a child had been born to him? But no, to his amazement, the nurse took his outstretched hand and led him to a room where Dr. Moncrieff was waiting for him.

"Good evening, Mr. Jewel," he said. "I have very bad news for you—"

"It's dead," said Art dully.

"No. But we have to choose between saving the child's life, or your wife's. Your wife is very exhausted, but she wishes to see you before you give your decision. Will you come at once, please?"

Martha did not look exhausted and dying in Art's eyes. Her cheeks were deep pink, like rambler roses, and her eyes burned.

She seized Art's hand and he noticed that hers was very hot, with the texture of a withered leaf, and felt quite unfamiliar.

Just outside the door Art had said, "Does *she know* I've got to choose? I mean, have you told her?"

"No. She told me. She knew."

He heard Martha's voice, as unfamiliar as the touch of her hand, like the voice of a stranger: "Choose the child, Art. You've got to, the Church says so."

The whole thing seemed quite unreal. Art turned to the doctor. "The child," he said and he felt as if he was being strangled. His whole being was crying out, "Martha!"

The nurse and the doctor glanced at one another. In their view they had been told to murder a woman. They felt utter contempt for the weak thing who had given the order.

"That's religion for you," Dr. Moncrieff whispered to the nurse; then he looked up and saw Martha Jewel's burning eyes fixed on him. He never forgot those eyes, like black stars that scorched his soul.

He fought for that infant, and he fought for the woman with that terrible flame in her eyes, and she fought for herself. Art, too, was fighting at last.

Martha lived. When at last Willie was born, Dr. Moncrieff hoped that he would die, and hinted that it would be a mercy. This was not within Art's hearing but there was a terrible moment in which he thought that there was an unspoken agreement between them to let his child die. People had told him of such things.

They had put Art's misshapen infant into his own hands to hold, and he felt sure that they would not have done that if they meant him to live. It was only for a moment, however, and then the nurse took him. That was a black, agonized moment for Art Jewel. In it something fierce and primitive awoke in him which never died. He desired his son's life as a thirsting man desires water.

And that son's life was a tiny atom, a spark against which the whole force of what we call civilization, conspired, the whole force of it, past, present, and future. Out of the past, a towering mass of evil cast long shadows across him—the greed, the selfishness, the cruelty, the lust, the infidelities of generations of human beings. A multitudinous procession of murder and innocence cast its fire and shadow on the wizened little face, as on the face of all children born into our world.

First of all, as if they swept past the Christ Child sleeping in the stone manger, the flock of Holy Innocents with jubilant cries like wild birds migrating, wild birds winging to the sun of eternal light, the first martyrs, baptized only with the baptism of blood, with crimson stars tangled in their burning hair. After them, all through the ages, came the martyrs whose death and resurrection seem the inevitable co-incidence of Christ's birth, of the birth of life into the valley of the shadow of death. And always dark on the burning brilliance of martyrdom, the shadow of murder, of the sevenfold evil that is death in man's heart fighting against life.

The shadow of Herod's swung sword: the shadow of Tyburn tree; of man's hand black over the golden pyx in the act of sacrilege, desecrating the body of Christ, violating the sanctuary of his own ancient faith: shadow of man's hand first striking down the Virgin Mother of God with her child of snow upon her heart. Shadow of factories growing higher than Cathedrals. Of tall chimneys, encircling towns that fall into slums. Shadow of cities growing larger and larger, and obliterating the cottages that once were homes. Shadow of machines stretching up nearly to the stars, nearly to the star of Bethlehem. And where before, in this procession, there had been the Holy Innocents, flashing through the arch of Herod's swords, there was now a multitude of wizened, twisted children, with no gateway even of swords to go through, moving slowly, mechanically, blindly, through a bewildering labyrinth of shadows of machines, like a shot in a modern film of Frankenstein horror. From the beautiful swift bodies of the first little martyrs in their swallow flight to the sun, the bodies of children had changed to bowed grotesque gnomes.

Death had ceased to be swift and clean like a flash of silver, as evil murder itself had ceased to be open and instantaneous, but an evil of crimson and steel. Now it had become something so furtive that it hid, not only from its victims, but from itself, covering its face with a mask of benignity, its stench with cheap scent so that at length it could look into the mirror unabashed—whether it looked into the mirror of the heavy overmantel of an Edwardian drawing-room and saw itself masked in the expensive mask of complacency, or whether it stared back from the dingy mirrors of tawdry seaside hotels and saw itself in the mask of cheap vanity that has frittered away the power to love by lust.

Shadows of swords and fists, of chimneys and machines. Shadow of fear, of murder grown timid, grown sentimental and righteous, disguised and hidden, until at last evil is seen only as a projected thing, projected on the bodies of the innocents to cry to Heaven for vengeance, as the death wounds of the first born of Bethlehem cried out in scarlet.

And all the time against this weight of death, life fought and prevailed, from generation to generation, because love is stronger than death, and love and life are the seal and sign of God in man. And the battle was fought all through the centuries by those who dared to love. By the boys and girls who faced the immense ardours and endurances of purity, who wrestled with their own flesh and blood and would not fritter away the capacity for passion, who dared to suffer the withering thirst of heart and mind, body and soul, that they might ultimately drink the water of life from the source, who defied misery, oppression and tyranny, whom the machines could not crush, and the wheels could not grind, who were not overcome by poverty, by hunger and cold, who were not afraid of hard work, who were not abject before the herd, who in the multitude remained themselves, two who could carry the world's burden and stand upright and say, "I love." Who in the midst of death, gave life from generation to generation, in a kiss.

There is a likeness, even in outward things, between the unconquerable life in broken humanity, and that in Christ's Body. For sin tried to batter life out of the innocent Son of God just as it tries to batter it out of the world, taking that perfection, that flawless beauty and scourging it and driving it with thorns and spears, bruising it, overloading it, bending it double under the load, pushing it down in the dust and spitting on it and crucifying it, just as it has done to the bodies of innocence ever since. Pitting itself against love, against the likeness of God in the heart of man. Crying out, against the primal instincts that waken like dawn even in a twisted humanity, that life must be extinguished in the forms that evil has forced upon it, because man must not be asked to look upon what he has done. Yet it is in the poorest, the weakest, the frailest, that life triumphs, for when sin had disfigured even the immaculate body of Christ beyond recognition—so that it was said, even of Him, He has no comeliness whereby He shall be known—it was in that same Body, no other, that He rose. In that same Body, with those same wounds, that the risen life began.

Neither the procession of evil and love through the centuries nor the awareness of that shining Body of ultimate suffering and ultimate love, rising again and again from the tomb of the human heart, came in words or pictures or in any conscious thought to Art Jewel. But obscurely they were there: and they welled up in immense love for this little deformed creature whom the doctor thought better dead, and in wonder at the power of life, that could fight against the whole world and all its evil, and prevail in such weakness, such defencelessness, and such helplessness as this.

Prevail it did. Art watched the first physical struggle for survival in that tiny creature, he saw it twitch and try in vain to thrust with its powerless clenched fists. He saw it wrestling visibly for a breath, a heartbeat, a world, a life, an immortal destiny, an eternal Heaven, the vision of God—and it won. Art Jewel knew that it was his own life that won.

The child suffered. A new experience came to Art, an experience that grew in him all through the years of Willie's life.

He saw his own eyes looking at him from the face of his dumb child, not with reproach for his life, but with love; he saw in those eyes the terrifying joy of innocence crucified. And Art Jewel, being made in the image and likeness of God, learnt something of the secret of the Eternal Father, when His Only Son looked at Him from the Cross.

The miracle which took place on the night of Willie's birthday was lasting. Art went to work, loading and unloading freight from ships. He was not trained for anything else and his broad back and strong arms fitted him for that. He was there regularly, early in the morning and often enough working overtime in the evening. At first the employers were sceptical, then they learnt to trust him, and finally to rely on him.

There are two kinds of poverty, the holy and the unholy. The unholy is like damp rot, it is the poverty that men should not accept. It is forced upon them by evil and injustice. Everything that it touches rots and decays. It is verminous and dirty, it breeds bitterness, fear, and hatred, it is the misery generated into the world by the union of fear and greed.

The other, Holy Poverty, is different. It is the poverty that flowers in frugality, it teaches men the glory of working for those whom they love and lifts their minds to contemplation, they discover in it God's Fatherhood. This poverty does not ask for rest, it possesses peace. It is content with necessity. It has the vision which enables the heart to discern between the essential and the unessential. It has the humility which makes it invulnerable, the freedom which goes with having nothing, the gratitude that goes with having everything. It is Poverty made lovely because Christ has taken it to His immaculate heart.

For seven years the Jewels had kept a home, and it was blessed with this holy poverty. Art had to work hard for money, sometimes, even now, he had to struggle with himself to go on working hard and regularly for it. But he won. For money was no longer connected in his mind only with torturing anxiety and sordid scenes. It was food and drink, and warmth and sleep for their little son.

Their one room became beautiful. Willie loved bright colours and glittering sounds, Art painted what furniture they had, a lot of it made out of packing cases. He rubbed these pieces down, smoothed them and painted them blue. He framed some bright prints out of books and hung them on the walls.

Martha made curtains of flowered cotton, and a patchwork quilt for the bed, and on Willie's first birthday, they bought him a glass chime that hung in the window and tinkled whenever a breeze came up from the river.

CHAPTER 6

SET IN THE MIDST
OF THEM

And Jesus calling unto
him a little child, set him
in the midst of them.

The sun was going down when Father O'Grady reached the Jewels', and in the warm light the man and woman looked as if they were made of bronze. But Willie, even in this light, was a child of ivory.

He was as fair as his parents were dark, and his fairness, with its contrast to his own flesh and blood, added to the unspoken and perhaps unrealized impression among the people that there was something supernatural about the child. An innocent, who is visibly destined to die young, could not fail to have a certain radiance for people of simple faith. A little creature shining as purely from the waters of Baptism as on the day when they were first poured on him, and soon to be in the blue fields of Heaven. But when, as in Willie's case, such a little creature also suffers, and suffers with a smile on his face, then indeed it is hard to measure the awe, the sense of mystery, with which poor people approach him.

For those without the means that riches give for hiding, drugging, and disguising sorrow, or the ways that more sophisticated people have of finding at least temporary escape from its realization within themselves, suffering is not in itself a thing to be dreaded, as it is dreaded by those who imagine themselves to be more fortunate.

To those who have always been, and have had to be, on intimate terms with it, who know it as a friend is known, who have lived side by side with it and dared to look into its eyes, suffering is not the dread that it is to those who have never had the courage or perhaps the opportunity to accept it, unreservedly, as a fact which cannot ultimately be denied or mitigated.

The poor do not see it as only misfortune, certainly not as the supreme misfortune, but as a mysterious title to honour. Those who suffer always are the aristocracy of the poor. So Willie Jewel was unique in the love and reverence of the people of Riverside. Not indeed that they wanted to see a child suffer, but they did want to be constantly easing his suffering, bringing him their gifts, seeing his sudden radiant smile, and a flush of pink on his white face. They came to him as simply as the shepherds did to the Child in the manger: not exactly glad that their God shivered in human flesh and lacked all things, yet glad that, since He chose to need, He needed the gifts that *they* had to give: since He chose to shiver, He shivered beside *their* pastures and they with Him; since He chose nakedness, He chose to be covered by the wool of their lambs.

The impression that Willie gave was of joy and of sweetness, he had more delight in a primrose brought to him by Rose O'Shane than many a healthy son of a rich man has in a fairy cycle or his first pony.

It was natural and loving—not as it seemed to outsiders, unnatural and callous—that the people should pray to old Father Malone, not for a changed Willie, who would be one of the countless other tough little boys, who joined the wolf cubs for free buns and annual outings, but the unique, mysterious, and lovely Willie Jewel.

Fr. O'Grady saw at once as he came up to them that the child was very ill. He was six years old now, but smaller than a child of five. His face was old in spite of its simpleness, old and grave and very sweet, like the face of a Bambino in an Italian Primitive.

He was sleeping and Martha put a finger to her lips, and rising greeted the priest in a whisper. He sat down on the step beside her and they spoke in low voices.

"Is he worse, Martha?"

"Yes, they want him to go into Hospital, but we won't let him. He is better with us, we understand him better than nurses and doctors."

"Tomorrow," Art said, "the Novena starts. Everyone is joining in, even some of the Protestants."

"You know, don't you, that sorry though I am, I cannot allow public prayers to Father Malone in Church?"

"I know, Father, but that's all right. We shall all start together at six o'clock, some at home—and if some are just paying a visit to the Blessed Sacrament, no one would forbid that."

"No indeed, or want to."

Willie stirred and opened his eyes, when he saw the priest he smiled and then looked past him and smiled again at Rose O'Shane who was coming down the street. She had an iced cake in a bag for Willie, a cake shaped like a heart with a hard pink icing.

"Is he allowed to eat cake?" asked Fr. O'Grady.

Martha nodded, "The doctor says, just give him anything at all that he likes."

"Dr. Moncrieff is very devoted to him."

"So devoted," said Art, with sudden bitterness, "that he thinks it sinful of us to have the Novena. Yes, Father O'Grady, he told *me*, the child's father, that he would be better dead, and mark you he doesn't believe in anything after this life."

"He is a poor man without Faith," said Rose, and her voice was as soft and warm as the falling of summer rain. "He can see nothing at all to live for if you have not the use of your limbs. But he is the more to be pitied for that, poor thing."

"Yes, and he doesn't really mean the hard things that he says, Art," said Martha, "though they hurt just the same. It is because his whole life is lived for curing, and trying to make people strong, and he sees how happy some are when they are better, and has no idea at all of the joy that there *can* be in suffering. He has been very good to Willie and done all any man could do for him, and he just can't bear to see him in pain."

"Ought we not to be careful what we say?" said the priest and he glanced towards the child.

Art smiled. "He understands," he said. "But you don't

need to worry, Father. Willie isn't a bit afraid of dying, and he knows that we are all going to Heaven soon if we are good. It doesn't worry him any more than another child would worry if he knew that he was going to the seaside."

"I think," said Martha, "that dying will just be Willie's First Communion."

But they were drawn away from the subject nevertheless by a young seaman who was coming down the street with a little monkey sitting on his shoulder.

"Ah, Bless him!" said Martha. "This is Jim Smith. He comes every night to show Willie the monkey. It is good of the lad, he brought the monkey home from foreign parts, for Willie, but I couldn't do with it in our room, so Jim brings it to see him every night instead. He is joining in the Novena too, although he is not a Catholic, and he did not know anything about prayer until Rose here explained about the Novena and asked him to join in."

Jim Smith knelt down, as if, Protestant or no Protestant, Willie was holy in his eyes, and Willie made strange little sounds of joy, rather like those that the monkey made himself. "Have you ever heard anything like it?" said Jim, "he is talking monkey talk to him! Why even sailors that have been to Africa can't talk monkey!" And he took Willie's hands that were as soft and helpless as the petals of white roses and stroked the monkey's little round brown head with them.

Presently others joined them, factory girls with thin young bodies like hairpins, dressed as much like Greta Garbo as, a few skimpy pieces of material, third-hand finery, cheap cosmetics and consummate artistry could make them.

They walked with the slinkiest walks and drawled with

the huskiest drawls that they could achieve, but the kindness on their small sharp, painted faces was a lovely thing to see, and Willie loved them just as they were, he loved the gaudy colours that they wore, and the brightness that they brought into the street, as if a flock of coloured butterflies had suddenly invaded it.

They all had gifts for Willie, and Martha rebuked them. "Father," she said, "every day they are bringing Willie things and I tell them they should take their money home to their mums, if they have no use for it themselves."

A wild chatter of protest broke out, "But it is only a painted button they gave me at work—it is nothing but the sweets we are allowed as perks—it is only one of the artificial flowers we make ..."

"That may be," said Art, whose whole face beamed proud gratitude to them. "But you will be spoiling Willie, all of you."

"They couldn't do that," said Rose O'Shane. "God made him as he is so that he couldn't be spoilt."

They were silent and then they began talking about the Novena, and Father Malone, and as they talked it seemed as if the old priest was very close, sitting among them, smiling; as if his shadow must be hidden among their shadows that were lying dark on the pavement in the last glow of the sunset.

"Do you think," said Jim Smith, "that a Catholic priest would answer a Protestant's prayer?"

"Of course he would," said Father O'Grady, and he got up to go.

When he got to the corner of the street he turned to wave to them. He thought again of Bethlehem. There was just something about the way they were grouped around the child, drawn inwards to him, concentrated upon him, and he the white immaculate centre. Something about the reverence of the kneeling sailor, the curve of his back, his bowed dark head, something in that whole group on the steps reminiscent of the first simple people, discovering God's secret that the Word was made flesh. But perhaps, more than in all that, the reminder of the Incarnation was in the way that his parents seemed to be showing him, *giving* him to the people, that his weakness might be their strength in a selfless love.

"Ah! Patrick Malone," said Father O'Grady, and he looked towards the last golden rent in the blue sky, as if he could speak through it to Heaven. "Patrick Malone, grant our petition, let the child stay with us to teach us to love one another."

CHAPTER 7

THE PRESBYTERY

Here you have no abiding
resting place.

On the first day of the Novena, Willie Jewel became critically ill, an acute attack of pain racked his bones and when it had passed he lay still in his bed, too exhausted even to open his eyes. This did not in any way discourage the Faithful, on the contrary they declared that it might well be an arranged thing to show up the Glory of God. After all look at Lazarus, he was allowed to get to the point of stinking to make the whole thing more convincing and glorious.

On the same day, and oddly enough at the very moment arranged for the opening of the Novena, Father Perivale arrived on the doorstep of the presbytery and rang the bell. He had come as special preacher for Sunday morning, and at the suggestion of Monsignor Frayne had arranged to sleep the night in Riverside, acting as a kind of self-appointed spy for a Devil's Advocate to be.

The Archbishop seemed to have done nothing. He might

possibly have given Fr. O'Grady a mild warning, but if he had, it was *too* mild, for rumours of Father Malone's alleged sanctity were increasing every day. Miracles, which were not really miracles at all, were feeding the popular sentiment as rain feeds fungus.

It seemed that the child, who was known in Monsignor Frayne's circle as "Father Malone's victim," was coming in for a kind of secondary veneration himself, without having even enough grace to be dead.

Indeed there was already this first result of the devotion to Father Malone, which, whether he worked the miracle or whether he did not, could not now be stopped. The attention focussed on Willie Jewel.

Riverside, like every other slum, was full of ailing children, but now, all because of the cult of Father Malone one of them was singled out, and pointed at, as if the suffering of children was to be set up before the world for contemplation. It was almost as if there was a conspiracy between the old priest in Heaven and the young child on earth to make mock of the wisdom of the world.

On the stroke of six Father Perivale rang the bell of the Presbytery. At precisely the same moment all the Catholics and a large percentage of the Protestants in the Parish went down on their knees and started the Novena. Among them Jenny Doolan, Father O'Grady's housekeeper and Tim Hoolihan, his man of all work.

Jenny was cooking when the hour struck, and like many another woman, planked down on to her knees still holding the saucepan in her hand. Had Father Perivale been able to see through the walls and roofs, he might have supposed himself suddenly translated to the lost city of Pompeii at the tragic moment when its citizens became static, only this would be a less tragic Pompeii, for everyone would be prepared for death, and taken in the very act of prayer.

Willie Jewel himself lay motionless on his bed, Father O'Grady, Art and Martha Jewel kneeling beside him. In all the houses around, radiating from the child's bed, life stood still for a moment in prayer. Women like Jenny Doolan knelt with saucepans and kettles in their hands, mothers knelt by the children they were bathing, and the children knelt up in their baths and folded their hands. Men home from work knelt down by their comfortable chairs, or put down their cups of tea and knelt down by the kitchen table. Men knelt down by their spades in their patches of garden, pulled up their lorries and folded their hands on their steering wheels, dockers unloading the ships' cargoes put down the great cases from their backs and knelt by them as if they were altars.

Boys and girls kissing by the dust bins knelt on the pavement in their hiding places, and prayed with their faces on one another's shoulders. People closed their eyes and clasped their hands in the cinemas, a few defiant old ladies, feeling really wicked for the first time in their lives prayed before the Blessed Sacrament in Church.

People of all ages and shapes and sizes, of all trades and races and colours prayed for Willie Jewel, Negroes with eyes as black as damsons and souls as simple as primroses, gentle golden-faced Goans, Chinamen, Japanese and Mulattoes, and a multitude of Irishmen. Red-haired Irishmen and blackhaired Irishmen and sandy Scots prayed for Willie Jewel. Dark-haired, dark-skinned evasive Welshmen prayed for him. English sailors with hair bleached the colour of straw and flaming red patches of sunburn on their necks and noses, old men with rosy wrinkled cheeks prayed for him.

Old men and women in the workhouse, who could not go down on their knees any more, folded gnarled hands like the roots of trees on their laps, people lying flat on their backs in hospital lifted stiff hands and folded them painfully on their breasts, people in prison knelt down in their cells and prayed for Willie Jewel.

They prayed with fervour that measured the struggle of their own souls for life, strong as green shoots, cutting their way up out of the hard dark earth, forcing a way to the light, driven by sap that had drawn its power from an unseen sun in an unknown Heaven.

They were praying for Willie Jewel, but they were praying, too, that Father Malone would prove himself their saint, that the door he had opened in Heaven would not be slammed in their faces and that the light of glory that shone in their hearts would not be put out.

When Father Perivale rang the bell he did not expect it to be answered, for he knew that Presbytery bells do not ring excepting in the case of urgent sick calls, when they are rung furiously by the holy souls in Purgatory.

As a matter of church etiquette he rang two or three more times and finally gave a timid knock and squared his shoulders to face whatever the result of it might be. For he knew well that those who open the doors of holy houses are often a race apart, chosen, one must suppose, rather for their unsuitability than for any other qualification, unless they are chosen not by man at all, but by God to test the faith of the callers.

Tim Hoolihan was no exception, indeed he was known to the Riverside clergy as "the Test of Faith," for they agreed that any convert who got past him had Faith indeed. No one ever knew for certain if he was half-witted or uncannily shrewd. But everyone knew that he suffered from adenoids. His mouth was always open, he always blinked. He had a very small head and an infantile face on top of an enormous body. His huge size, far from giving an impression of power, gave an impression of helplessness that was dangerous because he was so big, like a bus without brakes or an elephant on roller skates. His speech had a swooping, diving quality which veered up and down, from a sound as contradictory as a roaring falsetto to a rushing husky whisper.

The "Test of Faith" it was who flung open the door to Father Perivale's discreet knock. He had already reached the door when the Angelus rang out the signal for the Novena. He was kneeling against it, while Fr. Perivale was ringing and knocking on the other side, consequently not even the sound of his approaching footsteps warned the caller.

Tim Hoolihan, who expected Father Perivale, indicated by hisses and gestures that he was to go into the parlour and wait. This suited the young priest very well for to tell the truth he had for some days now felt a growing attraction to Father Malone himself and was no longer certain whether he hoped that his investigations would increase his devotion or his suspicion. At all events, he thought that he might learn something of the troublesome old saint's character from his environment. But only two things could be certainly learnt from a tour of the presbytery, one that it was still exactly as it was when Father Malone took over, fifty years ago, and the other that he had neither attempted to lay up treasure for himself on earth, or to disperse the rubbish which lays itself up.

The Riverside priests might well have put over their front door "Here we have no abiding resting place," for the presbytery was like a railway station on a neglected siding, which was nevertheless a junction for Eternity, where travellers who had lost the way could get back on to the main line for Heaven.

The parlour was a dark dingy room looking on to the street and over the well of the area. On winter evenings the street light just outside the window gave it a wan yellow light of a curiously depressing quality, which must surely have increased many a slight uneasiness of conscience to overwhelming anguish. The mantelshelf was edged with a frill of scallopped leather, and over it hung an immense framed print of Pope Leo XIII looking very ill. All round him, like satellites round their guiding star, were long dead priests of the parish painfully reminiscent of stuffed birds.

Facing the Pope from the opposite wall, with a smile of almost brazen piety, considering the obvious licentiousness of her torturers, was a Virgin Martyr of the first century, who like many a film star of our own days had already been through fire and water without disarranging a single strand of her permanently waved hair.

So much for the walls. The floor space of the parlour was crowded with furniture which seemed in each case to be there rather to defeat than to achieve its own purpose. Along one wall, a row of straight, hard chairs, eminently unsuited to a room frequently used for confidential talk between two people, never for meetings. There were, however, two other chairs, apparently intended for use, equally hard but more pompous, placed one on each side of a large highly polished table of ginger wood, which seemed to be intended, if it was intended for anything, as a protective barrier between the priest and his caller, or perhaps merely to support the brass-potted aspidistra which at all events could serve the useful purpose of hiding embarrassment when necessary. Beside the aspidistra was a dry ink pot and a corroded pen, lying ironically on a pen wiper. But most depressing of all was the book shelf, only half filled with books that leaned sadly together, with frequent gaps, like missing teeth in an old man's mouth. Volumes of the Catholic Directory, accumulated through the years, fraternized with the *Catholic Who's Who* of so long ago that it must surely have become the "Catholic Who Was," ex-library copies of the works of Father Faber bought from a second-hand shop, because some long dead priest was sorry for them being among so many heretical books, *Fabiola*, slumping in bulky dereliction against a rather shocked biography of an impossible French nun, *The Holy Man of Tours* standing on his head. And fierce with the pitiful pride of decayed gentry in a charity home, Burke's *Peerage* clothed still in faded splendour of scarlet and gold.

Poor, never read, never handled, unloved books, growing shabby and old and dying, not from the sweet wear and tear of friendship, but from being unused, unwanted, and forgotten.

When Father Perivale had been in the parlour for about an hour, the door suddenly opened letting in the unique presbytery smell, a composite of Irish stew, paraffin oil, pipe smoke, and oilcloth. Following the smell, came Jenny Doolan.

"Bless your heart, Father," she said. "Fr. O'Grady is out."

"I thought he might be," said Father Perivale politely.

"No doubt," said Jenny. "He is being persecuted."

"Dear me," exclaimed Father Perivale with some alarm, "I thought that Father O'Grady was greatly loved!"

"So he is, it is those that are loved that are persecuted. Killing him, that's what it is, downright wicked I call it, killing him on a Saturday too, and him the only priest sitting." She spoke, Father Perivale thought, as if she spoke of a hen. "You'll see," she went on, "he'll come in late, bolt his dinner, and before he shuts his mouth on the last bite, he'll be down in that draughty church, catching his death in the box. They'd have killed him outright but for me long ago, though I say it as shouldn't."

Father O'Grady came in stiff and tired, he had walked a good distance since he left Willie Jewel's bedside, to hear the confessions of his old bedridden parishioners, the Hospital, the Workhouse, and the Convent; but it was not the walking or the cold or the tedium that had wearied him but something else. The Novena had only just started—and yet, already something had gone out of the music. That lyrical quality of joy, almost visible, since Father Malone had left open the door into Heaven, was overshadowed, only slightly, but enough for the priest to feel it. Before, there had been an almost indescribable expression on people's faces, like the expressions on the faces of children on Feast days, a certain wonder and joyful expectation of delights, not of their own choosing but lovelier for that. Now the muscles had tightened a little. Where there had been eagerness to receive whatever joy God gave, as birds receive crumbs, and flowers receive light, now there was a specific want for a particular favour, and everyone's whole attention was concentrated on that one thing. There was no longer the awareness of every whisper and gesture of Divine Love that was already given and was being given all the time.

Now that he had come in, there was nothing that Father O'Grady would have liked better than to relax, to eat enormously of Jenny Doolan's stew, put back a couple of pints of beer, turn the gas fire full on, put on his slippers and his old coat, fill his pipe, and sink into a delicious coma.

"Lord make haste to help me!" he said, and he poured half the beer which Jenny had left to tempt him on to the aspidistra, and put half his allowance of tobacco back into the jar.

It was just in these moments when his resistance was weak that he had to do concrete things like that, things as simple but as big as a child giving his toys to his mother because he likes them so much himself, things which helped him in the way it would help a child to hold his mother's hand in a dark passage.

If he gave way an inch to nature when he was in such a mood, although there was no actual sin at all in anything that tempted him, he felt sure that he would, as he put it, go down the drain, and end up like one of those poor priests he had heard of in Catholic countries, where priests are two a penny, and sit drinking sweet red wine until they are too heavy to move off the chair, and smoking cigarettes until they are black all over from nicotine in their blood, and who, no doubt, would end in Hell, but for the great army of unknown, sweet old nuns, who having served their sentence of usefulness have come to be regarded as a little "queer," and who, though they would not so much as lift their eyes to look on those black, bloated faces, now give their whole lives to making reparation for the sins of bad priests.

Jenny came in with the dinner tray. "The young special priest from the West End has been in the parlour going on for two hours," she said.

"Heavens! I had forgotten him!—"

As Father O'Grady hurried to apologize to his guest, he said to himself, "I must offer him up," and Father Perivale was added to the black tea, the interminable scruples of the lady boarder in the convent, the obstinate rudeness of the impenitent old stoker in the Hospital, the hole in the sole of his own shoe, the half-pint of beer in the aspidistra, and the twist of tobacco in the jar.

At the dinner table, Jenny Doolan was to Father O'Grady what the devil was to the Curé d'Ars. She put salt into his stew when he wanted to offer saltless stew for the parish gluttons, and beer into his mug when he wanted to offer tepid water for the parish drunkards. One holocaust alone she could not cheat him of, she could not prevent him from offering *her* up, for all the maternal, childless parish spinsters.

Only when coffee was served, black and stinging to keep Father O'Grady awake in the Confessional, did Jenny leave them, enabling Fr. Perivale to speak of the subject uppermost in his mind.

"Is it your opinion, Father," he said, "that Fr. Malone is in Heaven?"

"It is indeed, but all the same I never would take anything at all for granted with Holy Church. Besides it would be a terrible thing if Patrick Malone was in Purgatory all the time, and not a prayer said for his soul because of us thinking him a saint—I know of a case myself, of a nun who was looked upon as a saint in her Community and not a prayer was ever said for her until one day, she appeared to a lay sister all covered in barnacles like the bottom of an old barge."

"How really frightful! But surely we may take this nun with a pinch of salt?"

"Well, you might the barnacles, but not the nun."

"Tell me, Father O'Grady, had Father Malone any Little Way of Holiness something like the Little Way of St. Teresa of Lisieux?"

"He did have lots of little ways, disconcerting some of them were, but I shouldn't think they were little ways of holiness."

"But had he no theory, no special message, so to speak, which could be preached to the modern world."

"I never heard him say anything about it—I think he just preached the same thing as Jesus Christ—love one another."

"And there was no special kind of sanctity?"

"Isn't all sanctity much the same?"

"But surely not Father! Isn't it a fact that star differeth from star in glory?"

"I suppose they do, but I must say they all look exactly alike to me. Perhaps it is simply because I have to look up to them from so far below—it's the same with the saints, I have to look up to them from a vast distance below, and living in the house with one doesn't make any difference to that, so it may be that I only see what shines brightest in them."

"And that is?" asked Father Perivale, feeling suddenly very humble.

"Oh, I suppose it is that they all have a genius for love, and they all give all they've got, so that it does not matter much what it is."

"And Father Malone left you no secret?"

Father O'Grady knocked his pipe out on the side of the fire place—"No, at least, none that we don't all share. But he did leave me a heavy burden, the sins of his people and it's time I went to hear their confessions. Will you make yourself at home, Father, until I come back."

CHAPTER 8

SATURDAY NIGHT

... and blessed is he, that
shall not be scandalized
in me.

There is something mysterious about Saturday night. It is a
night of quickening, of the heightening and raising of psychological temperatures. It is pay day, when, whether one
should spend it or not, for a few hours one has money to
spend, and for a few hours there is freedom from office, factory and shop. Whatever happens on Saturday night can be
slept off on Sunday morning. Tomorrow morning there is no
work, there is no alarm clock, no shout of "time to get up."

Tomorrow no one will be a cog in a machine, a voice in
a chorus of voices, a face in a multitude of faces, tomorrow
everyone will be himself or herself, even if only by dropping
out for a few hours.

On Saturday night the streets come alive, the routine is
broken, the tension is off, there is the chink of money, the
public houses are lit up and noisy. On week days the same

public houses are there too, but they are quieter, different, some of them have even a kind of secrecy; they are places where it is sometimes possible to get away, to be warm, to be alone; there are some down the side streets that are furtive. But on Saturday night, they are loud and light and noisy, kindly and quarrelsome. After a few drinks, feeling runs higher, human nature is more vulnerable, more defenceless, sentiment flows over and spills into indiscriminate love-making. A spark of anger blazes up suddenly into a fire that is out of hand.

The darkness on Saturday night has its own quality. It is no longer a cover laid silently over the ardours and sorrows and sweetness of the world. It hums and throbs and sings, it is splashed and fretted with light. The doors of the pubs swing open and shut, gusts of sound and light spatter the pavement, there are sudden glimpses of men and women dark upon a glow of gold, and sudden bursts of laughter or of noisy weeping. Sometimes all the darkness of the night and all its laughter and all its sobbing are gathered and swung between the pavement and the stars in the music of an accordion.

The boys and girls out of the factories walk hand in hand in the streets. They are lovely with the slender loveliness of the poor when they are young. The girls blossom in just the way of those "Japanese Flowers" that children drop into water, as a tiny round circle which immediately wriggles and puts out tendrils of yellow, vermilion, emerald and blue, that twist and writhe and sprout into fantastic little flowers.

Hair that has been in curlers all the week comes out, cheeks that were white are made pink, lips that were faint coral are scarlet.

The very young factory workers walk hand in hand through the gold fretted darkness, dreaming and shy, shaken with the glory of one another, breathless with the swift new passion of innocence on fire.

There is also intense activity in the Catholic Church. Saturday night is bath night. It is also the bath night of souls. Of course people go to Confession on all the other days and nights too. But Saturday is an accepted night, when every Catholic, everywhere in the world, knows that he will find the church buzzing with a business-like activity, that is no outward showing of the unutterable mystery that is taking place, and is often shocking to the uninitiated. No wonder, for even in its holiest acts, human nature is imperfect and there is shoving, pushing, muttering and gate crashing, even in the queues outside the Confessional. Since the Lord commands that the tares and the wheat be left growing together until His coming, you must, until that blessed day, have your viciously pious old lady, who prods her neighbour with her umbrella in Confession queues, side by side with the lowly and humble of heart who is prodded, and the penitent, who unconscious of the mote in his brother's eye, prays undisturbed and unnoticed, his whole being withdrawn into the stillness of love.

When Father O'Grady hurried into church, his penitents were already waiting for him like a hungry and impatient bread line. He had hardly time to put on his stole before the first two were in, one on each side, like two hungry birds waiting for their crumb of Heaven.

They were simple people, who understood very little about the grace that they were receiving, some of them, if they *had* understood, would have fought shy of the torrent of light that was being poured over them. Their ears were tuned to the undertones of this world, their eyes used to its grey twilights. They could not have borne the splendour of the God who came to them in this narrow box, but for the divine ingenuity of His love, which used their very blindness and deafness and denseness for His disguise and came to them clothed in their own limitations.

Father O'Grady understood his people, he knew that they were coming to be fed. Penance is sorrow for sin and forgiveness, but it is much more too. It is the Good Shepherd feeding His sheep, feeding His lambs, and a crumb of the Bread of Life is the whole of life.

He closed his eyes and murmured the first blessing. A scruffy little acolyte told the usual story on one side, a very old woman told it on the other. After them came the long line of pious women hankering after consolation, the emotionally starved hungering for a little sweetness, a little taste of sugar on the living Bread, the young men who found it so difficult to make a firm purpose of amendment and to try to avoid the dangerous occasions of sin, the boys and girls, the devout old men, the ageing children of Mary who were eager to confess their neighbour's sins as well as their own, the sailors who had met temptation under bluer skies and in lovelier guise than it is met in Riverside, the mothers who must hurry so that the fathers who were minding the children could come after them, and the children who had only lately made their First Confessions and still came quite simply to receive the embrace of their little Lord.

As time wore on, a few drifted in from the streets, who if

they were not drunk, had as the Irish say, "drink taken" and when they had said "Bless me, Father, for I have sinned," they were apt to begin to weep. Father O'Grady told them to go away and come back when they were sober, but he feared that they would not come back, and he grieved over them; for he felt that they were drifting away, but that they would always know the drag at the heart, and that wherever they went, whatever they did, whenever anything touched them, be it a glass of beer or "Star of the Sea" played on a barrel organ, they would be homesick.

Half an hour passed, an hour, an hour and a half, Father O'Grady grew stiffer and colder. He was cramped in the tiny box and could not stretch his legs, the chair was hard and straight backed. Little points of rheumatism in his shoulders and in the back of his neck, first began to ache and then to burn. His head ached too and the air ceased to be air, and became a cold fetid stuffiness.

The penitents whispered the miserable little stories of sin on breath that was rotten with garlic. The priest had to make repeated acts of Faith that the murmurs of attrition, which caused such uneasiness in the pit of his stomach, also caused the angels of God to rejoice—" But then," he thought, "Almighty God in His Providence has given them no stomachs to turn."

He leaned towards each one, offering up the discomfort, the nausea, the boredom, because he knew that in these people Christ had His will. In them, on this Saturday night, He renewed the life of the whole world, in this little box, the impact of love between God and man happened again, the world kissed the Holy wounded Feet in the dust.

The priest thanked God that it didn't matter at all, that his own soul was dry and his body aching; that it was only with an effort that he could concentrate on each confession, not letting his mind wander for a second, so that he would be obliged to ask some poor child of God to repeat something over again; that it was harder and harder as each one came to the end, to think of even the most obvious platitudes to whisper for their encouragement.

He knew that it wasn't himself that mattered, though since God chose it to be so, he had to be there, just as the clay made of earth and spittle that Christ chose to put on the blind man's eyes had to be there.

He was glad that he had the cramp, the headache, the rheumatism and the nausea, because he had nothing else to offer in co-operation with God's huge intent of love.

The Humanity of the Son of God is too big for men, it scandalises them. That He should pour the waters of life over souls on their weekly bath night, that He should renew the life of the world, not only in the inspired, the saints, the prophets, but in the maimed, the halt and the blind, in the inarticulate, the uninspired, the short-sighted, the dogged Saturday night regulars, that on the night of the sharpening of physical life, of the heightening of human emotion, with its taking hold of the heart and its sudden pang of desire, He should quicken His own life, His own Immaculate Passion of love, in the hearts of sinners.

That He the Omnipotent, the Immaculate, the Eternal, should become part of Saturday night—that is too much for the littleness of men.

Half an hour, an hour, an hour and a half, two hours. The

scuffling and bustling in the church had subsided. Now the remaining penitents were those last in the queues, who will surely be the first in the Kingdom of Heaven.

There was silence now, so that the drifts of sound from the street came in, but they sounded far away and inside there was only the inaudible whispering from the confessional, like the rustling of sleepy birds in the boughs of a great tree.

At last it was over. The last Absolution given, the last kiss on the hem of Christ's garment, and Father O'Grady could go.

CHAPTER 9

THE WATER OF
THE THAMES

Save me, O God:
for the waters are come in,
even unto my soul.

When the house was still and Father Perivale had gone to
bed, Father O'Grady lit his candle and went to his own room,
the room which had been Father Malone's. He occupied it
because he supposed that it was his duty to. He was Rector
now. He had inherited the burden of a saint. He did not feel
worthy to breathe the same air that the old man breathed.
He thought that this room should be closed until the glorious day, when peals of silver bells in Rome should proclaim
the Saint to the whole world. When that day came the room
should be thrown open to pilgrims. But he had no right to
behave now, as if the thing he longed for was an accomplished fact. So Father O'Grady used the Rector's room and
in it he kept a guilty secret. In a locked cupboard he had a
few relics of Father Malone, for the future veneration of the

Faithful. There was his Rosary, mended with string in several places, his breviary with its thin pages worn to a feathery softness, his old hat shabby and mossy beyond description. There was the pair of shoes that he had got when he changed his own with the derelict man in the street, and most precious of all there was his foul old pipe, of which he had often said himself that no man could smoke it without a special grace.

It never would have entered Father O'Grady's head that he could be a saint himself. But when Father Malone died and he had to take his place, it had seemed that the only way to avoid letting his people down was to copy the saint they loved just in exterior things. He told himself that he must walk in the old man's shoes, but humbly, walking only a few steps at a time to start with. Those first few steps set his feet on the stony path of holiness.

Metaphorically as well as actually, Father Malone's shoes were stiff and full of nails. They let in the water, they fitted only into the footsteps of Jesus Christ, scored on the hard paving stones of the London streets.

The holiness of Father Malone had been a thing of tremendous, simple reality. It started at his mother's knee, when he was a barefooted Irish boy and it never lost the clear objectivity of a child's heroism. It was concerned, not with fine shades of spirituality, but with flesh and blood, with such concrete things as food and drink and tobacco and clothes. Such things as daily mortification of the appetite, of human respect, of sleep, and of countless harmless indulgences that make life tolerable to most human beings.

There is nothing so definite, so searching as the sanctity of children. It asks no questions, has no doubts, it dares everything, but expects nothing of self, therefore it is incapable of delusion. It is sacramental, offering its substance of flesh and blood, for daily, hourly transubstantiation.

It is an uncompromising little measure of the will-to-love, as hard and straight and well defined as a wooden ruler in school, marked with inches and half inches and tenths of inches. Turn to the miracle workers, to certain of the saints who lived long ago in the enchanted woods and magic mountains of sanctity, and you can find escape, or think you have found it, from the personal responsibility of holiness. You can delude yourself with the comforting thought that it is a presumption to expect wonders and miracles from yourself, to hope that the intricate refinements of your spiritual life should give as much faith as a grain of mustard seed.

But the Sanctity of Childhood, which happens to be the characteristic sanctity of the twentieth century, is an unanswerable challenge, or rather a challenge to which the only answer is, "Yes."

It is plainly within the capacity of every one who has a body and soul, and the ordinary limitations and weaknesses of human nature: nothing else but that—and the Grace of God which can be had for the asking—is required.

It is in the eyes and ears and the tongue, in the hands and the feet and the tips of the fingers. It is in the narrow kitchen, the office chair and the low bed. It is in the food on the table, it is in the milk or water or wine in the cup—"Can you drink the Chalice that I drink of?"

"Yea, Lord, we can!"

Father O'Grady put down his candle on the table, and opened the window on to the night. Another Saturday was passed, it was dark now and still, Riverside slept.

All day long he looked forward to this hour from midnight to one o'clock, he thought of it as the time when he would gather himself together into one whole, complete act of adoration.

Nothing in the daytime ever seemed complete. Everything that he began was interrupted and cut short. No action, no thought, no conversation, no prayer, ever seemed to be whole, completed, finished. Everything was broken. Everything was hurried or interrupted, or left with untidy loose ends. Even things that *had* to be completed were disintegrated by distractions.

The lives of really holy people seemed to be so different. They wrote out neat time-tables, including luxurious hours of solitude, of meditation, half-hours before the Blessed Sacrament, prudent recreation, and so on; and when people called on them and made demands on them, they were, as indeed in these circumstances they might well be, calm and charming and able to give an impression of having unlimited time to give, and no preoccupation in life so absorbing as the trivialities of this individual's mind.

Father O'Grady had tried writing out time-tables too, even including time to answer letters, and to write an occasional one to his brother in Dublin, whom he was devoted to, but had not seen for a matter of ten years or more; but his time-tables were never adhered to for as much as a single day or even a single morning.

There were people at the Sacristy door waiting to break into his thanksgiving, people in the hall of the Presbytery asking him to hurry over his breakfast, people calling at every hour of the morning, afternoon and evening, and every one of them had some urgent matter that could not wait, or some burden that could no longer be carried alone, or some secret which they could not live face to face with by themselves, and to each and every one of them the priest belonged.

There were sick calls day and night, there were accidents in the docks and the broad road that swept through Riverside from the water's edge to the West End, and over and over again the priest had to hurry to one of his poor crushed and broken children with forgiveness on his tongue and in his hands, and the Eternal Love in a golden pyx over his heart.

There was the endless business of the Parish. The debt on the church, the fund for building the new schools, the endless red tape of the County Council about the old schools, the Parish Bazaar, the whist drives, the socials, the meetings, devotions, quarrels and snobberies of the Children of Mary; the societies, groups, guilds, movements of "Catholic Action" constantly being founded by visitors from the West End and dropped again; the endless complications caused by the undisciplined fervour and unmortified zeal of the visiting Faithful, and the disciplined apathy and bored fidelity of the local Faithful.

There was the Presbytery that was in constant need of repair, the slates falling off the roof, the chimney smoking, the drains going wrong, the pipes bursting, everything always corrupting and coming to pieces, human nature most of all. Men's souls and minds had to be constantly washed, bound up, propped up and repaired, or they lost in the fight with corruption and fell to pieces.

The priest had a haunting sense of disintegration all the time. Everything was always being broken up. The work of all the priests before him for Christian Education, the work that the nuns and school mistresses did on the souls of children, who drifted into faithless ways so soon after school days ended. The buildings, the people's homes, the church, the presbytery, always falling down—as if sin, the most disintegrating thing that there is, had even entered into brick and wood and stone. So too with his own thought, even his own prayer, from without and within, this process of breaking up, pulling apart, scattering.

He went on cherishing the illusion day after day, that the late night, with its solitude, must bring integrated prayer, that he would be able to gather his thought into a circle of light, into the unity of a shining ring, a crown of prayer, and in that prayer his whole being, body, mind, heart and soul would be one still, concentrated act of adoration.

He often thought of Our Lord's prayer at night and reflected that He, even He, felt the necessity of going away, to be alone to pray.

But he did not reckon with the limitations of his body. When he imagined that hour of wholeness, that solitary ring of light in the darkness of night, he forgot that he would be cold and sleepy, and that the very first act of contrition for his own sins and the sins of his people would scatter, that the words would fall away as if they were seeds scattered in a drift of wind.

He blew out the candle, opened the window and knelt down in the middle of the room. He covered his face with his hands, but no words came to him, no thoughts, not even an aspiration or any centre or point of stillness that even the vainest wishful-thinking could have mistaken for the "prayer of quiet." He tried to examine his conscience, to make at least formal acts of contrition for himself and for his people, but the words fell away like dust. He was only aware of sin as a wound, a wound that afflicted his people, and bled in him. The words of contrition were bleeding from his brain and his mind was left white and wordless.

He heard the ships' hooters deep and mournful through the darkness, they at least gave a voice to the loneliness of man.

It was so still that the river itself was audible, dark water, gently, gently lapping against the dockside.

Father O'Grady resigned himself once more to his limitations. He offered what he called the prayer of the body. The empty mind, the aching limbs, the struggle with sleep, the longing to be in bed. The effort of will that kept him on his knees, for the endless hour, which was no longer, even in his own mind, the hour of completeness which he had thirsted for, but an hour to be adhered to with his will—"offered up" with the countless other things that he offered up in every twenty-four hours, from the irritating wheezing of "the Test of Faith," to the sense of the sins of the world heavy on his own soul.

He longed for the hour to be over, the hour he had reached out to, with hands of light, all day long! He longed for the warmth of his bed and to have his head on the pillow. He was numb with cold. His head rested on his arms on the table and only one phrase went through his mind, over and over again like a broken down gramophone that repeats half an inch of the record over and over again.

"Save me, O God: for the waters are come in, even unto my soul."

He had wanted his prayer to be a draught of the shining water of Life, clear and sparkling, a fountain springing up from the dry dust of his heart, but the water that entered into his soul was the dark mysterious water of the Thames.

The water that carried men away to other lands, that brought them from distant, unknown worlds to London, that carried merchants and sailors and travellers to and fro on errands that sometimes separated, sometimes united men for ever. The waters that flowed with the tears of old mothers and lonely lovers. The waters that ran strong and black with tides of longing and of destiny, bringing men and women to one another's arms or sweeping them away over seven seas. The waters that carried food and wine and merchandise to and fro between the cities of the world. Cargoes of fruit, grapes and oranges and golden pomegranates, sugar candy, candy peel and spice, tea and coffee and sugar and nuts, bales of cotton and wool and silk, dyed vermilion and emerald and blue, and rugs from Persia and China and Egypt and India, and treasures of ivory and teak wood, metal and copper and jade, all the full measure of delight for the feast and splendour and laughter of living.

The water that whispered dark secrets down its tides, drugs that passed swiftly, silently from hand to hand, from thin yellow fingers in far off lands, to hands tattooed with flowers and hearts entwined with roses, to hands already crimson with blood, and black with the touch of evil gold, to terrible soft hands white in the moonlight, with scarlet nails.

Waters that carried outcasts and derelicts and the lost and the forgotten, all the flotsam and jetsam of wrecked humanity to and fro, to and fro through time to the ultimate harbour. Waters that caressed strange little wooden wharves, running furtively beside ramshackle warehouses and taverns, where here and there, a light behind a blind in a window cast a shower of golden petals on the dark ripples. Water that carried rats along the side of the wharves, and into the ships and cities, water that knew dark and lovely secrets, water that is the soul of London and brings the world to her heart.

Water that is part of the darkness of humanity flowing forever round the mystery of its light, water that is, with all its whispering and weeping and seeping darkness, symbol of the water of Life.

Water of the Thames, dark and lovely water, gently, gently lapping against the dockside, chug chug chug of the river Thames against the wharf, and Fr. O'Grady rocking, rocking, rocking, into the sleep of the dark water. Now his deep breathing too is woven into the lapping of the river and the rest of his prayer is sleep.

"Save me, O God: for the waters are come in, even unto my soul."

CHAPTER 10

ROSE O'SHANE

If I ascend up to Heaven,
Thou art there:
If I go down into hell,
Thou art there.

Every evening at six o'clock, Rose O'Shane walked slowly down Mimosa Street to the "Cat and Fiddle."

She was beautiful with a large and splendid beauty, beautiful in face and body, in her slow majestic movements, the honey of the words on her tongue, in her tenderness to weak and helpless things. Beautiful above all in the charity which glowed in her like a heap of red embers, which a mere sigh from any poor creature at all could fan to a bright flame.

Her progress down Mimosa Street was magnificent. She wore a feathered Gainsborough hat on the back of her head where it had slipped as her dark red hair fell down in locks on her shoulders. Her fur coat swung open and sagged from her arms. Her blouse and skirt, bored with each other, yawned apart in a wide gap, indeed it seemed that only her dignity kept any of her clothes on her body, as if it acted on them like a magnet.

It was common property that Rose O'Shane had known better days. The fur coat, the astonishing hats, the quality of her thought, even the way she walked, told of better days. But no one asked her anything, for there was that about her that made even the most insensitive pretend not to see the bald patches like mange on the old fur coat, the antique style of the feathered hats, and all the rest of the rust and tarnish on her glory. Above all everyone by unspoken consent pretended not to know that Rose O'Shane took too much to drink.

Not that this was considered very shocking in Riverside, or that it was a rare thing. But the people felt that in some indefinable, but positive way, Rose was a superior being. She was their aristocracy, their personal royalty, and they identified themselves with her in this, although it was this very quality which set her apart, in a strange inevitable loneliness, despite the fact that she was given to these people, spent for them, even squandered on them, by a positively profligate charity.

It would have been personal humiliation to her friends to think of her as a tippler—like any of the other tipplers who shuffled along Mimosa Street in carpet slippers and their hair in curlers, for their pint of beer, or to admit that her feet could possibly be set on the same road as those wrecked old women who were dragged shouting and sobbing and laughing with the terrifying laughter that is out of control, to the cells, every Saturday night, as regular as clockwork.

Sometimes they met her coming back from the "Cat and Fiddle," still steady for she was always steady, but with her face a little smeared. Then they did not look into her eyes. Because of that courtesy, mixed as it was with their own vanity and shame, they were spared seeing those wise and gentle eyes looking back at them through a heavy mist and the warm intelligent beauty of that face, smeared like a soft pencil drawing that someone has rubbed with his fingers.

She was the subject of endless rumour. It was said that some worthless fool had let her down, that she once had a lover who had died, some even said that she had a husband whom she supported, hidden away somewhere, but no one ever knew, and no one ever asked personal questions of Rose O'Shane.

Of one thing every one was sure, somewhere in the story there was love, for only love could have awakened compassion, like the compassion that Rose O'Shane gave to all the world. She ought to have been the foundress of an order of mercy, to have mothered countless orphans, succoured prisoners, tended the sick, administered vast fortunes to the poor, as it was, without an outlet at all for the magnificence of her nature, pity was her undoing.

No one knew what Rose O'Shane did. She was gone every morning at eight, and back again at six, that every one knew, what they did not know was that she was a washer-up. Between nine and five she washed up greasy dishes, greasy plates, greasy pots and pans, in a West End Restaurant. In the morning she washed last night's dinner things, they were the worst. They had been piled up by the sink all night, and the grease was congealed and hard. It also had little tracks of the feet of mice all over it, and the fat and gristle left on the plates was always nibbled by mice. The lunch was not so bad, there was a chance to rinse the plates before the grease hardened, and sometimes she was able to drink quite a good glow into her, by draining all the dregs of the glasses as they came out. On very rare occasions, the waiter Josef brought her out a whole glass of Chianti. Josef was a Catholic like herself and therefore she felt able to discuss things with him more intimately than with the others, but he was permanently disgusted by the sight of people eating and so obsessed by it that he could talk of very little else.

"These English," he was for ever repeating, "these English have put all their emotions into eating. It is because of Queen Victoria—no, I am not laughing, I am in deadly earnest, Queen Victoria and the Protestant Religion have made the English afraid to be natural human beings; in their lives they try to kill every emotion because every emotion is embarrassing or improper. Why, an Englishman thinks that it is improper to be in love with his own wife, and what does he do? I will tell you, for I see it every day of my life, he puts all his grand passion (which he cannot kill, because he is after all a man), he puts it all into the eating of a beef steak, or a goulash, and his tenderness, what does he do with that? I will tell you, for I know. It is bestowed on a dish of young duckling and sweet green peas. I do not know why I am not dead, why I have not died already from a permanent disgust!"

"But," Rose would answer, "eating can also be beautiful. Once, as a child, I heard a remark about it which I have never forgotten, it was from a Protestant clergyman too: Every time we break bread, he said, we should do it in memory of Jesus Christ, and every meal should be a Communion with one another."

The chef, a French atheist, was impatient of these discussions: he would put a face as red as a turkey cock, crowned with a towering white cap, round the door and shout:

"Allez oop, Josef, Allez oop ! Everything is spoilt if you don't hurry up. Not that I care, these English are as much pleased to eat a boiled flannel as the most per*fect* goulash or mousakka."

And he would spit neatly all along the top of the soufflé (for which the house was famous), for that, he said, was the secret of a good French soufflé—"Allez oop."

And then there was Armand, who was a Turk and who picked pockets on his day off, because he was paid a starvation wage for making a thick black treacle called Turkish coffee and giving tone to the house. He would look with a slow smile which could equally well have been an expression of amusement or hatred at each of the others in turn and say: "It is well for the English, those who can most eat tasteless food win wars, therefore the English will win the war that is certainly coming. If you are accustomed to just the right seasoning, the right piquance, well—you have no power to endure, for wars now are wars of the stomach. If you can enjoy to eat boiled flannel, very well you are lord of the world, no one can conquer you."

The Restaurant was cosmopolitan and that was one reason why Rose O'Shane was able to endure it. To this one fetid, verminous little building, came people from all over the world.

Indeed, Rose often thought as she made her way back to Riverside, weary from those long hours standing by the sink, there are many lost lands in London—a little homesick Italy;

a few streets that are France; a teeming Commercial Road, with its homes hidden behind it like a market woman's children hiding in her skirts, that is Israel; a few narrow picturesque streets running down to the water's edge, that are a lost little China.

It reminded Rose of the Tower of Babel, for she knew that though everyone spoke English, and some had grown up never knowing their own language, there is a confusion of hearts that has succeeded the confusion of tongues, and these people living side by side in one city could not speak, or understand, or learn the language of one another's souls.

In Riverside they all came to Rose O'Shane with their sorrows and their joys. They came as naturally as a thirsty man goes to water to drink, or a weary man lays his head down on a pillow to sleep. Sailors who had come home from long voyages to find their wives gone away, or worse, to find themselves fallen out of love with faithful wives. Girls who could not get any young man to look at them, though they were prettier far than some others who had followers like a queue for a cinema. Boys and girls who were truly in love and saw no hope at all of getting married. Boys who were out of work, and so bored that they almost wanted to break in somewhere and steal, to break the monotony, and some who had.

Many derelicts of the Catholic Church came to her too, and began to look again at the pitiful face of God, because there was someone in the world as holy as Rose O'Shane, whom you could nevertheless have a drink with, and crack a joke with. That people came to her with their joys as well as their griefs tells more than anything else of the character of Rose O'Shane. Few people have fingers so sensitive that they can touch other people's joys without taking off the bloom of them. It is here that the touch of love can be recognized, the touch that increases joy, the touch with which Christ changed water into wine at the wedding Feast at Cana.

She listened too, to the endless litany of little ailments, and she had no contempt at all for them, for a back that ached over the wash tub was the same to her as a back that ached under the Cross. It was so because in a way that words cannot tell, she was at once Rose O'Shane and Ireland.

That sorrowing love of Christ that has sent Irish men and women, fasting and barefooted over sharp rocks and through icy water, on St. Patrick's pilgrimage, was incarnate in her. In her too, as if her whole race lived in her, the hopeless glory and despair of generations of young Irish soldiers, beating themselves to death against England's iron chest. In her the objective, disinterested love that is Ireland's unique grace. The holiness which seems inconsistent to our illogical English minds, that rejoices in the beauty of God, forgetting self, and self-perfection. The Irish open their arms to Him, just as they are; and it would no more occur to an Irishman not to rejoice in the beauty of the Lord, because it is a sinner who rejoices, than it would occur to him not to rejoice in the crimson of the roses.

If it were possible for a man who loves God to perish, and if that man were Irish, he would quite naturally kiss the feet of Christ on the Cross as he passed by on his way to hell.

There is no debit and credit and calculating of merit, no double entry for the Recording Angel in Ireland. Ireland, like all the world, is heavy with sin, but Ireland is in love with God. Filled up as she was with pity for the world's sorrow,

weary as she was from long hours at the sink and the endless demands of her friends, carrying within her the generations of her country's love and bitterness, Rose longed for the
blessed moments of relief and irresponsibility in the "Cat and
Fiddle," the easing of tension, the laughter rippling through
the mind, the easy tears.

She was going down and down was Rose O'Shane—and
what a glory it was that was going down!—like a great Spanish galleon adrift on the sea, battered and ready to sink, but
still magnificent, her purple sails no less beautiful for being faded by burning suns, her burnished figurehead no less
beautiful because its gilding was worn thin by the caresses
and the lashes of many salt seas.

Like a great ship with crowding sails, she moved slowly
down Mimosa Street to the "Cat and Fiddle," followed by a
stray kitten, like a little black barge in the wash of the great
ship. And that one evening, for the first time since she had
come to Riverside, she went past the swinging door. Not once
only, but several times, to and fro, to and fro, with the little
black cat going to and fro, to and fro behind her, until the
sun went down and darkness began. Then she succumbed and
went in.

No one looked into Rose O'Shane's eyes when they were
misty, no one, that is, but Willie Jewel. Several times she
had visited him after going to the "Cat and Fiddle," and she
thought that there was a look of dread in his eyes. Now that
may not have been so at all, for Rose was haunted by the suspicion that everyone thought of her secretly as a drunkard.
She was always watching for the slightest confirmation of
this. It may therefore have been imagination, but she *thought*

that the accusation was there in Willie's eyes, in the worst form that accusation can take, fear.

She never went to see him, mind you, when she was not sober. Rose was always sober, and like all her countrywomen, she distinguished between being drunk and merely having "drink taken." But she walked with more dignity, rather more care than usual, enquired with a little too much precision how Willie was, and stooped to kiss him. Then it was that she thought she saw fear, not ordinary fear, but the kind of dread and shock, which afflicts a child who has learned something sad or corrupt for the first time, which no one could possibly have prepared him to know. A grown-up crying, a dead bird on the path, the inward certainty that Father Christmas does not come down the chimney.

This look of fear, real or imaginary, haunted Rose. The defenceless blue eyes of the dumb child looked at her from the rosy dregs in the crystal glasses in the Restaurant, from the pile of dishes and the dingy cloths, from the paving stones of the street, and alone in her room at night, they watched her through the darkness.

A man stood by the pavement with snowdrops in his hand, he was gaunt and dark, and darkly clad and his hands were red and chapped. Rose looked at the flowers and thought "How small and white they are, to be in those sad dark hands, it is like the white Host in the hands of the sinful world."

She thought of the woods of her childhood in Ireland, and remembered that Willie had never been to the country.

"If I kept off the drink," she said to herself, "I could often afford to buy him a bunch." She made up her mind that she would give it up, starting that very evening.

Yet once again that evening the battered galleon sailed down and down to the "Cat and Fiddle," passed the door once, twice, three times, then came back a fourth time, and the fourth time it was dark, the hooter on the river sounded nearer in the darkness and very mournful. Rose seemed to be the only person alone in the streets, people were walking home arm in arm, or standing chattering in little groups. From time to time the door of the "Cat and Fiddle" swung open and a gust of laughter and singing streamed out on a beam of light, and then the door swung back and the night was empty again.

Rose pushed open the door and went in. There was a warm sweet smell of rum, a sailor was leaning over the bar, telling the story of his voyage, he had just come in from the sea and everyone was standing him drinks, everything was glowing and warm and friendly.

The wine entered into Rose O'Shane like a stream of crimson ease, softly it filled her veins with rest, wave upon wave of peace. Ease flooded through her, a warm, rising tide.

On that night with its failure began a long struggle for Rose O'Shane. But there came a night at last which marked the first of many triumphs spaced out between many failures, when she did not go into the "Cat and Fiddle."

She had imagined that when this at last happened, she would experience a sense of exaltation, but she did not. She felt like something torn up by the roots, like someone who has denied a friend, and realized that to her drink had been company as well as comfort and peace. But she took a bunch of early snowdrops to Willie Jewel.

CHAPTER 11

BENEDICTION

O, Saving Victim,
opening wide
The gate of Heaven to
man below.

On the second day of the Novena, Willie became so much
worse that Martha sent word to Father O'Grady asking him
to come. A rumour had already gone round that the child was
dying and the prayers of the people rose in a crescendo. They
crowded to the weekday Benediction to pray together.

Father O'Grady sent Tim Hoolihan to carry a note by
hand to Father Smith, assistant priest of the next parish, asking him if he would forgive the short notice, and could he
oblige by coming over to take Benediction, as he himself was
called out.

The next parish was a long way off, but Father Smith
was in sympathy with the cause of Father Malone. He was
a young, simple, red-faced priest, who had burnt candles in

front of Father Malone's photographs on the side, and was joining in the Novena.

Benediction was at four, at half past three the church was full, the benches crowded, the people kneeling in the aisles. Even on Sunday nights or on the great Feasts there were seldom so many, although it is in Benediction that hundreds find the only visible beauty that shines out on the drabness of their lives, like stars burning into a grey twilight. It is an easy and sweet ceremony, with the singing of hymns, and the relief of prayers spoken out loud, a sweetness, a gentleness, a goodnight to the little flock.

The church was noisy, the people had come early because they were restless and unsettled. How could they remain quietly at home or at work while waiting for a miracle? A miracle that was to break upon a moment of crisis.

Everyone was whispering. Some stood at the back of the church in little knots, talking in murmurs. There was a continual tramping of feet as more and more came in.

Each one who came was stopped in the aisle by an outstretched hand from the benches, three, four or five times on their way up to their seat and plied with eager, breathless questions.

"How is he?"

"Have you news?"

"Is he worse?"

"They say he is sinking, have you heard?"

"Lord spare the child to us."

"Lord pity the dying."

"What is the news of him?"

"They say he is in agony—have you news of him?"

"Christ be with him."

"Mother Mary comfort him."

"Sweet child Christ be with him."

The organist, Miss Mulliger, an eccentric old lady, whose want of balance was charitably attributed to her talent for music, was blowing up the organ. She invariably put ribbons in her hat, according to the liturgical colours of the day. But for Benediction, white.

The organ wheezed and panted, like a dragon coming round from an anaesthetic. Now and then when a sudden gust of enthusiasm took Miss Mulliger, it lingered in a long wheeze, so like her usual tremulous opening bar to the "O Salutaris Hostia" that everyone flung on to their knees, only to find that there was nothing happening at all.

The school children, allowed out early for the midweek Benediction, came in whispering and jostling one another, and fidgeted in the front benches like flocks of quarrelsome sparrows.

Behind them the Sisters of Charity with their great white coifs followed, like a fleet of sailing ships riding proudly on calm waters.

Presently a boy came in bearing a star on a reed, and began to light the candles on the Altar. It was Jimmy Hogan, a tough child respected for his punch, and the terror of the lads of his own size (not much of a size), for miles around. But the friend of stray cats, dogs and sparrows, and known to the Riverside sporting world as the best tiddler fisher of the century. But now he was indistinguishable from a young angel, blue eyed, flaxen haired, his face scrubbed to a glossy, apple rosiness, vested in a snowy white surplice over an unrubrical but beautiful cherry red cassock.

One by one he lit the multitude of candles. It was as if he touched a million buds in a celestial meadow, with the Star of Bethlehem, and they bloomed with its holy fire. Now and then he had to return to one that faltered, one that winked and flickered and must be coaxed and petted into light. And everyone watched with absurd suspense, as when people listen to a singer, in terror of nervous apprehension that his high note will not come off.

When the stars were lit, the tensity, the expectation in the church was almost unbearable. The people could hardly wait now for the door of the Tabernacle to be opened and the Lord to be borne out among them and lifted up.

They were waiting with the same desire, doubt, hope, faith, with the same longing to believe, to be convinced, to see, with which the crowds in Jerusalem waited the coming of Christ in their narrow streets. The beating of their inarticulate hearts hammered on the leaf light door of gold:

"Lord, that I may see!"

"Lord I believe, help thou my unbelief!"

At last the bell rang out, a sudden clatter of silver over the heads of the people, and they flung down on their knees, to stay on them.

Books and rosaries and pennies were dropped, some last comers clattered in at the double, and threw themselves down with such violence that it seemed that they must have broken the bench.

The organ with a sustained wail, like the escape of a captive beast at the last gasp of life, began the "O Salutaris Hostia" in earnest.

The congregation were not singers. Usually there would be just one robust old man letting off his rage at the tepidity of the others, in a tuneless roar, and one tremulous old lady, quite unconscious of the others, uttering a quavering solo, but for the rest, only a few moans and false starts.

Father O'Grady, who would have liked a good volume of sound, had to console himself with the wise old saying, "Where there are many hymns, there is much heresy."

But to-day everyone sang. It was the loudest, the most tuneless, the most reckless, the most unselfconscious, the most fervent singing that had ever been heard in Father O'Grady's church. It swept over little Father Smith as he came in with his eyes shut, his biretta on the back of his head, and his alb bunched up in the manner so distressing to Monsignor Frayne. It seemed impossible to him that with such intensity, such wheezing and roaring and sighing and sweating in prayer, the miracle would not be granted this afternoon.

He unlocked the Tabernacle door and lifted out the Sacred Host. Walking carefully and slowly, as St. Joseph might have done when Our Lady put the Divine Child into his arms to carry, he went behind the Altar, up the tiny steps, and set the great Monstrance on its throne.

Again there was a lurching forward, a rattling and creaking and dropping as the congregation plunged and dived down into adoration.

The heads of the children went down, the rows of the boys' heads, like round knobs of unpolished wood. One tiny little girl, a First Communicant of the year, squinted through her locked fingers, and screwed up her eyes, to see the gilded rays of the Monstrance blurred as if they were real glory.

Father Smith began the recital of the Joyful Mysteries. The people gripped their rosaries tighter, seizing the beads so hard between their fingers that their fingers cracked. Their lips moved faster and faster, some whispering, with a hiss like kettles spitting at boiling point: some with their muttered prayers caught in a kind of loose, grumbling rattle in their throats: all gathering speed as they went on, their lips moving faster and faster and faster, as if their prayers were running, rushing to God. Trying to race death, and to throw it back from the very gates of eternity.

Now they sang again, and the singing rocked and swayed with the movement of the sea, and it gathered in love and in sadness; but it was a sadness full of relief, for they were singing the Litany of the Blessed Virgin, and it gave a voice and words to the sorrow, and hope, and love, that was their daily bread and the salt of their lives.

It rocked and rocked their hearts with the movement of the sea. To the people of Riverside the sea was always present. Present in the hope, the fear, the waiting, the patience, of the mothers and sweethearts of the men who were out in ships. Present as they swept, and washed, and cooked. Present in their dreams in the night. And the Mother of Christ was both Mother of men and "Star of the Sea." She shone above the tall masts of the storm-driven ships, and the waves of the sea rocked in her light, and at home the cradles of the seamen's children swung to and fro to the rhythm of the waves, rocked in the hands of the merciful Mother of Christ.

She was their pride and their joy. The drabness and smeariness, the mediocrity of life, slipped away in the thought of her. She stood before the throne of God, their own and one of themselves.

> Tower of Ivory!
> Gate of Heaven!
> Morning Star!
> > Pray for us.

And in the city street and the narrow dark house, she was the white flower in the woods to them. The poetry and loveliness of their lives.

> Mater purissima.
> Mater castissima.
> Mater intemerata,
> > Ora pro nobis!

The cadence of their love rocked to and fro, and flowed like waves round the foot of the Monstrance.

The girls who had skimpy, washed-out clothes, tawdry finery and cheap rings, rejoiced because she, their Mother, was a queen, Queen of Heaven, robed in its blue, crowned with its stars.

The mothers, the old women, and the men, put their cares into her hands and the rhythm of their singing rocked them into rest.

> Salus infirmorum,
> Refugium peccatorum,
> Consolatrix afflictorum
> Auxilium Christianorum
> > Ora pro nobis.

Almost in the same breath, the Litany flowed into the "Tantum Ergo."

Again the bell rang out, loud and sweet and solemn, the

bell of Benediction. It shivered into silence. Silence possessed the people. Silence possessed the whole of Riverside.

Not the silence of emptiness, but of fullness, of a crescendo of expectation, like a towering wave, gathered to the whole of its strength, lifted up to its full height, pausing in the moment of its utmost integrity, before rolling on, to fling itself forward and break upon the rocks.

Father Smith lifted the great Monstrance above the bowed heads, held it up for a moment before his plain face, suffused with love, as if he held the sun up, burning in his hands. Slowly he made the great Sign of the Cross with it, lowered it on to the Altar and knelt before it.

The flowers on the Altar breathed the shimmering breath of the candle flame. The incense rose in straight blue lines through the haze of gold.

"Blessed be God," said the priest, and the wave broke, surging, tumbling, rushing forward in a torrent of praise.

"Blessed be God," roared the people.

Blessed be God.
Blessed be His Holy Name.
Blessed be Jesus Christ, true God and true man.
Blessed be the Name of Jesus.
Blessed be His most Sacred Heart.
Blessed be Jesus, in the most Holy Sacrament of the Altar.
Blessed be the Great Mother of God, Mary most holy.
Blessed be her holy and Immaculate Conception.
Blessed be the name of Mary, Virgin and Mother.
Blessed be St. Joseph, her most chaste spouse.
Blessed be God, in His Angels and His Saints.

Now the "Adoremus" rose, gentle as a caress and flowing over the Sacred Host, as Father Smith lifted It from the Monstrance, put It back into the Tabernacle and locked the door.

Benediction was over, but Miss Mulliger maintained the fervour of the people as they crowded out into the street, by thundering an improvisation of her own on the organ, a triumphant pot-pourri of piety, incorporating all the most loved hymns with the most familiar marches, a number of indescribable chords and discords, sudden, almost frivolous trills, and melodies suspiciously like the popular song hits of the day.

Someone was waiting outside the church with news. "Willie is a little better."

CHAPTER 12

TIMOTHY GREEN

*... He had compassion
on them, because they
were distressed, and lying
like sheep that have no
shepherd.*

On the day of Father Malone's death, when Timothy had stepped down from the bus into Riverside and unexpectedly into a crowd of Angels and men exulting in an hour of sorrow, he had gone there for a paper on whose staff he was then working. The episode had nearly cost him his new job, for he came back without the "story" he went to collect and with another instead. But while the one wanted was of glamour spinning downhill to degradation in a dope shop on Riverside, the other was of human nature lifted above its weakness and misery to exultation; it had no newspaper value.

Had the dead priest worked a miracle, he would have gone straight from last page obituary column, to front page news and heavy type. But the only thing he had actually *done* was to die, important no doubt from his own point of view, but much too usual from the point of view of the paper.

Now, if he had sat bolt upright among (the editor supposed) sheaves of Madonna lilies, and granted the reporter an interview, *that* would have been news, as good as an interview with Lazarus, or very nearly, but—the editor put his pencil behind his ear, a habit peculiar to self-made men, and looked at Timothy. "No doubt," he thought, "a very clever young chap, and he will be useful to us in time, but it won't do for him to get Religion."

"It looks as if you have a slight attack of crowd hysteria," he said aloud. "Very catching you know, crowd hysteria."

"Yes, but it is over a week ago and thinking it over calmly hasn't dulled my impression at all; crowd hysteria doesn't work in retrospect, on the contrary it brings on an immediate reaction, that's why people so often go wrong immediately after a revivalist meeting. The impressive thing was not simply that the people were so exultant, but that their joy was caused by bereavement, the wonderful sense I told you about, of intense life, was actually the result of a death. I can't help feeling that there is something big in my idea of articles on the testimony to truth springing up spontaneously in the hearts of the people—or something like that."

"Too vague m'boy—and anyhow it does·not make sense. Bereavement causing Joy, death giving a sense of life—no, it doesn't make any sense, and it hasn't got any newspaper value."

"Perhaps I haven't put it simply enough," Timothy turned scarlet. "I should say, Sir, that the genius of running a paper, is not giving people what they *want*, but what they *need*, for when people get what they want, they get a surfeit. No one can be surfeited with their *need*. They may want to be told that this life holds out real happiness, but they *need* to know that there is another life, that goes on for ever after death, and gives a meaning to things, which to the poor anyhow, are meaningless without it—In fact, sir, they need saints. Give the people a saint, who proves in flesh and blood like their own that they are *more* than flesh and blood."

The editor smiled, pursed his lips, gave a low whistle. "You've got it badly," he said, and he thought "presumptuous young puppy. But I rather like presumption in a youngster, it *gets* them somewhere."

He leaned across his desk, tapping it with his forefinger to give force to his remarks, and feeling a sense of his own power surging happily in his veins, admonished Timothy—

"So you think you know all about running a paper—What *genius* would do. Well, m'boy, I have edited this paper long enough to know something about it too, and let me tell you this, the genius is not in giving them what they want, or what they need, but what they'll pay for, and people *hate* paying for their necessities. They'll pay for delusions and luxuries, and gladly. Look what an emotionally starved woman with a face like a bus will pay, to delude herself she is Greta Garbo!—If you want people to have salvation, you have got to give it to them free, paying for it is like paying your light bill, in fact most parsons find people have got to be bribed to take it. Of course m'boy, we cater for the religious sentimentality that's inherent in us all, and we give them a bit of uplift from time to time—here, hand me that file, thank you—er—yes, here we are, two series last year, well known parsons on 'What is emptying the Churches' and well known film stars on 'What I believe.' But it's no good as a regular line, or without a name behind it that's a kind of box-office draw, so to speak. Take Saturday off m'boy, and get it out of your system. What do you do Saturdays? Play any games? No? Oh, well. Get out into the air anyway, and out of London."

Timothy did take Saturday off, but he did not go out of London. On the contrary, he walked about her streets with his mind in turmoil. He went back to Riverside and visited Fr. O'Grady's church. He was appalled by its tawdriness, and by the first sight of some of its plaster saints, the effeminacy of its St. Aloysius, the sentimentality of its St. Teresa of Lisieux. He sat in one of the benches and watched people come in and pray before these two, and he watched, amazed by *who* came, dock labourers, and sailors, girls made up lavishly, policemen, mothers carrying babies and followed by little hordes of children who played in the aisle while their mothers prayed, and children who came alone to pray themselves, tiny girls who could only just walk, and rough little schoolboys who flung down on to their knees at a run. Timothy stared, and wondered what was the strength of this strange pair of saints that could draw men and women and children from such hurried breathless moments of love, from such hard, matter-of-fact lives, to pray like this, with clenched hands and screwed up eyes, like children who screw up their faces to pray harder!

He went back to the West End, and from one church to another, and he always encountered this young man with a lily and this young nun with roses covering her crucifix, and always people coming to them, looking to them for strength, for help, for hope.

He thought of the boys and girls he knew, whistling to keep up their courage, snatching at every sensation, frittering away the love of life in the lust for life. He thought of the old people he knew, who dreaded their old age because they could not believe that they could be loved for anything but beauty and strength of body, and now that these were ebbing they could not face life with no love in it, stretching out into loneliness that only the dreaded death could end.

How soon all these people would be forgotten! and when their brief struggle and unrest and torment were ended, it would be as if they had never been.

But these two—the young man with the lily, the girl with the roses, one dead for hundreds of years, the other for half a century—were alive now to all these people who brought them their hopes, their fears, their sorrows, and they would remain, a live, immeasurable strength on earth, long after they too were forgotten.

What was their secret? What crystal water did they give to the world's fever?—What was their answer to the cry, shrill on the lips of the boys and girls, confused on the tongues of the aged and dying, the cry on the lips of the rich and the poor from cradle to coffin. "Life, Life, Life."

At dusk he found himself in Leicester Square, and his environment suddenly became charged with the quality of nightmare. From every side, from behind him, in front of him, above him, flared one idea, sex as the object of life. Not sex that is an expression of love, of youth, of something pure and joyful springing spontaneously from the loveliest in life, but something thrust upon the people by the avarice of men, cynical men, who manufacture it in reels of gelatine, in tablets and potions, who sit back in their clubs and offices and comfortable homes, made rich by exploiting the starved emotions of factory girls and clerks, of frustrated spinsters, and frightened old people.

Sex, sex, sex, it stared at him from every hoarding, every shop window, assailed him at every few yards on the pavement, blazed down on him from a thousand electric lights, scorching him like shafts of fire. For the first time he saw it objectively, as if he were outside of himself, as one is sometimes outside of oneself in a dream. He saw the young men of all the cities of the world, defenceless against avarice, with their pitiful wages that promised no home, no family. With their hungry souls that asked for bread and were given stones. With their starved nerves, driven through with temptation, sweeping like flame down their spines and through the marrow of their bones.

That was London, part of London, part of her evil, that flared up suddenly to burn in the blood like a fever.

But Timothy belonged to London, he belonged to her mists, her blue twilights, her lights like floating stars, to those serene, more distant stars, set widely apart in the dark vault of her disregarded skies.

He belonged to her city, to her old grey buildings, her ghosts, to her towers and spires, and her courtyards with their hidden lawns and flowering trees. To her river with its swift murmuring rhythm running through the city of Southminster, with its sweet and bitter secrets of life on London docks, with the lights of the Houses of Parliament glittering across its tiny waves like a fall of burning leaves, with its stout little barges chugging up and down, its gaudy pleasure steamers, and its Police Boat, sinister and silent, ploughing to and fro, past Cleopatra's needle and the great black lions, patrolling the dark waters for that pitiful human drift for whom civilization had proved too cruel.

He belonged to her hotels, her restaurants, her bars, her factories, her shops and power stations, her ships and warehouses, her pavements swarming with life.

It was strange that the people who swarmed her pavements at night, were the same as those who sat at ledgers, behind cash desks and counters, crowded into restaurants and swung from straps by day. By day the office world possessed them, took them to itself in a kind of horrible transubstantiation. Each face became a face in a row of faces that were all alike, which mirrored in the shop windows, was a multitudinous inane smiling face, accepting civilization as it is—despair.

Each voice became a voice in a chorus of voices, a chorus of voices talking about food and girls and beer and cinemas. But at night each one became himself. When London, like a magnificent old lady, put on the diamonds of her lights and stars, her children put on their own faces and spoke and wept and laughed in their own voices.

Timothy turned away from the crowds and made his way to his lodging. He crept up the carpetless stairs as silently as he could so as not to disturb the other lodgers. The house was dark and whispering. Below him down the well of the stairs he heard a door open and shut, and as he went into his room, another, close by him, opened and closed again gently like a secret. Footsteps passed his door, slippered footsteps, there was a little sighing through the house, a stair creaking and silence.

Silence that was taking possession of London as it took possession of the house. Gradually subsiding sounds, a broken drunken singing, rambling further and further away, note upon note of the passion, the tenderness, the loneliness, the despair of men, note upon note falling into the darkness and lying still. The only sound at last, the slow steady footsteps of the policeman on point duty.

The lights went out of the windows one by one, until at last only the street lamps marking long regular rows remained, and here and there a dull patch of gold or orange behind a drawn blind.

Timothy thought of all the people he had noticed during the day, gone home now. He wondered what kind of homes they had. He thought of the homes of families, kind and solid, built on the rock of love, the home that is one small room where someone has taken root, or has made a shell that is his armour. He thought that in this city even the homeless have homes, for it is the Londoner's unique gift to be able to make a corner in a doss-house, or a chair in a workhouse, or even a bench in a park his own.

Yet there were some, real vagrants, to whom just London herself, her skies and streets, were home, those who wander from doss to doss, those who drift in the haze of drugs and go from one doubtful lodging to another, vanishing long before the house wakes in the morning, never twice in one place, nameless, homeless, drifting, always shadowed by the police who take them, when it becomes mercy to take them.—And those poor bundles of humanity roused from the blessed oblivion they had found on the embankment and woken by the policeman to the cold, the hunger, the craving for drink, for company, for something, anything to stir the blood, and told "Keep moving—move along—keep moving."

Now the people who stood out from the daytime in Timothy's mind, passed before it in procession, to disappear into the darkness, moving down the shadowed alleyways and dark streets to sleep, the Italian with the barrel organ and the little monkey in a red doll's frock: the old, almost sub-human paper seller in the City, who looked as if he must live underground, the tumblers and jugglers who entertained the theatre queues; the man, not seen but heard as a harsh beery voice under the Punch and Judy show in Edgware Road; the lovely old "Mas" who sold flowers at Oxford Circus, wrapped in their shawls, wearing gents' straw boaters and sitting by great bonfires of chrysanthemums; the long miserable line of young men with jutting Adam's Apples, who stood day after day in the Labour Exchange seeking the work they would loathe; the mincing foxy faced film extras, all the flotsam and jetsam of the world that haunts Wardour Street, the chestnut vendors of Tottenham Court Road, rubbing their red, half mittened hands together and keeping up a fidget that was almost a tap dance behind their glowing braziers; the poor old drunks, pitiful because they seemed lost and helpless, taken away by tolerant kindly policemen and locked up, now laughing, weeping or sleeping, as the drink took them, in the Police Court cells.

People sleeping, lying in all the revealing, heart-breaking attitudes of sleep. People awake as he was awake in the night. People who were reading, sitting in the ring of a lamp's light, bowing beside the star of a candle's flame, leaving their sad, material worlds, the empty grates, the dreadful washstands, the chipped enamel cans, the smeary tooth glasses, the thin patches in the middle of the threadbare mats, entering into realms of pure and holy thought: of philosophy, poetry, science. Their minds expanding, ring upon ring of light.

He thought of the lives that would be revealed to one another if men could see through the thin walls that separate them, through the drawn blinds that hide them in the night. In his imagination he saw them, the families huddled together in overcrowded rooms, lying close to keep warm, the workers sunk down into their welcoming narrow beds, the aching weariness of the day seeping out of them, their clothes shaped to the shape of their work, the backs and shoulders of the coats rounded, the elbows worn thin, the alarm clock beside the bed ticking on relentlessly, counting off the seconds of the blessed oblivion. The drunkard sleeping fully clothed, sprawled across the unmade bed in his untidy room, mice fearlessly nibbling on the greasy plates left over from the last meal. Husband and wife lying side by side content in the love that is whole like harmony in music. The shy, half-frightened boy and girl awake in the new wonder of passion, drowning reason in its shining torrent. And illicit lovers, separated from the respectable matrons sleeping the heavy sleep of the well-nourished and unimaginative, only by thin walls of brick and plaster, trying to snatch moments of security, moments of release from loneliness, from homesickness, from frustration, from starvation of body and mind, tormented, cowering under the darkness as if it were a cover that could hide them from the morning's irrevocable crimson fingers, that will tear them apart.

And he thought of the ugly loveless "love making"; the travesty in Mayfair, in airless curtained rooms pranked out with gilded cherubim: fetid and furtive in Soho, in ornate back rooms behind rat-ridden, narrow passages.

He thought of children lying asleep—children in night nurseries at the top of narrow Georgian houses; children turning in the moonlight to see the reassuring bulk of the old Nanny in her bed beside them; children with nightlights burning in white saucers, comforting as the Star of Bethlehem; children clasping ugly old loved dolls, dolls with noses flattened out by continual embraces; children sleeping with their mouths slightly open, their flushed cheeks warm and rosy, their soft hair, like curling sprays of golden fern upon their pillows; parents coming in to the quiet rooms where children are sleeping, looking down on them with meditative eyes of love, shading the candles with hands like small dark wings; children in hospitals, side by side in rows of cots in long white wards, the nurses smelling of linen and verbena, passing silently from cot to cot, observing each one in turn.

Timothy thought, while I am here, secure and alone in this sleeping house, the hospitals are awake, the ambulance is hurrying through the streets. In the hospital there is hard white light. The surgeons are at work, masked and gloved and gowned, working under the great arc lights in the theatre. In the waiting-room men and women live through their life's agony. The old mother, dazed, tremulous, woken suddenly in the night. The young husband dumb and white. The friend huddling into her coat, the agony of suspense aggravated by the cold. Their mouths are dry, they cannot speak even to one another. Silently, swiftly, efficiently, the surgeons are working.

Out there in the darkness, in Bloomsbury, in Kensington, in Bayswater, blameless old ladies sleep, with wide open hands, like children who have placed their trust in God.

The dark colour of the night is ebbing away, the hour at which human life burns down, at which man's vitality sinks to its lowest ebb is close. Innocence lies sleeping and evil wakes. Thieves enter closely shuttered rooms, move on silent feet, work swiftly with gloved hands, look down unmoved on the defenceless faces and silver hair of innocence asleep.

Out there in the muffling, velvet silence, in the hour before dawn, when, just before its ebbing, darkness thickens and clots, murder is done. Behind one of those blind windows, someone unsuspicious, unprepared for death, is being murdered.

Darkness thins, diluted with faint silver, shadows gather round lights that are burning out as darkness moves slowly into light; someone's life moves gently into Eternity, surrounded by those they love. Someone is dying—and someone is being born.

So the life of London passes through another night, swiftly, secretly, irrevocably, like sand falling silently through a dark hour glass.

Sitting at his open window, sometimes falling asleep, sometimes wide awake, Timothy's mind reaches out to his fellow men. He is conscious of his kinship with them, of his oneness with them in the suffering common to them all, the fear, the loneliness, the thirst and hunger common to all men; in the common need to love and be loved, to forgive and to be forgiven.

A loud cry goes out from his heart, though his lips are

silent: "Let me go down into the depths with you, give me my part, my heritage in your pain, your struggle, your dreams, lift me up on the wings of your ultimate longing, sink me in the depths of your deepest misery, brand me with the brand of your shame, receive me, because I am a man, into the heart of mankind."

Unknown to him, other young men had risen in the night, from hard narrow beds, from tranquil sleep, sleep as white and pure as the shadow of light on milk. Contemplatives who have offered themselves to receive the world's wounds, who know all mankind in one man, wounded with all men's wounding, the Man, Christ on the Cross. These young men, unknown to him, have offered his inarticulate heart. At dusk, at midnight, at dawn, in the ordered loveliness of measured agelong song that hushes the Seraphim before the throne of God.

When drift of silver and weaving shadows gradually gives place to the unbroken light of dawn, when the stars have burnt out and the austere heavens, bleached of the colours of the night, fill with morning light, wide and unbroken like slowly welling, shadowless water, Timothy lies down and sleeps.

As he drifts into sleep he remembers the plaster saints again, standing alone now in the dark locked churches, the flames and the flowers withered at their feet, the boy with his lilies, the girl with her roses, still withholding their secret from him. But the secret is nearly told, already its radiance shines faintly in his mind, it already touches his heart with its warmth, like the light of the sun touching the flower it is just going to open.

Timothy sleeps, he is alone and yet there is a presence in the room. A Presence that expands in his heart and fills the silence, a Presence as elusive as soundless music remembered in the mind, yet as close and tender as two hands covering a child's eyes, and a voice of tenderness saying: "Who am I?"

"Guess who I am."

"Guess who it is."

"Who loves you?"

CHAPTER 13

THE GREEN LEAF

*Now of the fig tree
learn ye a parable. When
the branch thereof is now
tender, and the leaves are
come forth, you know that
summer is very near.*

No sooner had Timothy informed those few people, who
might have felt injured had he not taken them into his con-
fidence, of his intention to become a Catholic, than he found
his soul, the existence of which he had himself but recently recognized, the centre of a whirlpool of indignation and
distress. Godparents, relations, old family friends, known to
him until now only as faded photographs in albums mate-
rialized in the shape of pompous letters of warning and re-
monstrance. Countless reasons were offered to explain, or in
the case of the more charitable, to excuse his conduct. Had he
been crossed in love? Spent an unhappy childhood? Was he

anemic? Was he not carried away by emotion, by the music and the incense? Had some Jesuit got hold of him? Was he eating too little? or an ill-balanced diet?

One however, a sister of his mother's whom he had not seen since he was six years old, blamed herself. Had she, she wrote, given her nephew a Bible before he joined a religion which forbade it, he might have been saved. As it was both he and she were damned.

His father discovered that in spite of his own apparent lifelong indifference to all religion, he was devoted to what he now called the "National Church," though not indeed so much from motives of loyalty to God as to the Conservative Government. He saw in Timothy's conversion, however, exactly what he had always foreseen. It was to be expected from his lack of enthusiasm for football. It was, moreover, besides an act of disloyalty to his country, a flagrant violation of the commandment to honour your father and your mother. (Mr. Green looked this commandment up to make sure that it existed while writing the letter.)

As to Timothy's mother, she remembered tearfully that *her* mother was a devout churchwoman, and herself went to church on the Christmas day of that year, and shed a few tears of self-pity because of her son's curious conduct.

Unable to formulate any arguments herself, she insisted on his coming to tea with an old family friend, who having spent a few holidays abroad, knew all about the abuses of the Roman Clergy in the Southern climate. She would, his mother hoped, snatch Timothy as a brand from the burning, while enjoying her home-made muffins.

She did her best, poor lady, both to snatch the young man

from perdition, and to enjoy the muffins. In both attempts she failed.

She told him of the vast quantities of tobacco smoked by priests in Spain, the vast quantities of red wine consumed by priests in Italy, the vast quantities of rich food devoured by priests everywhere. She mentioned the huge sums of money spent on absolution and candles, and the cruelty of Roman Catholics to ponies in Portugal, to bulls in Spain, and to dogs everywhere—except in England, where of course, Roman Catholics, and even Roman Catholic priests, are not quite so bad as everywhere else.

None of this seemed to be effective, so she lowered her voice, and reaching a blue-veined, ringed hand, for a second muffin, introduced the sale of indulgences, the Borgias, the rumours about the Vatican Choir in the middle ages, walled-up nuns, the skeletons of infants under convent floors and "Pope Joan."

When Timothy had gone, she turned her attention to consoling his mother. "You worry too much," she said. "After all there are some good points in Romanism. Take this fish on Friday business. It is very healthy, as a nation we eat too much meat—far too much."

But that which afflicted Timothy was the attitude of his own friends. He discovered them capable of unimagined bigotry and narrowness, he was a coward they said, afraid of life, afraid of thought. Eric raved and called him a traitor to humanity, but bitterest of all was Peter.

The first friend Timothy had made after he left home, was Eric Jacobs, who lived in the same lodgings, and flattered him by trying to indoctrinate him with the idealized Communism that was his own creed.

He assured Timothy that the future, and particularly the inevitable revolution, was in the hands of youth. Youth would march into the future to lay hold of, to grasp, to seize its glorious heritage of light. For this they must be willing to deny themselves, to live at present in the most hazardous and uncomfortable fashion. That however, was good, everyone was too soft, and everything they suffered made them realize the brotherhood of man. Eric said all this with such passion that Timothy, delighted by the flattery of his saying it to *him*, had accepted it without thought or question; but the phrase, "brotherhood of man" kindled a fire in his mind.

Eric had many magazines from Soviet Russia, illustrating his points. They showed photographs of mass formations of strapping young men and women, forming living emblems of the Soviet ideology, the Hammer and Sickle, the Red Star, the name of Lenin, and so on. There were seldom fewer than a thousand or so in one photograph, excepting when it illustrated collective farming. Then there were smaller groups, in order to leave room on the film for the action of "huzzaing," or giving the salute of the clenched fist, or embracing a girl in a frenzy of enthusiasm for a mechanical plough.

It was Eric who had whispered to Timothy that Peter—Pyotr as he was called by his friends—was the founder, leader, and inspiration of a secret organization of Communists.

There was no need to whisper as the two young men were alone, but Eric's monotonous life was invigorated by the sense of mystery, indeed of conspiracy, as a tired man's blood is invigorated by strong wine. He thrilled to it as a schoolboy does to his secret society and it gave him the pathetic importance of a child, who says to the others, "I've got a secret," and whose only secret is that he has none.

He took Timothy, after swearing him to secrecy, to Peter's studio, a room up four flights of carpetless stairs, at the top of the house, furnished true to convention with packing cases and a camp bed.

Opposite the door as they came in was a long window that framed Peter against a deep blue sky and a blaze of stars. Standing there against the night, a scarlet handkerchief knotted round his throat, he looked like a painted saint in an old Russian ikon. His darkly golden face was long and thin, he had the luminous almond-shaped eyes of the Byzantine saints, and the lock of black hair falling over his forehead; but contradicting the strength of his ascetic face, his hands were the ineffectual but beautiful hands of a neurotic.

An oil stove, smelling atrociously, filled the room with a thick treacle of heat. Round it, Peter's disciples sat on the floor. Timothy never forgot his first impression of them. The little half-caste Burmese, the West Indian girl singing to herself in a whisper, and rocking to and fro as she sang, the old German street musician who had once played his fiddle to adoring audiences in Berlin, the minute Japanese waitress with the face like a flower, who sat always in the attitude of bowing, the Scotch pavement artist, with chilblains on every finger, the handful of Italian models of the old school, wearing huge rings bought in the Caledonian Market, and half a dozen or so more, all of different races and colours as if they were carved out of different beautiful woods, mahogany, walnut, chestnut, beech and maple and lime, and one that looked like pale polished ivory.

They were misfits and outcasts. In time Timothy came to know them all and to think of them secretly as "lost children," for even the old among them were held at some point in an unhappy childhood, at which they had become dislocated from their own happiness for ever. Children, for the most part, of loveless, lost homes, of divorce. Children whose faith in God had been shattered long ago by a father or mother who was God to them, and had broken faith. They carried through life the betrayed hearts of cynical children. Rootless, carrying homelessness within themselves, imparting loneliness even in their affections.

On that night, as on every night, they were round the stove eating the watery stew that was always to be had at Peter's, for, though he was poor himself and often hungry, he worked the little miracle of always having something to give, by giving all he had. But it was not only stew that Peter gave to his followers, he gave them a spark of belief in themselves, he gave their poverty an honourable place.

When Timothy first saw him, he was standing making a little speech, indoctrinating them with his dreams, and his dreams were a soothing drug to them. They who were failures, were to master the misery of mankind. From their ideals a world would come, a new world, without poverty—the rich, magnetic voice went on and on. Meanwhile there was comfort here and now in one another's company, and in the warmth of the stove and the goodness of the stew. What was the secret of the power that Peter had over them all, even over Timothy?

It was surely that Peter, who denied the Spirit, who defied and despised religion, who was obsessed by the material ideal, was in fact dyed through and through with the colour of the Christianity that he denied.

He was by nature ascetic. It was not alone easy, but inevitable to him to deny himself, to suffer cold and hunger, to lie on a hard bed, to belong to no one, though he was given to everyone.

He had within him, though he would have been astonished to know it, the instinct that has sent generations of pilgrims from Russia to Jerusalem. The call from illimitable distance, heard as if it were a whisper within one's own heart, mysterious as the migration of birds, that makes all things as nothing compared to the sweetness of the hard way, that is the incommunicable secret of pilgrims.

In an overcivilized world, he had the primitive soul of a Russian peasant, who, if he is deprived of the knowledge of the true God, makes his own idols from whatever looks bigger than man—machinery, for example, transformed by a capital M to "The Machine," and so given the mystery of vast, inhuman personality.

He had, too, the instinct of the Russians of the old school even of the degenerate among its aristocracy, to go down to the humiliated and the oppressed, to discover the humiliated, suffering Christ in the dregs of humanity. He did not recognize who it was that he sought, but the drag was there at his heart in unappeasable, gnawing compassion. He was burnt up by a bright and terrible fire, which, starved for fuel, consumed itself in the blaze of its own beauty.

Timothy spent nearly every evening in Peter's studio. There he listened by the hour to Peter's talk, and it swept through his mind like blown fire.

He came also to love Peter's disciples, and to delight in their company. He laughed with the Italian models, who were for the most part out of work, or used only by Art Schools.

"Artists nowadays," old Antonio told him with a contemptuous gesture, "artists nowadays do not wish to paint the miracle, the beauty of the human body. No, they prefer to waste many tubes of paint and many miles of canvas on their own subconscious!"—And had Timothy seen what the subconscious of the artists is like? It is a mix-up of faulty geometrical instruments, severed limbs, and decomposing fruit, at least, so it is in the case of the more lucid, but most of the artists are worse even than that. They are paranoiacs. Now can you believe it, they prefer to paint a paranoiac nightmare to the beautiful body of his little daughter, Violetta!—"Now look at her, is she not pure, and young, and lovely?—Is she not like Venus rising from the sea at dawn? Can you not see the ripple of the shallow waves in her every movement? The drift of the virgin light of dawn in the sweet mobile face?— pah—these so called artists—Where can you find me one who could look Botticelli in the face—?"

The Burmese, who makes beautifully lacquered boxes, with such conscientious craftsmanship, that they take too long to do, and can only be sold at a loss, breaks in irreverently:

> In the parlour
> Auntie Nellie
> Dusting down
> Her Botticelli

Antonio sighs and goes on: "And how, then, do we live, we models of the old school, of the great tradition? By collecting and selling old bottles. Yes, Violetta, the despised Venus, goes round all the studios collecting empty bottles, and believe me these paranoiacs have plenty of empty bottles—On the sale of these we must live—Alas—!"

And Timothy goes over to the corner where Pyotr is trying to comfort the little Japanese girl. She has a contract to
remain three more years in London, it is not that anyone is
cruel, she has plenty to eat—but it is so ugly, she does not
think that she will live for three years without seeing the almond trees in bloom. "There are," says Timothy, "almond
trees in St. John's Wood," but she does not answer. Shall he
take her to see them on Saturday? She shakes her head, but
thanks him, tears flow silently down her face, like little drops
of crystal flowing over gold. "You see," says Timothy to Peter and Eric, "that little creature has security, but she is pro-
foundly unhappy. It seems that her own personality is a kind
of flowering and cannot be conditioned to this ugliness. Her
life is withering. When she goes back to Japan she will be
withered up—dead!"

Eric says "Don't imagine that capitalism is not destroy-
ing Japan too. Go into our big people's stores and look at the
cheap flimsy garments and things that are made in Japan and
look at the price of them, and ask yourself, who made them?
and how? and for how much?—Sweated labour, that's what
we import—Flowers!"

But nevertheless Peter brings a huge bunch of flowers to the
little waitress, and though they disagree more and more, he
and Timothy never quarrel. Peter is hard and determined,
but Peter nurses his friends as tenderly as any woman when
they are ill. Peter believes in the sword, in "realism" but he
has the urchins of the whole district on his knees and tells
them stories that spring out of Russia, out of the old "Holy
Russia." Stories of bears. Dancing bears, talking bears, think-

ing bears, in the tall green forests. Peter believes in utility and
he sees that the aged are no longer useful, and are a drag on
the State; but he meets the old blind beggar every night and
brings him in. He puts his one basket armchair by the stove
and reserves it for the old street musician.

Peter believes that Christianity is a drug for the people,
but he wipes the blood and sweat and tears from the Eternal
Face that he does not recognize. From Peter at least, Timothy
expected tolerance, but he was the most intolerant, the most
pitiless of all. Wholly illogically, he took the conversion, not
only as a betrayal of the poor and the outcast, but as a personal offence. A wound inflicted upon himself. It was, he said,
an absolute breach, the end between them. The studio door
would be shut to Timothy.

But what had made him do this? Timothy had longed
for someone to ask that question, instead, as they all did, of
answering it and answering it wrongly. But now that he was
asked, he could not answer. Peter stood in front of him, his
hand flung out open, waiting as it were for Timothy to put
the answer into it, and Timothy, longing to give the incommunicable secret, stood before him mute.

⌒

Near the offices of Timothy's paper there was a tree. A little
stunted tree, black with soot and ringed by a circle of iron
railings, put up long ago in the reign of Queen Victoria.

There must have been a board meeting about it at which
pompous gentlemen in black coats decided that the little tree
was worth preserving, that it had value for the City of London, that it belonged to her children, and to her children's
children, that it was in fact a sacred trust, like an orphan.

For these reasons, and for the further reason of a secret, incomprehensible fluttering, like a flutter of butterflies in the pompous gentlemen's blood, it was worthy of the cost, the labour, the red tape, involved in providing it with the support of iron railings.

What positive lyrical grace breathed in the souls of the gentlemen on that occasion, ruffling the surface of their complacency like breeze on an April morning, urging them to action—which, though somewhat ridiculous in itself, as the little tree needed no support but its own life, was nevertheless an act of faith in life and loveliness, and in man's response to life and loveliness.

Their faith was a million times justified. Since they themselves had entered into eternal life, generation after generation of men had lifted their hearts when they passed the little tree. Among them Timothy's fellow workers. As they passed on the morning when the first spark of green showed on the black twig, they looked up, and one by one their faces lit, like white candles that a spark has suddenly made beautiful with flame.

Hunger for life burnt visibly on their lifted faces, and Timothy had an answer to that hunger in his soul, for on the very day that the green leaf broke into life on the stunted tree, he had been received into the Catholic Church.

After the warnings of his well-wishers concerning the avidity with which the Catholic hierarchy would "fall on" him, Timothy met with what, perhaps, only in view of his expectations, was discouragement, even from them. He had of course, the usual experience of waiting on the Presbytery steps, and ultimately, just when his courage was faltering and he was meditating a retreat, of being confronted by an apparition that bore out all the lowest and softest whispers of the family friend, someone between a policeman and a monk, confronting him almost menacingly.

"Can I see a priest?" Timothy said feebly.

"Which?"

"Anyone."

"They're at dinner."

"I could wait."

The apparition paused and peered down into Timothy's face.

"I'm short-sighted," he said. "Are ye by any chance a sick call?"

"A what?"

"A sick call—are ye in danger of death?"

"Oh, no—at least, I wasn't—"

"Well, that's a pity for ye, if ye were in danger of death, I could tell Father before the pudding."

When the priest came at last, he was a gentle, rather remote old man, so white in the face and hair, so pink in the nose that he resembled a white dormouse. He looked permanently cold and no wonder, for the house was fireless and chill. He peered sadly at Timothy, as if he were very sorry for him before speaking, and then, "Well now," he said, "what is your trouble?"

"I want to become a Catholic."

"Dear me—dear me. You do?—well now, what has put *that* idea into your head?"

"I—I—don't exactly know. At least I can't put it into words."

"Well, well—never mind. Do you know who made you?"

"God."

"Now that's perfectly correct. It was God. There isn't a

shred of doubt about that. And now, do you know *why* God made you?"

Timothy was silent, he had not thought of that. At last he said sheepishly, "No—I can't say I do."

"Well now, never mind, to tell you the truth there are a great many people who do not know why God made them. That is why there are so many unhappy people in the world. You take this little book and learn the answer—and don't worry, take it easy."

Timothy went away with a penny Catechism in his pocket, lonelier than he had ever been, even as that loneliest of all creatures, a little child.

Three months later he was received into the Church.

On the night before, he set his alarm clock and woke at every hour until morning, in case it did not wake him. But it did, and it seemed strange, though in keeping with everything else, that an alarm clock, not a peal of bells or Song of Angels, should call him to be born again.

The charwoman who swept and dusted the church witnessed his reception. She was an old hand at it, having stood side by side with many a solitary convert's Guardian Angel, a foster mother of waifs and strays on the doorstep of Heaven—

So reassuring was she with her poor orphans, that it was almost alarming, like the alarming brightness of the dentist's assistant whose work is to coax the patient to the ordeal and to face the agony; to end agony manfully.

"Don't worry now," she said. "You'll feel better when you've made your Confession, and mind you tell the whoppers first, and when it's all over you shall have a nice cup of tea, as you won't be going to your Holy Communion until tomorrow. Oh, I've seen many young men, and a few old ones come into the Church. Same as I've seen lots of people come into the world, and go out of it. My mother had a real devotion to the dying and it's many a happy death I've helped her to lay out."

Timothy nodded. He knew with emotionless joy that the candle of faith that the priest put into his hand, was the candle that would be burning by his coffin, that the hands he folded now he folded over his dead heart, that the will that he pledged was the gift both of his life and the homage of the dust.

He said his act of faith like a child reciting a lesson, and when it was all over, and he made the sign of the Cross on leaving the church, he realized the wonder of the sign, and marvelled, but still impersonally as if he was thinking of another man. He was going back to the office now, in the name and the power of the Trinity!

He, the hollow man, who an hour ago had no power at all. He looked and felt just the same as before, but before he was powerless, now he was going out in the power of Christ's love!

He saw the significance, the shape and the size of the sign of the Cross as he would not see it again, covering him, his mind, his shoulders, his heart. He saw it now objectively, as we see what is new to us, as we see new faces, new people whom, when we know and love or hate, we shall see changed by our own conception of them, or shall not see at all, because they have been taken too close.

Now he saw the shape of the Cross, man's mind the shaft of it pointing heavenwards, and he saw his shoulders tak-

ing on the world's suffering in Christ's power, and his arms
reaching out to left and right in the stretch of his mercy, and
his heart—the centre of the great rood, and the source of his
love, the horizontal beam driving down into the earth, and
the sap of life rising up from its roots.

He walked to the office, and no red flowers sprang up out
of the pavement where he walked, and there was nothing at
all to mark the wonder of the day.

But on that day the leaf pierced the hard wood of the little black tree with life, the tree that was rooted in the poor,
sooty earth of the London square, and there was a voiceless
"Sursum Corda," "up with your hearts," in the City.

CHAPTER 14

SOLLY LEE

*How shall we sing the
song of the Lord in a
strange land?*

I

"If you also should forsake me, my little Carmel, I should then be quite altogether brokenhearted. I should die. You would not have your poor Solly to die, would you, my little girl?"

Carmel Fernandez made no answer and Solly went on desperately—"Don't you love old Solly a little bit?—Ah you do not, I know it, no one ever loves me. You hate my ugly body, that is what it is. You do not see my soul. You think I have no soul. You, a little Roman Catholic, should see my soul—but no, you do not, you see only the outside, the pig hide of me. Oh yes, I have no illusions, I know I am like a pig. Some little girls are not so kind as you, Carmel. Lily Ping, my little Chinese girl, she told me—'You are like a pink pig, Solly'—and Hetty, my sweet Hetty, do you know what she said to me? She said to me—'Solly, you are like a bladder of lard with sunstroke'—but I bore no resentment and I was good to them. Yes, I gave a hundred pounds to Lily Ping, think of that, a hundred pounds and a string of Ciro pearls. And I was generous to Hetty too. No one can say that ever I am mean, I may be a Jew, but I am a generous man, you know that, don't you, my little Carmel?"

"Yes, Solly, I know that you are." Carmel looked at her own hands lying in her lap. She had only to look at them to know that Solly was generous. A month ago they were chapped and grimed, now they were white and soft, with red enamelled nails. Her clothes were quite different too. Before they had been washed out cotton frocks, so skimpy and shrunken from washing, that she had had scruples about whether they were modest to wear. Now she had suits of fine thick cloth, cut and made by Solly himself, and silk underwear. It would be harder, if she had to give up all this, to give up the silk underwear than anything else. The touch of it was caressing, it soothed her, it made her feel precious, that she was valued and loved.

Above all it made her feel that she was a different person. When she had just bathed in warm scented water and put on her silk underwear, she was not Carmel Fernandez any more. She was someone grand and glamorous, like the rich girls in the films.

When she had made up her face and looked in the glass at the stranger there, it was impossible to think that this was Carmel Fernandez, who was named after Our Lady of Mount Carmel, and had once, not very long ago, had scruples about the modesty of her dresses.

This was someone different. Someone for whom it was not sinful to be like this with Solly. Not Carmel Fernandez, for whom it would have been sinful even to think willingly of what she was now doing.

Solly looked at her and he was proud, she was beautiful and she was his. That warm, olive-coloured, sweet oval face was his. Those dark eyes like damsons were his. That dark curly hair was his. Yet he already had misgivings. Was she really his at all? There was some part of her that he could not touch, something that he could not reach, which made her self-possessed, her own, which gave her a baffling, sorrowful integrity, even in humiliation. And it was at present his own humiliation to know that she *was* humiliated, she was not really happy, she would go away and leave him as everyone else had.

It was an obsession with him, this fear of losing her, he could not leave it alone. He tried, as he had always tried with everyone, to buy her love. He knew that no one would ever love him for himself and he would be grateful even for being liked—very much liked—for his gifts—even in the last resort for pity—yes, he would have been grateful for pity from a factory girl.

"Don't I make you happy, my little one?" he asked.

"Yes, Solly," but she looked away and he knew that it was not true.

"But no—you are not happy—you want something? Tell me what it is. Solly will give you anything you want. Is it a new dress, a pretty hat, a little puppy dog, or would my darling little girl be happy if Solly bought her a lovely string of pearls?"

Carmel looked at him with compassion as well as misery

in her eyes and touched his arm with her unfamiliar white hand. "No, Solly dear, I don't want any more things, you have given me so much, I don't want you to give me anything more."

At her touch, Solly's weak, pink-rimmed eyes filled with tears of self-pity.

"Ah—so—I am your *dear* Solly?—perhaps you care a little bit then—eh?—now Lily Ping and Hetty, both would have wanted more, no matter how much I gave. Always it was more and more, and then all the same they left me. You know what it was, my dear little girl, I made them so attractive that other men came after them, and they had no use for the poor bladder of lard with sunstroke. Why, when Lily came she was so thin and yellow, so insignificant, I thought, I can *make* her love me. She will be my little girl as well as my mistress, I will fatten her up and dress her up—ah Carmel, I did that, and Hetty too, she was so white, so plain, like a piebald rat when I got her—and what happened?—Both of them grew plump. Ah, what curves they had! All given to them by Solly. What dinners I gave to them, at the very best restaurants, Carmel, and in the morning, breakfast in bed. Never a hand's turn did they do. No, it was their old Solly, who got up in the morning, lit the fire and brought them their breakfast in bed, and they got so plump, so pink, so pretty, and then—Poof!—like that, they were gone."

"You must not keep thinking about them," said Carmel. "You only upset yourself."

"Are you jealous, my dear?—I hope you are, then I will know that you begin to love me—but you need not be, for I am faithful. Everyone forsakes *me*—I, never. It was so also with my wife, Ella."

Already at the very mention of Ella, tears were running down Solly's face. Carmel knew that nothing now would stop the story of his unhappy marriage, of the treachery and cruelty and infidelity of his adored Ella. Of his subsequent loneliness and wandering homeless from place to place because without Ella he could find home nowhere on earth—of how he had cared for her, the clothes and the jewellery that he had given to her, the way he had waited on her as a servant, and nursed her as a sick nurse—but alas!—

Carmel folded her hands in her lap and listened, or pretended to listen. Really she was thinking, "This is the third day of the Novena for Willie Jewel. If only I could join in with the others—if only I could go and see Willie and Rose O'Shane and Martha and Father O'Grady—"

II

Solly Lee was doomed to loneliness before he was born. His doom was in the heart of Moses Levi, his grandfather. For generations the Levi family had suffered persecution, tyranny, grinding taxation, contempt. Moses inherited the accumulated memories of generations of fear, pogroms, exile, separation, hunger. His soul wearied, the chains of the ghetto corroded his heart. He dreamt of peace, of an old age spent in the tranquillity of a distant land, of his sons growing up around him in security, of his sons' sons in the twilight of his years, his seed multiplied like the stars.

One night, in peril of his life, he fled, with him his wife Naomi and their three young sons. For many months they were homeless wanderers. Ultimately they settled in the East End of London.

Solly was born in his grandfather's house in London. His

earliest memory was of his grandmother's hands spread over the flame of a candle on the evening of the Sabbath; long golden hands, transparent in the light of the flame, the blood glowing like rubies round the dark filigree of bones.

Solly sat very still while grandfather read the portion of the Scripture allotted for the Sabbath day in Hebrew. He did not understand Hebrew, and he did not try to listen. He watched grandmother's hands, fascinated by the slightly crooked bones in the fingers, and the large knuckles. He thought "grandmother is very old. She has very old hands."

Grandmother's face was not old. When all other beauties grew dim in after years, the grave beauty of that holy face haunted Solly. The high cheek-bones, the long sweet curve from brow to chin, the warm olive colour, the deep-set mournful eyes.

It was grandmother who mixed a strange aromatic beauty into his daily life. She who imbued the house with a sense of mute mystery and made him aware, at least when he was a very small child, of some tremendous Secret Person, to whom he must be beholden. She knew far less of their religion than grandfather did, but it was she who was the centre of the little rites of the home, bringing sweet, sensuous things into his life, which were informed with a significance beyond his comprehension. Diminishing rows of candles, which, if you looked along them with screwed-up eyes, were like a burning dagger of light; long green, rustling palms, and the fragrance of citron, and spices, and warm melting wax.

Just before the beginning of his troubles, Solly used to follow grandmother about like a little dog. He went round the house with her and to the market with her, and watching her face he saw that her lips often moved.

"Who are you talking to, Grandmother?" he asked one day.

"I am blessing our Lord God."

And he learned that she blessed God many times a day. She blessed Him when she ate the fruit that grows on trees, when she smelt fragrant wood or flowers, when she smelt fruit or spice or oil. She blessed Him when storm broke, when she heard the roar of thunder and saw the flash of lightning. She blessed Him when the first white bud broke on the tree. She blessed Him when a wise or learned man came to the house. She blessed Him when they saw beautiful animals, dogs, cats and birds, and the gulls sweeping over the bows of the ships in dock, on wings like the wings of angels. She blessed Him when she used anything new, when she put on new clothes or dressed Solly in new clothes: when she ate any kind of fruit for the first time in the season, and when the new moon rose over the chimneys.

Solly felt close to grandmother, especially when she blessed her Lord God for beautiful dogs and cats, but he felt miles and miles away from grandfather, of whom, though he did not fear him, he stood in awe.

Although grandmother's life was filled with her religious rites, they seemed homely, they brought her closer to Solly, they were domestic, sensuous and tenderly devout. But grandfather was set apart by his prayers, his soul seemed to be soaring away, outside of their little house. Solly watched him, half in awe, half fascinated, he watched him wrapping himself in a shawl to pray, binding thongs of leather on his forehead and arm: heard his voice reading the scripture in Hebrew as a voice from another world. He sensed both sorrow and emptiness in the old man. Sorrow that was oppressive, and emptiness that was as frightening to a child as it would be to suddenly find himself alone in an empty house.

Moses Levi, in self-sought exile, did not find the promised land that he had dreamed of. Although his memories of it were dark, blood red and black, and sodden with tears, he found that after all he could not tear out his roots from the ghetto he had forsaken. There, the people, the chosen people of God and his own people, were one in the solidarity of suffering. Their oneness set them apart and excluded the rest of the world. Their unity was not one that could be broken even by death. It was like hard rock made of multitudinous grains of sand, that has been washed in the salt of deep and bitter seas.

Here, in London, there were also faithful Jews, who frequented the Synagogue and kept the laws of diet and the Fasts. But there were also many who betrayed the agony of the centuries, who betrayed the blood and tears of the children of Israel, who betrayed their age-long glory as Jews, by compromise and infidelity. Old Moses Levi raged inwardly because they betrayed Israel and mixed their flesh with the Gentiles, not even for the rich savoury flesh pots of Egypt, but for the tasteless boiled stews, the saltless mediocrity of the Gentiles, who in their turn were faithless to their own God. Faithless even to their poor crucified Jesus Christ, though they professed to believe that He was in their midst, His heart bleeding for them!

More and more did Moses Levi seek escape in the past. As he grew old and his vigour seeped from him, he thought less and less of the coming Messiah and more and more of the past glory of Judaism.

While grandmother unconsciously greeted Messiah, blessing the first flower on the tree, grandfather turned more and more to outward forms, to the long ceremonies and exactitudes of the law. The ancient Liturgy had worn deep grooves into his heart like the bed of a river worn into hard rock. Through these grooves in his heart flowed the torrent of tears and blood that is the glory of Israel. In the empty twilight vaults of his mind the harp of David, strong and pure, hymned the One God.

He was a weary, self-exiled old man who had borne the suffering accumulating in the heart of successive generations of Jews for six thousand years, and now desired only to be rocked to sleep like a child on the heart of God.

Solly used to stand spellbound, watching grandfather sitting in the doorway, as still as an old man carved out of limestone, his hands lying thin and straight along his knees. The lids of his eyes, like crumpled tissue paper, hardly veiled the fire which had not yet faded out of the eyes that burnt like two stars in unfathomable darkness.

Solly's mother, Rebecca, and his father, Abraham, had far less hold on his imagination, and far more hold on his body than his grandparents. Long before they left the parents' house they were unfaithful to all that was sacred in it. Solly sensed this as a vague, persistent uneasiness in himself, though he was really taught nothing about God, whose Presence was his environment.

He felt uncomfortable when his parents took him, from time to time, to another part of London to eat in a big Restaurant with Gentiles eating all round them. Here there was, it seemed, no Law about what you ate, and a few slices of ham speedily acted as a poultice to soothe his troubled conscience, which indeed, since he was then only about six years old, would probably not have pricked him at all, were it not that Rebecca told him not to tell grandmother anything about it.

At home when the great Fast was in progress, Solly's uncles and his two cousins who were over twelve years old grew white and strained, their faces looked sharp, and the grandparents, themselves bloodless and drained, watched them with quiet exulting pride. Solly had sometimes envied his cousin David, when at the end of the Fast, grandmother had taken him into her arms and held him close to her, as if she folded the purity of Israel to her breast. Then she was not an old woman, for all the renewal of her race sang in her blood, and she greeted Messiah in the pure young David, as she did in the taste of the first fruit, the fragrance of the cut wood, and the first flower on the tree in the children's park.

At these moments Solly felt unhappy, because his mother was always popping sweets into her own mouth and his during the Fasting time. Because he knew the significance of the furtive smiles exchanged between his parents, and because he knew that they really took no part in the poetry of grandmother's tender love of God.

In a way the child, taught only by the interplay of his own imagination and his senses, felt *himself* to be shamed. His attitude to his mother began to be wholly sensual, she conditioned him to expect some sweet or savoury morsel to be popped into his mouth whenever they were alone, even her kisses were sticky with boiled sweets.

The young uncles gradually filled the house with treasure,

everything was valuable, everything was beautiful, everything was chosen with the taste of connoisseurs, only there was too much of everything. The parlour smelt of beeswax and sandlewood and musk.

Solly's father, Abraham Levi, had a little tailor's shop at the corner of the next street. One day when Solly was nine years old, his parents packed their personal belongings into three bundles and moved into it, to live.

The child was homesick, he experienced in his own way that which Moses Levi experienced as he rocked to and fro mourning his native land. He wanted grandmother. He began to imagine going into the room and finding her alone, with her arms open to take him to her heart as she took David after the Fast. But he never attempted to go to her, fear lay like a shadow across grandfather's doorstep. There was a bucket there with a straw in it, and every one who came in and out dipped their fingers into it to wash away the contamination of the house.

Once grandmother passed them in the street, she was dressed in deep mourning like a widow. She was looking down and did not raise her eyes. Solly did not cry out or run to her. Something stopped him, made it impossible. He soon found that grandfather, his young cousins and all the Jews from the Synagogue cut him in the street. He was at the beginning of the shame of being the child of an apostate, but only at the beginning.

Abraham Levi had forsaken the faith of his fathers. Rebecca his wife had never been true to it. Jewish in origin, her family had long ceased to practise. Only when she married Abraham did she realize the complete domination of a Faith which demands not merely that you should give your heart, but that you should give your stomach to God.

She was a large, florid woman with a vast, crude sense of humour, an immeasurably good nature, and not a spark of poetry in her soul. That she dearly loved her husband is certain, had she not she could not have endured the atmosphere of Moses Levi's house for ten years. Two things helped her, a love for her child bordering on idolatry which made her ready to suffer anything to secure some of the family's prosperity for him, and the frequent relief of the unrestricted meals and countless other petty indulgences that she secretly shared with Abraham.

Abraham fell readily in her hands. He was not naturally devout as his brothers were, and he greatly preferred the company and the custom of the whole world to the exclusiveness of Israel.

"Look here, my dear," he said to Rebecca, "we've got to make our own way. Why, we might just as well be pieces in a museum, the way we live. I'm sick and tired of the old man's misery and his prayers."

"That's right, Brammie—so am I, and not to eat this and not to eat that. What's the good of it anyway?"

"I fancy we'd be wise to move out, Becca."

"Yes, anyway you know best, Brammie."

"And become Christians."

"Oh Lord, Brammie, we couldn't do that."

"Yes, we could. We could get baptized, that's all you got to do, then we'd get the custom of the Gentiles."

"I wouldn't fancy that—after all we got Jewish blood in our veins, we don't need to pretend to be Gentiles. Just got to show we are broadminded, that's all."

"That's nonsense Becca, we don't need to practise, all we need to do is to rent a pew in the church, and maybe turn up at the service now and then, just by way of advertising we are Christians, and get the Gentile custom. You've got to edify the Christians if you want their patronage."

"Yes, you're always right Brammie, but why need we be *baptized*? Wouldn't it do just as well if we went down to the 'Pig and Whistle,' and blew ourselves out publicly on sausages? I reckon most English folk would find that more edifying than being baptized."

"Now look here, Becca, being baptized doesn't hurt you, it wouldn't hurt so much as vaccination."

"It isn't that—only it just seems kind of insincere."

But Abraham had his trump card up his sleeve and he played it successfully.

"I'm thinking of our son, young Sol," he said. "If we aren't going to do our best for him, we might as well stay here and get his share of the family shekels, but judging by the way the Lord is looking favourably upon Jacob and Ezra, I should say the dividend is going right down to nothing at all. They've got five sons between them now, and if we aren't viewed so favourably by the Deity"—he winked hideously at this point—"it's our job to go all out to give our *one* boy the best of everything. Now I mean him to be spared what I've gone through, I being a foreigner, a Jew boy, son of a queer old madman, don't fit anywhere, don't feel right anywhere, it's not good enough, Becca. Our Sol is to be an English gentleman, see? He's got sandy hair like a Scotch boy, and he don't understand a word of Hebrew, or any other language but English. I mean to make good and send him to Oxford University for education. With all that and Christian baptism, what is there to distinguish him from an English gentleman?"

"Well, if it's really best for young Sol … all right. But Brammie, don't you reckon Levi don't sound much like the name of an English gentleman?"

"It's not going to be Levi," said Abraham triumphantly. "It's going to be Lee."

So they moved out of old Moses' house to the shop, changed their name to Lee, and after several unsuccessful attempts to impress ministers of Religion with their good faith, found an honest little Protestant parson who clung to the thirty-nine articles of Religion to which he was vowed, and in consequence had lost nearly all his congregation to the adjacent High Church parish. He, brimming over with gratitude for what he believed to be a conversion from Judaism, baptized all three.

"Now," said Abraham, "we are all things to all men and we shall have the custom both of the Gentiles and the Jews."

Things did not work out according to Abraham's plan. He did not gain the custom of the Gentiles and he lost that of the Jews. After his father's death he was regarded not only as an apostate but as his murderer. He had to sell the shop and leave the district.

The grief which took possession of old Moses Levi was not simply grief, it was death. The frail body which had withstood hunger and thirst and flogging, for the faith that his son had denied, was broken by Abraham's treachery. Within a few weeks he died.

No one ever knew what was in grandmother's heart. The two sons who were faithful, and their children, surrounded her like a bodyguard and cherished her. Excepting for the one occasion when she passed him in the street, little Solly never saw her again.

In all his life Solly was loved by one woman only, his mother. And her love found but one form of expression, to feed him. And feed him she did, even in the lean years when they were once more strangers in a new district and Abraham, no longer a master tailor, was working as a cutter for a small wage.

Rebecca wrapped her son in a blanket of suffocating motherlove. Even when she had only a gas-ring in a lodging house bedroom to cook on she managed to produce rich hash, curry and savoury stews, goulash, bliny, and chowder, until Solly was shapeless in mind and body.

He was not bullied at school. He was simply left alone. The school bully said he could not kick him, because his flesh was too soft, his foot would sink in and get lost in it.

Solly tried to win favour by giving presents. His parents denied themselves even necessities to provide him with pocket money, and with it he tried in vain to buy the friendship of other boys. He was always alone.

At fourteen he was apprenticed to the tailor where his father worked, and soon after that Abraham died. Rebecca outlived him by seven years. Seven years of unbridled spoiling of Solly, who was fed and fed and overfed, until bis mother died in her turn from a complaint of the liver, aggravated by continually leaning over the hot stove.

Solly had hardly mourned his father but he sat all night by his mother's dead body, rocking to and fro with grief.

He followed her to the grave weeping like a child, and her burial brought home to him as nothing had ever done before, the fact that without his mother he had no environment. He was exiled from his own flesh and blood, he was harbourless but for the harbour of her love. The bitterness of Abraham's apostasy was brought home to him by the fact that even the little piece of earth that makes a grave did not belong to them.

The Jews he knew would not take back this poor Jewish clay to rest in its own earth, and he felt himself to be an imposter in asking for a plot of Christian soil. More so, as since Abraham died Rebecca had not set foot in any church, and Solly never had, so that now the clergyman was asked to bury someone who was a complete stranger to him.

Solly was left helpless. Rebecca had softened all his resistances. In him the vitality which had swept the Levi family on through generations of·hardship had grown soft. He could not deny himself. He was completely dependent on material comfort. But the instinct, frequent in his race, to possess the beauty that is admired came to his aid.

One day he saw a little carved ivory figure of a woman in an antique shop and he desired her. It was not enough to look. He must hold that roundness, that smoothness, that glossy creaminess in his hand. He must feel it, stroke it, hold it, possess it. Moreover, he must buy it. Even if someone had been willing to give it to him, he would have said "no."

A gift could never be sufficiently his own. He would be beholden for it; that would give the donor a certain kind of ownership himself. Long ago his awareness of the Secret Presence, whom grandmother had blessed for the gifts of beautiful things, had grown dim and faded out. Now he wanted to possess absolutely in his own right, so that no one could come into it at all, even a giver. He thought that only money could give the kind of possession he craved, as if money could separate the thing from its maker. And certainly there are some things which by being bought or sold are separated from God.

The little ivory figure obsessed him. She haunted his sleeping dreams, growing in them to the full stature of womanhood. A warm, white womanhood that humiliated him with a morbid consciousness of his own futility. It challenged his manhood in a way that he could not have imagined, as if this woman in his dream was womankind, challenging all mankind in him, forcing him to realize his softness, his dependence on comfort, the servility of his approach to life. She humiliated him because he knew that he was capable of answering her challenge only with sensuality and sentimentality. But she was a white virgin of ivory challenging the pure passion of love that makes the world glorious with life. Her arms were open to him in his dream, but he could not get up from his soft bed and go to her, and his cousin David came, his face drawn from the Fast, burning with the fire and elation of sacrifice. And the ivory girl changed slowly and became Naomi, his grandmother, in that moment long ago, when she was not an old woman, but Israel taking Messiah to her heart.

Solly stayed to work overtime day after day. He gave up his entire leisure. He touted private customers for himself and sat up right through the night making costumes for them. He saved every penny, even denying himself food and smokes, and walking instead of riding on the bus until he had ten pounds saved, the price of the little figure. Then he bought her.

The fact that he possessed her, that she was his, bought with his own money, gave him a new self-respect, a new sense of power. Money had a new meaning in his eyes.

He made up his mind that now he must get a wife, a real woman of flesh and blood, but first of all he would have a home for her.

For five years he drove and sweated himself, for five years he denied himself. At the end of it he had a shop of his own in Riverside. He had lost weight and looked more attractive than he ever had done before, or ever would again. He had made himself a smart-waisted suit. His face had acquired a foxy sharpness, for a short time he was self-confident.

At least one virtue Solly could claim. In spite of his mother's persistent spoiling he had been a good son to her. He used to get up in the morning and make early tea for her, and then go back to bed. He used to buy presents for her and pay her countless little attentions. When he was married he did the same and more for his wife. Nevertheless, without one word of warning or explanation, and after a very short time with him, she ran away.

It was after this that Solly gained his unsavoury reputation. At first he was driven by vanity, he doubted himself too deeply now to rest. He craved for reassurance and in a wretched, futile hope of attaining it tried to seduce every girl he could. He no longer made any attempt to deny himself. He had enough money, and he knew that it could not buy the thing he wanted.

He filled out again and resumed the ugly contour that Rebecca had given to him. His hair got thin and showed his bald head under wisps, his slight bow-leggedness increased.

He took to dressing in a frankly vulgar style, and to wearing diamond tie pins and rings on his fingers. His small eyes became smaller and pink-rimmed. After a time he grew used to humiliation. The servility which was his characteristic as a schoolboy returned. A new fear gripped him, the fear of loneliness. He had now neither family nor race nor country nor faith, and since no woman would ever love him, loneliness became a spectre that stalked and obsessed him.

Long before Solly Lee persuaded Carmel Fernandez to come and live with him, mothers refused to allow their daughters to take work in his shop or workroom. His sense of frustration was intensified by the difficulty of getting workers and by the almost certain fear of losing them when he had. They were better paid than any girls in Riverside. They were never sweated. Solly gave them pretty clothes and took them to dinners and theatres in the West End. Usually he asked nothing in return, but that he might keep the same familiar and pretty face in his workroom, and perhaps be liked a little bit. But actually the girls treated him with contempt. They themselves were treated with contempt by their friends, who refused to believe that huge boxes of chocolate creams and Ciro pearls are ever anything else but the wages of sin, and though very far from being angels themselves, they had nothing but scorn for sin involving so repulsive a little man as Solly Lee.

The only women whose attitude to Solly was frank, sweet and unsuspicious, were the two nuns who called annually to collect for their home for unmarried mothers. The obsequious manner that offended others delighted them. They were truly grateful for the hot syrupy tea that he made for them, for the magnificent donation that he always gave, and his obvious pleasure if they rested from their long tramping round the streets from house to house for the space of a little chat with him.

It was really a chat between Solly and Sister Francis Patrick, the superior of the two, for Sister Ann Veronica was only allowed to speak at all when Sister Francis gave her permission, and as she knew that Ann Veronica was usually suffering from indigestion which demanded the total concentration of all her faculties, she refrained in charity from adding the obligation of joining in the conversation to her other difficulties. Besides, she knew that Ann Veronica offered her indigestion up for the babies of the unmarried mothers in the home, which gave it the status of a prayer that should not be disturbed.

But when they were alone on their rounds again, the two nuns had nothing but praise for Solly Lee, praise mingled with a feeling of proud and possessive maternity, because they had so often been told by others of their patrons that Solly Lee was a terrible sinner. They were confident that God had given him to them for his salvation, and that he was almost wholly dependent on their prayers, and Ann Veronica's offered hiccoughs.

"You would hardly imagine," Francis Patrick would say, "that such a nicely mannered gentleman would be a sinner at all."

"That you would not, Sister, though they do say that the devil has very pretty manners."

"Ah, but Sister, the devil never gave a cup of tea to a nun in his life."

"That is true, Sister, and I have often thought that if only he had been a girl, Mr. Lee has all the makings of a perfect novice."

"Well now, Sister, let us say a decade of the Rosary for the poor dear man as we go along."

And so they would go along, saying the prayers out loud in turn, and feeling as responsible for Solly Lee before God as they did for the helpless babies in the home. Rocking him in their pure maternal hearts, as proud, in the way of women, of their sinner, as the unmarried mothers in the home were of the innocent fruit of their sin.

CHAPTER 15

THE CATHOLIC CHURCH

Who is this that
cometh from Edom, with
dyed garments from Bosra,
this beautiful one in his
robe?

One day, a little while before his association with Carmel Fernandez, Solly Lee happened to go into the Catholic church. He went in simply from curiosity, to see what it was like.

It was just after Benediction; no one had remained in the church but from the candles on the Altar thin blue lines of smoke were still drifting. The air was heavy with incense and another smell which brought a rush of memory to Solly, of his childhood. The smell of warm wax and of flowers in the heat of flames.

On either side of the Sanctuary, in the chapels of the Sacred Heart and of Our Lady, votive lamps burnt in little thick glass tumblers, encrusted with oil and dust, so that the tiny flames were blurred and magnified, and the lamp glass looked as if it were cut out of a great lump of rough topaz.

Father O'Grady's church was a riot of vulgarity. It had all the worst characteristics with which ecclesiastical craftsmen, co-operating with the clergy and popular devotion, could endow it.

All round the church, as Timothy Green had observed, stood plaster statues of the saints most dear to the people of Riverside, and for that matter to the people of the whole world. St. Teresa of Lisieux, with eyes of real glass, and tears of real varnish on pallid cheeks, showing at one glance her predisposition to tuberculosis and her gift of tears. St. Joseph in yellow because all the simple people of the earth insist that yellow is "St. Joseph's colour." St. Anthony of Padua, with a sugar mouse pink face of exquisite sweetness, laid against the rosy face of the Holy Child, sitting on his open book. St. Aloysius Gonzaga, so faint with prudery and anaemia, that the lilies clasped to his breast might well have been there for his funeral.

There was one redeeming feature, which had been insisted upon by old Father Malone, a life-sized painted crucifix over the High Altar.

At first Solly had only a general impression, clusters of candles in the shadows, like secret patches of burning flowers. The circle of lamps around the feet of Our Lady and the Sacred Heart, the thin flames burning out among withering flowers at the feet of the saints, the smell that brought back his childhood so poignantly.

Next he became slowly aware of Our Lady in her Chapel,

crowned as a queen and holding the Little Christ King in her arms.

Solly had received no instruction either in the Jewish or the Christian faiths. Of Christianity he knew only what can be gathered from living among English Christians, almost nothing at all. His emotions were rooted in his own race. Because that was so, children had a supernatural quality in his mind. To the Jew every child is an object of wonder and awe. "He who is childless," says the Talmud, "is considered as if he were dead." In every Jewish family the little son is the little Messiah of the home.

The supreme injury inflicted on Solly by his faithless wife was that she had gone away leaving him childless. Had he had a child of his own, he could have overcome his morbid self-consciousness in approaching the whole world of childhood. But as things were he was cut off from that world, too; he was afraid of seeing an expression of repulsion or ridicule on a child's face; he could not imagine any child who would not feel one or the other for him. He preferred to deny himself the sweetness of even a passing word with one of them rather than to risk so bitter a humiliation.

Now he stood looking at the little crowned Boy and saw that he was turning, not shyly away to His Mother, hiding His face in her breast, but *outwards* to himself, with an eager face of welcome and His arms held out.

He had never thought of Christianity in terms of a little son, given to man. Now he saw it just as that. The Mother stirred him too, something in himself answered to the glad show of her ornate beauty, her dull red robe painted with stars and flowers of gold, her blue cloak, deep and vivid as

night, her great crown and the crown of the Holy Child, burnished and encrusted with glass jewels, garnets and emeralds
and pearls, the lily sceptre in the hand that was not holding
the child, and a halo of stars lit up by electric lights, shining
round her head.

While he stood gazing at the Queen of Heaven, "the Test
of Faith" came shuffling out of the Sacristy to put out the
stars. Instinctively, Solly stepped back into the shadow of a
pillar. Here, too, in this church, he felt that he was trespass-
ing, the apostate's son who was everywhere a usurper, whose
dead body would trespass in the earth that covered it. But he
only hid himself until the peculiar-looking man who turned
out the stars had gone again. Then he came out stealthily
and stood in front of the Sanctuary, because for the first time
since he left his grandfather's house he had the experience,
both elusive and compelling, of having found somewhere that
was familiar, of having come back—come back to something
so like his first home that he could almost taste and touch
and smell the forgotten beauty of it. If this place did not belong to him, in some strange way he belonged to it.

A wave of homesickness swept through him, homesickness not only for grandfather's house, not only for his own
kith and kin, but for kinship itself: solidarity with his own
Race. To belong to his family, yes, but by virtue of that to belong to the family of the whole human Race.

Solly Lee was not used to thinking, he could not now
translate the impressions that came to him into coherent
thought. They did not come to him as a co-ordinated pattern.
They did not come with the swiftness and unity of intuitive
learning, flowing through him like a passage of music as intu-

itive knowledge does: but slowly, painfully, with long pauses, striving against deep-seated resistance, yet bringing sweetness of relief as his defences crumbled, like difficult tears forced from the eyes of one who has forgotten how to weep. They came in fragments, in pictures out of the past, sense impressions, memories, longings, stabs of remorse and self-pity, moments of apprehension, of beauty. Without his knowing it, as his own life passed before his mind, it was a mosaic picture of the Jewish Race.

Now that the electric stars were put out, the church was nearly dark. The candles had burnt down low and were guttering at the feet of the saints. In front of him in the darkening Sanctuary, the lamp burnt, a solitary flame, like the forgotten heart of love.

In the darkness, the smell of warm wax, incense and flowers grew more pungent. Solly saw a little Jewish boy, devout and gentle, who went about touching the simple things that belong to every home, and everything that he touched was informed by a secret beauty. The invisible was given to him in visible things, the intangible in what he touched. That little boy was Solly Lee, or rather Solomon Levi, who had been mourned as dead, and who was dead, because he was no more.

In that child there had been a flame, the real flame of life, it had burnt out. There was still a boy, a boy who grew flaccid and puffy and white, who never knew hunger or thirst or any sharp desire, because hunger and thirst and desire were always sated, even before they were a pang in his flesh. It was this sated, flaccid boy who had grown into the grotesque man with the unsavoury reputation, who did indeed handle and fondle the material things about him, but who had lost that divine touch, which was a kind of communion through the senses, or at least through sensible things, with Heaven.

He knew now what it was that made him discontented with everything, and with every human relationship. Nothing yielded its secret self to him. That was it. Nothing gave him its secret self. The mystery remained wholly dark. Now when he touched anything, only what was tangible was his, the inward beauty eluded him.

Was he lost for ever, that little boy whose hands were laid gently upon the secret of the One God? It almost seemed as if he was present now. Certainly here there was a quality in things that there had been for the child long ago, as if here in the Catholic Church the outcast had found the lost beauty of the Jewish home. Flames and flowers and linen, incense and oil and gold, impregnated with love.

Solly moved back and sat down, the bench was hard and it was getting chilly. "Pity," he thought, "that religion is always so uncomfortable. There might be something in it, after all, we need a bit of colour and poetry in life—good Lord, you can't get away from it, this church glows like a jewel in these dirty grey streets." He sighed and shifted on the hard bench, then he caught sight of the Crucifix hanging above the Altar. The lifesized, painted figure of Christ on the cross.

The cross was red, against the red ground. In the twilight the figure was vivid in its whiteness, an attempt by an indifferent artist to copy the Byzantine style, the result was half archaic and formalized, and half naturalistic.

A long thin body, narrow hands curling, as if they curled

lovingly on the nails, a halo like a plate of darkly gleaming gold.

But it was the face that seized Solly, and caught his breath, a white, wedge-shaped face, with thin dark hair falling closely round it, and one black lock on the forehead. The closed eyes curved into a smile, a mouth of indescribable sweetness and pain.

It was the face of David, the young boy coming home from his first fast, it was the face of every Jewish boy who has come through the great fast, the first famine of the spirit, who knows the sorrow and glory of Israel because he has accepted the torment of the Chosen People.

Solly stood up again; he knew now why he had lost the power in his hands, in his words, in his whole being, the power to effect a communion with the invisible God in the visible world, the inviolate power of childhood. It was because he had lost the power of suffering, his birthright as a Jew.

His father and mother had betrayed him, betraying their forefathers, betraying their God; and he had betrayed himself. If he had overcome his flesh, if he had mortified his appetites, if he had chosen the austerities that refine like a pure flame, he would still have something of the power of the purity of a child. He would still be able to effect a communion with Heaven through his contacts on earth. Perhaps his wife would not have left him, if his caress had not lost the power to communicate love.

As he looked at this unfamiliar Face, the face of Jesus of Nazareth, for the first time, a procession of young Jews passed before his eyes. Those he had known himself, and those he had heard grandmother speaking of, in a hard low voice of grief. Jews who had suffered to the death in the Ghetto, Jews who had been killed in pogroms. Her own young brother Esdra, who had blood over his forehead. Solly looked at the painted drops of blood, like a fringe under the smooth dark hair. He thought of Esdra and all the Jews who had suffered to death, and then again of David, and the others. Of the drained white faces with the triumphant smile, seen for a moment, in the glory of knowing that in their coming of age, and their first fast, they had separated themselves from the faithless world that is falling away, disintegrated through a kind of soft rot at the heart; and had made themselves one with the Chosen People, who, though they were separated from the world by their divine destiny, were united with one another, in the solidarity of torment.

For a moment only, little Solly would see those pure young faces, then suddenly they would be hidden on grandmother's breast, as if it were insufferable that anyone should look on their naked pride and torment.

But this young Jew, for He *was* a Jew, this Face, in which all those young Jews' faces lived in death, was turned outwards to the gaze of the world for ever.

It was almost envy that Solly felt, envy certainly for his cousins, if they had been faithful, but stranger than that, envy for this poor, crucified Jesus, with blood painted upon His face, to whom the Christians gave lip-service as God, and who seemed to Solly to be a boy who had somehow gathered to himself all the inheritance of the suffering of the Jews from the past, and all the power of suffering that the faithless Jews would fritter and squander in the present and in the future.

"It's no use though," he said, "I shall always be rotten and soft and self-indulgent; it's too late to change."

He did not know that the little crowned Child, who had

so moved him, could come into his heart and give back the childhood that holds Heaven between its hands, or that in the crucified King of the Jews there lives for ever the eternal Bar Mitzvah of the Chosen Race.

Even while he wished to the point of self-pity, that he had kept a little asceticism, Solly found it too cold, too uncomfortable to remain any longer in church. He turned and went away, sorrowful.

The story of Solly Lee was the history of thousands of his race. Thousands who on that very night in London, all unknowingly, were betraying the unknown Messiah, in betraying the God of Israel. And in their midst, symbolized by the painted figure on the hanging Rood, He remained on the Cross. The Young Jew, in whom the Jewish Race has come of age. In whom the law, the fasting, the discipline that separated the chosen people, is miraculously transformed from an intolerable pride to an unutterable humility. In whom the suffering—a unity that excluded all but the few, who could endure endlessly—has become in His alchemy of love an inclusiveness, in which all men are one in the suffering of one Man.

CHAPTER 16

GRAVEN IMAGES

Thou shalt not adore them,
nor serve them.

There was a knock on the front door and Carmel got up quickly and ran upstairs to the room over the shop. From here she could peep through the curtain to see who was calling, without being seen herself.

When she saw Father O'Grady's black hat her cheeks flushed and her heart beat so fast, that at first she sat down on the floor where she was, under the window sill, and covered her face with her hands. But after a little while she recovered some of her composure and crept out to the banisters and leaned over to listen.

She felt sure that Father O'Grady had come to try to take her away from Solly, and she longed to run to him and tell him how she was at war with herself, torn between pity and the terrible loneliness that goes with having cut oneself off from one's own kind, and again the tormenting fear that she had wounded her father's pride too much and he would not take her back.

She leaned right over the banisters, her dark hair falling across her cheek like a black wing. She could see Solly from where she stood, standing with his back to the fire, and Father O'Grady's boot, and she could hear all that they said.

Solly too felt sure that the priest had come to take Carmel away, nevertheless he bowed to him, just as he would have bowed to a customer coming to be measured for a suit, and invited him to sit down.

Father O'Grady himself was as embarrassed as Solly, he felt that he really had no right to ask Solly not to make his holy cards, for although he and everyone else felt that Father Malone belonged to the Catholics, he was not, after all, their copyright, and what could Father O'Grady do? Actually nothing. What he had been advised to do was to persuade Solly tactfully, but he was not very good at tact or persuasion. Apart from this embarrassment, he felt that Carmel was hiding from him somewhere in the house, and that both he and Solly were really thinking of her. Her presence was vibrating in this very room. Again he was not only being watched from some hiding-place inside the house by Carmel's sad, lustreless eyes, but by other eyes outside the house, cruel sharp eyes like gimlets, boring holes through the brick walls: not eyes like Carmel's, wistful and full of unshed tears, but cold and curious, without pity. Eyes that had long forgotten how to weep. The eyes of the pious parishioners who took scandal because he visited the house, in which, they said, Carmel Fernandez flaunted her immorality. He knew that they were sharpening their tongues like knives to cut him, already adding a little more to the gathering cruelty in the world by hardening their hearts. He couldn't reason with them, it would not move them if he told them he was the humble servant of the Good Shepherd—though he could never as much as set eyes on the lost lamb, as it was always hiding behind the door.

"Good afternoon, Mr. Lee," he said. "I—er—hope I'm not intruding—that is to say, I have called about a … em … er … a rather delicate matter."

"I know that," said Solly. "And if you will pardon my saying so, Reverend, it is my business and no one else's. I don't pay allegiance to the Pope of Rome nor owe him any; though I wish him no harm as a matter of fact, but neither he nor any of his ministers is going to interfere with me."

"Of course—of course, and indeed I am sure that the thing would never get to the ears of Rome anyway. I certainly hope it will not, excepting of course much later on, when it will be possible to get the Imprimatur and go ahead with the Holy Father's blessing."

At this Solly was very much surprised. He had not the least idea what the Imprimatur might be, but he could hardly imagine the Pope blessing his union with Carmel—although without having the least idea how this had originated in his mind, or ever having questioned it, he took it for granted that the Pope was a very bad man, indulgent in the same ways as himself but with more and better opportunity. But that this should give him the fellow-feeling to interest himself in his little affair with Carmel seemed highly improbable. He began to think that the suggestion was guile on Father O'Grady's part, designed to flatter him into weakening. He said with the air of a defiantly sulky child. "Well, Reverend, if you will excuse my bluntness, how about getting to the point. What is it you have really come here to say to me?"

"Certainly, Mr. Lee, I will come to the point. It is the holy cards that you are publishing, and the point is the haloes."

"The holy cards!"

Solly's relief was immense and evident, so much so that he positively warmed towards Father O'Grady.

"Well, I never—the holy cards! and what about them, Reverend. Do you like them? Maybe you think you should have a royalty on them, eh? They are going like hot cakes and though the coloured are a halfpenny more retail, I can rely on selling them at three times the speed and quantity—but mind you, they are good value; *and* you should see the latest. So you shall, too; I had the proofs in yesterday. Gold haloes, Reverend; none of your yellow paint; shining gold as bright as gold leaf."

Solly paused, pursed up his mouth and made a gesture of kissing his fingers and tossing the kiss to Father O'Grady:

"Just one moment," he said, "I will show you the whole set out from the start." He chuckled and got down a large album from the shelf. "Here we are, now you look through that—and look here, Reverend, if you feel done in the eye in a manner of speaking, I don't mind coming to terms. Look at it this way, you are the idealist, all dreams and no eye for the main chance—though some of those Reverends abroad know which way to do the sleight-of-hand trick—but there, I don't want to hurt your feelings—but I grant you this, that you had the saint on the counter, so to speak. He is your proper stock in trade, and maybe I ought to have thought twice about cashing in on him without *first* approaching you with proposals of partnership. But I'm the lad that jumps on opportunity. I've got my fingers on the public pulse, Reverend. Yes, I know every flutter of the public's heart and just what to cash in on, and when. *But* I don't just jump in for profit. No, I'm bigger than that. I combine business with *pleasure*. And what's my pleasure? Giving happiness, that's what it is. Yes, you Reverends are out to make 'em good, but that's too dreary for me. I want to make 'em *happy*. Now I know just how happy these poor folk are, thinking of old Father Malone strutting round in Heaven with milk and honey and harps and all the rest of it. Mind you, Reverend, it wouldn't suit me. I prefer a nice little girl, and a pork chop, and a glass of good red wine on this earth. But poor old Malone he never did know how to live— now some of these Reverends in Spain—but there, I'll spare your feelings—" again Solly tossed a kiss to Father O'Grady, who took the opportunity of breaking in.

"You have quite misunderstood me, Mr. Lee—I am not complaining of not having been invited—"

Solly waved the priest's words aside and went on, "Well, Reverend, I see now that I made a mistake. You should be in on this deal. Why, to start with, we need a shop front. Now, how about your church as a shop window, eh? What could be better?—With your conscription Masses once a week, artful dodgers, you!"—Solly patted the side of his nose and wagged his head at Father O'Grady—"with your conscription Masses and a bit of red hot publicity from the pulpit, and the latest cards on sale in the church porch as the people come out— poof! We are millionaires!"

At last he stopped and Father O'Grady began again, "What I really came to ask you was, if you would withdraw some of your cards, or at least remove the haloes. Please, Mr. Lee, will you hear me through?"

"The haloes! But the haloes are the chef-d'oeuvres."

"The point is that the Church does not allow us to make, expose, or venerate pictures or images of persons wearing haloes, before she has given her approval by canonizing the person in question."

"Well, I'm blowed. But all the saints in your church have got haloes."

"They are all canonized, otherwise their images would not be there."

"Well, let them get on with it and canonize Father Malone."

"That is the point. Canonization is a long process; several stages have to be gone through before it really even begins, and during the initial stages, it is impossible to be too prudent. Any sign of hysteria among the people, or of presuming on the Church's final decision, would cause the Bishops to frown on the cause, possibly to close the whole thing down, and to forbid the devotion, and—well, Mr. Lee, I do believe that would break my people's hearts. Mind you, if Father Malone is a saint whom Almighty God intends to raise to the altars of the Church, even the Bishops could not finally prevent it, but they could delay it, and that would break the hearts of *these* people who knew and loved Father Malone."

"You're right there, Reverend. But how could your Bishops be so mean? It doesn't hurt them, if Father Malone is a saint. On the contrary, I should say it would send their shares up. What have they got to be so sticky over?"

"Truth. You see no one can *make* Father Malone a saint just because they would like to. What they have got to do is to find out if he *is*. There has to be a long searching enquiry into his life, to ascertain whether or not he really did practise virtue in a heroic degree."

"I should say it's heroic to practise virtue at all in this world. Look here, you tell the old Bishop to come and see me, ask him to come and have a couple with me. I'll give him all the dope he wants. I can assure him that old Father Malone practised heroic virtue, and what is much more than that, Reverend, he was a good man. There was none of that stuck up righteousness about him that there is about a lot of church people. Many a day he came round for a chat with me. Yes, Reverend, he would sit in that chair that you are sitting in now, and have a glass or two with me and a chat, not about religion either. He could talk about any man's interests, tailoring and antiques or anything you like. And mind you, Reverend, there were no flies on him."

"No, there were not, but—"

"Now look here, Reverend. You just slide your eye along that album. You will change your mind and come in on the deal. We will square the Bishops between us. If you are too hoity-toity to want the money for yourself, you can build a grand new church with it or spend it on some of your poor. I'll give you a straight deal. Now don't turn a good offer down."

Father O'Grady had already looked through the album. The first picture was a photograph, taken many years ago and "touched up" at the time. It had some slight likeness to Fr. Malone, but nothing, of course, of the beauty that long years of suffering and patience had engraved on the face when the saint was old.

The second picture was like an actor of the Victorian type,

that most macabre thing, an aged face without a line or wrin-
kle on it. After this each was progressively worse. The likeness
to Father Malone, even to any one aspect of Father Malone,
decreased as the artist's fancy increased. The black cassock
was replaced by a goffered white surplice. The introduction
of colour brought sugar-pink cheeks and coral lips, speedily
followed by palms, lilies and roses and finally the offending
haloes.

"Well," said Solly, "what about it? There is a distinct improvement since the first kick-off, eh?"

"No, Mr. Lee, I'm going to be perfectly candid with you.
In my opinion there is no improvement, you have lost every
trace of likeness. It is not Father Malone at all, it is not a man
at all—"

"But, Reverend, it is a *saint*, and that's what the people
want, a saint."

"No, it is not a saint: a saint *is* a real man, a man of flesh
and blood—This is not real—"

"Now look here, Reverend, I'll grant you it is not realism,
it is idealism. But so is the whole show. Heaven and all the
rest, religion itself, it's all just an idea; and I'll bet all you artful Reverends know it on the Q.T. too. But I think you are
right to stick to it and preach it, because if it is only a wishful
fantasy really, it's a good one, and it's one that makes people
happy, which realism does not do. That's why it interests me,
Reverend. I don't care a fig if people are good or bad, if they
go to church on Sundays or lie in bed all day, but I do care if
they are happy or not. I don't like unhappy people, don't like
'em around the place. And I reckon religion is the only thing
that does make them happy. Take the people round here,

their lives are just as dull and drab and uneventful as human lives can be, one long drudge from start to finish. Why some of them have never even had the thrill of buying a new dress, just take other people's old cast-offs, that's all. And what have they got to look forward to? Nothing at all. Just to be put away in a box and shovelled under the earth! Isn't it natural that they *want* to kid themselves that there is a place just round the corner, where they will all be dolled up in silk and velvet and diamonds and pearls, and hobnob with the King and Queen and have their own angels to do conjuring tricks whenever they tell them?"

"Heaven isn't a delusion, Mr. Lee. But your conception of it is, and it is not surprising, that as you told me just now, you would prefer the sensible pleasures that you know as reality now, to such a Heaven. You say you want to give happiness. Well, there is only one thing that really makes happiness, Mr. Lee."

"If you know the secret of happiness, Reverend, for God's sake cough it up, for we all need it enough."

"It is being in love."

Solly stared at Father O'Grady with round incredulous eyes. He had always supposed that church men frowned on love.

"Yes, being in love, whatever your circumstances are, that is what is needed to turn them to joy. Unless you are in love, both riches and poverty become burdens. But when a rich man falls in love his treasure is no longer a cause of worry and anxiety, because it is no longer something to be hoarded and hugged to himself. Instead it is something to give away, to give to the beloved. And who would not choose a lifetime of hardship if that were, as it often is, the condition for being with the beloved?"

"There is one point though, Reverence, which you have left out. I'll grant that being in love is the secret of happiness, but only when it is reciprocated, and even then provided that the other party stays faithful."

He felt tempted to tell Father O'Grady about Ella. But Father O'Grady went on: "Precisely. That was the point I was coming to. The secret of perfect happiness is being in love with God, for God always reciprocates. Indeed it is He who is always the suppliant. Heaven, Mr. Lee, is being in love with God; it is not something round the corner, as you put it, but something which—starts here and now, and makes everything in *this* life joyful, even its suffering."

"Well, Reverend, I suppose I'm a bad man, but I tell you straight, God doesn't seem real enough to me to be in love with. And as to the other side of the penny—His loving me—well, that just seems quite impossible to me, and anyhow I don't see what any of this has got to do with Father Malone's pictures."

"If you will be patient with me for a few minutes longer, I will tell you, Mr. Lee. You want to make people happy, so do I, and so does the Church. And she knows that the true happiness that lasts, and is not even broken temporarily by Death, can only be achieved through loving God. But many people like yourself cannot grasp that as a reality. If they believe in God at all, it is only as an infinitely remote Spirit whom they cannot approach, or as a hard judge whom they dare not. It was just to make men understand how wrong it is to think of God like that, that Christ was born of a woman and became man.

"Now imagine a wretchedly poor man, who has nothing at all but his misery. And to this man's door comes one who has everything, knocking and pleading to be let in. And when at last the wretch inside opens the door, the other tells him that he has chosen to leave everything, all his wealth and comforts in order to share every circumstance of the poor man's life. Would you say that this rich man loved the other and proved it?"

"Yes, but I don't see why he shouldn't ask the other chap to come and share all his riches with him, instead of the other way round."

"If he did, the poor man, who would judge by himself, would not trust him. He would always imagine some odd motive, always be suspicious and questioning, and he would never feel secure; he would expect at any moment to be thrown back to his former misery. Then if he got to love the other, as well he might, half the joy of loving would be wanting, because he could never give anything himself, but only take."

"Yes, I dare say he *would* suppose the rich man was a bit phoney."

"Quite, but he could not possibly fail to believe in the motive of disinterested love, the other way."

"Well no, not unless he thought he was barmy."

Father O'Grady smiled. "The Folly of the Cross, Mr. Lee, is often thought of as madness. God, in becoming man, did just what that rich man did in my parable, came to us, knocked on our door, shared in our human nature, lived our life, made all its griefs and hardship His own, hid His glory and power in man's littleness and weakness, even took our sins on Himself and hid His splendour in them, covering His divine face in our blood and our sweat, all in order that we should be able to love Him and that He would be able to love us in our way."

"And what has that to do with Father Malone?"

"This. Men forget. They cease to understand what the Incarnation meant, what God means by it, it has to be proved to them over and over again, in each successive generation. That is what the saints do, they live Christ's life again, prove His longing to be loved again in the medium of the particular people they live among, so that once again, men can *see* how God loves them and in responding to Him, lay hold of their own happiness."

"Maybe you're right. As a matter of fact, I think you've got something there. But all the same, I still don't see any harm in showing Father Malone in Heaven and idealized and all that on my holy cards. When he'd done being a saint on earth, why not show him tidied up a bit and rejuvenated in Heaven? After all you don't want to see a lined old man in Heaven!"

"When his body goes to Heaven, which will not be until after the Last day and the Resurrection of all the dead, he will have the beauty of his eternal glory, But what that will be we cannot conceive. It will certainly not be anything like these pictures. But for the present time the people want to hold on to the memory of the real man as he was, and to know that his holiness, which is now in the sight of God for ever, is made up of the life he lived with them and shared with them. Fr. Malone had deep lines on his face from suffering, his mouth was stern because he had to be hard on himself; but all round his gentle eyes, there were little criss-cross lines from laughing; and his hands were not smooth hands like this, they were gnarled old hands, square, and the joints swollen from arthritis, and they were always chapped in the winter. Now all that shows his people that his glory is made up of their own pain and laughter and struggle, from their own toil and ailments, their rheumatism, their damp foggy days, their fight with depression, even from the same hard water that they use. They want to turn to him in Heaven and see themselves in him, as they can become by God's grace, through nothing else but what they have and what they are now."

Solly was silent for a brief few seconds, then he said:

"Well, I can't say I have considered it that way. But then I wouldn't know, would I? I'm not a religious man, leastways, not like you would mean by religious, though I have my own religion. Kindness, that's my religion; do as you would be done by, that's my creed, though I'm bound to say it's hard to know how some people *would* be done by—the more you do to make 'em happy, the more mopey they get. But I can't get on with all this being miserable and going to seed that religious people seem to need to be happy. Still, one man's meat is another man's poison, isn't it Reverend? Have a glass of sherry now. Ah! that's better, you'll take a different view when you have drunk that. Mind you, that's the best, I don't give anyone anything but the best, that's real good old Bristol cream that is. Matured long ago by being rocked in the hold of an old wooden sailing ship, on its journey all round the world. There's beauty for you, Reverend. Think of that dark, dusty little bottle slung in its cradle, down below in the darkness, swinging to and fro, while the lovely ship sails on ... there's beauty for you, there's romance, Reverend, and it's all poured out for you in that little glass of red-gold amber. *That* could make me believe in God, Reverend, much more than a poor old man never having enough to eat, and never buying himself a decent pair of boots. All the same, Reverend, I bet this bottle has seen a thing or two. You know what I mean, the goings-on in ships!"

Solly stroked the dark dusty little bottle with a knowing look. "Yes, *you* should know a thing or two from some of these sailors' confessions, though it's more the traveller—a queer thing, Reverend, what one will do on a ship, things one wouldn't dream of on dry land. Come now, let me fill your glass up, come on now—"

"About the haloes, Mr. Lee," said Father O'Grady.

"Ah, yes—well, of course, it would put me at a dead loss. I suppose you are not thinking of offering any compensation?"

"If you just have authentic photographs done, without haloes, real memorial cards, those would be quite in order."

"Well, I've got to think this thing over. Now suppose you could give me a reasonable guarantee that Fr. Malone will get through the exam or whatever you call it, and be canonized pretty soon, I could hold on to my holy cards until the happy event comes off and then let 'em go; meantime I would go in with you on the variety you suggest, but of course there could not be too long a delay."

"I'm afraid the very least delay would be twenty-five years, and then it is not a certainty that he will pass the exam, as you call it."

"Well, twenty-five years is a pretty long time, but so long as the final profit is certain, and no hokey-pokey, I might do a deal with a firm I know, who could afford to buy my cards and wait that long. I'll be a bit too old to enjoy the profits myself after twenty-five years. Then, as you say, we might be backing a dead horse. Now tell me this, what are the odds on Malone? If there is a sporting chance I don't mind taking it. In fact I always say it's good business to take a chance. The man who will only bet for a place never gets to the top of the tree. But you've got to know your horse and your jockey. These old Bishops now, are they out to win, or are they going to pull the reins? Come on, Reverend, out with it. What's the Vatican tip?"

"There is no hokey-pokey, that I can assure you. There is a condition which has to be fulfilled, that is that through the saint's intercession in Heaven, a first-class miracle must be granted, a real miracle which could not possibly have happened by any natural means."

"And have you thought up any conjuring trick for the poor old fellow?"

Then Father O'Grady told Solly Lee the whole story of Willie Jewel and how the child belonged to the people, who had all grown in love because of him, and of the way they were all one through praying for him. And strangely enough, when he had come to the end, Solly Lee did not say as all the other faithless and some of the faithful had, that he thought it wrong to ask for the child's life. He only said, "That's very touching."

But Carmel, who was still leaning over the banisters, was weeping silently.

"Now I must go. And I must thank you for being so patient with me, Mr. Lee. You don't feel that you can give me an answer now?"

"Well, Reverend. It seems to me that I will have to do like the rest of you. If Father Malone does the hat trick with the poor little kid, I will hold my horses until Rome gets humming. If not—well, I suppose I'd better give up the cards anyway. Mind you it's a big loss and a bitter disappointment. But no one can ever say that I'm not a generous man."

"No indeed they cannot," said Fr. O'Grady, and he meant it.

As soon as he had shut the front door on his guest, Solly ran upstairs to find Carmel. She was in the bathroom washing the tear stains from her face. Solly found her there.

"Carmel," he cried, "my little Carmel. I thought he had come to try to take you away—"

He stopped short. Carmel was looking at him and trying to smile. With the make-up partly washed off by the soap and water and her dark hair wet and glistening, she looked an odd mixture between a woman and an unhappy child. Solly stood very still and neither of them spoke. When the silence was broken it was broken by Solly.

"He *has* taken you away," he said.

CHAPTER 17

THE FATHER

*Your Heavenly Father
knows well, what your
needs are, before you
ask him.*

Fr. O'Grady had an old hat, which promised to compete some day with Fr. Malone's and could be aptly described as a battle hat. There were rare days in his life, when this hat was worn lightly, almost jauntily, some of those early days, for example, when the rumour of Father Malone's sanctity was whispered as if by the breath of the Spirit, when canonization seemed as easy and certain as an untrained talent. Days when Riverside was blue and white, her skies painted by Fra Angelico, her streets dappled with pale gold. But more often Fr. O'Grady jammed on his hat, and on occasion, when a fight was indicated, he rammed it on. For he was all too well aware that his wrestling was indeed with "the power of Evil in high places." Sometimes, certainly, the places were only moderately high, he had now and then surprised it in the offices of

the County Council or at the Town Hall, but usually it was
in higher, subtler, more mysterious places than that. He had
met this spirit of evil, for example, draped in cobwebs, in the
towers of certain pious ladies' minds; he had come across it,
like a blind bat, trapped in a cloister; and to-day he knew that
he was going out to storm it in the proud, outraged spirit of
Francisco Fernandez.

The hat was well down over his eyes, his jaw was set, the
aggressive character of his resolution proved the task hateful
to him; but for days, ever since his call on Solly Lee, he had
been haunted by the thought of Carmel. What would become of her? She would not remain with Solly Lee, of that
Fr. O'Grady was certain. But would Fernandez take her back?
And if so, would he open his heart to her? And if not would
the bitterness of her life be more than she could endure? The
frost too bitter and hard for his shorn lamb?

He knocked gently, and waited. There was a sudden complete stillness within, it was not like the inevitable wait after a
knock at his own presbytery door, which at all events produced
no effect at all on those inside, and was filled by reassuring
sounds, footsteps passing the door, tuneless snatches of hymn
singing, suggesting at least utter indifference, cheerful detach-
ment from the presence on the doorstep, perhaps unawareness
of it, but not hostility. The pause on Fernandez's doorstep was
hostile. It was vibrant with the tension of a listening presence,
the stiffening and antagonism of someone inside, someone
close and hostile and bristling, who felt the knock as an in-
vasion, an attempt to shatter a brittle shell of solitude, which
had been built painfully with numbed fingers, round grief like
a sensitive nerve that could not tolerate exposure.

Fr. O'Grady knocked again, a knock which he knew fell like a blow on the mind of the listener inside, but even by its gentleness proclaimed a patience which could not ultimately be refused.

The door was opened, not by Fernandez, but by his sister, Teresa, who had kept house for him since Carmel's mother had died in giving her birth. Teresa was a monumental woman, her hair, though she was past middle age, black as a raven's wing, her face smooth, unlined, olive-coloured, handsome, and as hard and immobile as a face of wood. In such a face, with its deeply set eyes, slightly masculine nose, tall intelligent brow, and heavy chin, one expected a thin-lipped, unsensuous mouth, and was faintly shocked to find a full sensual mouth, which should have been mobile, which should have been beautiful, full of warm words and laughter and song: but was, in fact, compressed and rigid, and spoke of a degree of cruelty to self which could hardly have been maintained without equal cruelty to everything that was sensuous, amorous and gay.

Her greeting was respectful but hardly audible. Father O'Grady felt certain that she admitted him only because he was a priest, and a priest cannot be refused admittance to a Spanish household; her devotion to her brother shared his wounds and pride that is wounded is unreasoning and fierce in self-defence. She bowed him in to the parlour where Francisco Fernandez was waiting and left them alone together.

The resemblance between brother and sister was striking, the same handsome, sensuous, afflicted face, looking through the same mask of indomitable pride; the same revealing and disconcerting mouth, but in his case partly hidden by a fantastically long, black moustache.

The room was the right setting for the man. It was poor, but with the poverty of worn-out grandeur, faded splendour, beauty worn threadbare, poverty with a grand air of tragedy, in contrast to the noisy, swarming, generous poverty of Riverside generally, with its sharing, its humility, its laughter and its frankness.

The furniture was too big for the room and too much. It was oppressive, and spoke silently of larger, more spacious rooms, of greater expanses of light and wider skies, of more space even for human thought and human passion. It was old furniture, ornately carved in dark wood and polished by the constant touch of centuries of caressing, possessive hands. It was, however, wanting in comfort. There was no sofa, not a cushion, nowhere to relax. Behind Fernandez's dark handsome head hung a crucifix, which was surely an heirloom, and which to keep, and not to sell, the several last generations of the Fernandez's must have suffered many privations. It was made in ivory, mellowed to the colour of pale honey, and painted from head to foot with drops of blood, each drop inset with a tiny garnet. The loincloth was inlaid with flowers of gold metal, and shaped like a little petticoat, falling from the waist to the knees. The face had nothing of the mysterious joy of immolation, visible on many old English and even many Spanish crucifixes; the emphasis of a terrible beauty stressed only the torment of the suffering man-God.

In a corner on a bracket and covered by a glass case was a wax statue of Our Lady. This had a florid loveliness of its own, though it was more like a little lady doll than the English conception of what an object of piety should be, and was clothed in a dress of blue silk and a tiny lace veil.

Between the crucifix and the statue, hung a startling row of photographs, startling because they were faded and drab and Victorian in character, and yet from those faded faces an almost arrogant quality of life stared out. The family likeness was stamped on each one of them, and most of all upon the women; the grandmother, so clearly the arch-grand-matriarch, the mother, the many daughters, several of whom had surely died young as nuns; all wore the seal, that hard, noble piety, which, though the fact is quite inexplicable, so frequently stamps the features with a subtle but unmistakable resemblance to a horse.

"You wish to see me Father?" It was Fernandez who spoke first.

"I do, indeed; I am wondering how you are getting on. It's a long time since you have come along to serve my Mass now, Francisco, and you used to come daily. Indeed I never see you in the church at all, except right at the back, at Sunday Mass—and—oh well, what's the use of a priest beating about the bush? It isn't natural to a man as devout as you are to keep away from devotions that have been his life-long habit. You are doing it to avoid people, isn't that the truth?"

Fernandez's face had set harder, and when he spoke he spoke as if his mouth was stiff from a blow.

"It is possible, Father, that I prefer to keep to myself."

"Your sister is never at evening Service either. She used to come daily. It is a bad thing for women not to enjoy the sweetness of Benediction."

"I do not wish her to be exposed to the gossip of the parish. It is my wish that she goes among people as little as possible now."

"Because of your child?"

Fr. O'Grady saw, that though Fernandez did not move a muscle, the direct question was like the lash of a whip. He was like a man who will take the lash, without crying out, but without resignation.

"I have no child."

"Fernandez, do not let pride shut your door, and lock your heart against everyone. Suppose, that your child came back and asked your forgiveness?"

"I cannot forgive."

The answer fell like a blow on the priest's heart. He realized the hard set of the man's mould as never before, and as he sat pondering his next sentence, and praying inwardly to the "Little Flower" to give him some right and tactful words to speak, the memory of Carmel's First Communion came to him. The austere loveliness of that morning. The church transformed into a Paradise of children in love. A very small, fragile child, with little delicate bones like a bird, and large dark eyes, resembling, he had thought, an exquisite little monkey in a bridal dress. Himself, a young priest, new to the parish then, shaken with the beauty of the thrust of the green leaf into the light. He remembered now, how the Sister of Mercy, who had prepared the First Communicants, had shocked him a little, how he was faintly shocked then, because he was young, by what she said, and painfully shocked now, because he was older, by the *truth* of what she said: "The little Spanish girl is a problem, Father, and worry; she is a lot too pious, she does not know how to play or enjoy herself, brought up like a little nun she is. I sometimes feel I would like to turn that sanctimonious old father of hers over my knee and spank him, and that aunt who, God forgive me for saying so, looks as if she had swallowed the poker. They give the child everything but love, and love is the one thing she needs."

"Has it never occurred to you," said Fr. O'Grady out loud, "that you have some little share in the responsibility of what she has done. You—you have been very severe, Fernandez, perhaps there was too little love in the child's life?"

"Love"—Fernandez started as if he had been touched by a red-hot coal. "Love! I cared for her as the apple of my eye— my sister too, though her heart is in Spain, she has stayed here all these years to train up the child. I took her to church before she could walk, I denied myself everything humanly possible that she should be well fed, well clothed, and well educated—is it not love to care for her soul, for her eternal happiness?"

"Of course. But did she have any fun, any little treats or luxuries—"

Fernandez looked incredulous and made no answer.

"And later on—did she go out a bit, to dances, had she any young men friends?"

"Young men—dances! Father, is it a priest of God asking me? How could I allow her to mix with the young men here, Protestants or worse, or to dance in the low-down places on the wharves? She belonged to the Children of Mary, she attended their Socials; such things as the cinema, I forbade."

"And did you ever bring her a bunch of flowers, or buy her a pretty dress yourself, or make her an iced cake for her birthday—you or your sister?"

"Can I afford flowers? I am a poor man. And was I, her

father, to encourage her in vanity? As to her birthday, it is also the anniversary of her Mother's death. I cannot forget that."

"Poor little Carmel. You know, Fernandez, even in the slums, flowers grow wild, on ash heaps—"

He paused and then again, "I think, that soon the child will come and ask you to forgive her. I know how you suffer, man; I too am a father, I bleed for every child of my flock. A priest, Fernandez, is a father who must learn *his* fatherhood from God, because it is his privilege to be the instrument of God's forgiveness."

Suddenly Fernandez spoke with passion,

"I cannot forgive. She has sinned against me, her father, yes, but she has sinned also against the memory of her mother, she has sinned against the dead—" It seemed as he went on as if each word was acid on his tongue, like drops of some bitter medicine. "She has sinned against all the women of the Fernandez family—there has never before—before my child—been a woman of my line who was not chaste and holy. We lost everything, money, position, even the sun of Spain—but not this one thing, the honour, the integrity of our family. Here, in England, I kept aloof. I did not lower myself to mix with those who cannot understand the honour of a Spanish woman. I kept my child apart—as I believed, safe—and she has dishonoured my name—she has stained the name I gave to her mother. Yes, she has violated the dead. She has brought shame upon the women of my line, my mother, my grandmother, my sisters. She is bitter to me, my humiliation—my shame—"

Suddenly his voice broke, distressingly, ludicrously, like

the voice of an adolescent boy, and his shoulders drooped.
Father O'Grady waited. He saw that the tension was breaking down. Until now, pride had sealed his mouth and it had
hardened over his heart, like the crust of a scar, closing up a
wound before the poison has bled out of it. Father O'Grady
knew that unless the wound in a man's heart bleeds, his soul
will perish. He waited, saying nothing, bleeding himself, offering his own sense of futility, offering Fernandez's grief, in
himself, to God. He saw now that pride in his family was the
man's crucifixion, and now his heart had fallen, it had fallen
like a red fruit from the family tree, shaken down by a girl's
wanton hand, to be trodden into the dust of the streets of
Riverside.

It was nearly dark in the room, and easy to imagine that
the row of faded photographs of the equine-faced wom-
en of the Fernandez were no longer photographs, but living
women, whose presence caused the walls to expand, and vast
arches and vaults of twilight to open above them. Imperi-
ous women, walking in the pride of virtue in days that are
no more—in cathedrals that are far away. Women with full
and rustling silken skirts, mantillas like heavy fountain falls
of black lace, eyes like onyx and short cruel gemmed hands,
through which their rosary beads passed incessantly. Walking
from the shadows of the cathedrals to sun-baked quays, the
little stone walls at the water's edge hot to the palm of the
hand, the ships, moored beside them, galleons with crowding
sails, painted figureheads and decks of earth-red cedar wood.

The splendour faded, the gems slipped from their fingers,
the rustling silk changed to coarse cloth, the hands reddened
and hardened, the cathedral dwindled to the homely vulgarity

of the church on Riverside, the sails of the lovely ships melted with the light that shone upon them and faded. Instead of
them came the little tramp steamers and banana boats from
Spain, stout, and panting, and grimy, against grey water and
grey skies. The women of the Fernandez had nothing left but
this one thing, their passion of purity, white hot, like a lily
of burning fire that burnt a terrible purgatorial flame within
them—and Carmel Fernandez had scattered those white petals on the pavements of Riverside.

Once again Father O'Grady said:

"You must forgive her if she comes."

"If she comes—" the father's voice was low and husky
now. "But—will she come?"

"Yes, she will come. Listen, Fernandez, when she comes,
you must begin again, not only Carmel, but *you too* must
begin again. You must learn your fatherhood new, from the
Eternal Father, from God. You know, nearly every day in this
big parish, the priest is sent for to minister to someone who
is dying. He longs to make them understand before it is too
late to comfort them, that they are going to a loving Father,
who waits with open arms, longing to forgive all the folly, and
weakness, and sin of this world. But it is not so easy, for it
is not the poor words that the priest can whisper into their
ears, when they are already almost beyond hearing, that form
their idea of God, on which their dying happily or unhap-
pily depends—it is their earthly father who has formed that
idea long ago. You see, Fernandez, to a small child, the father
is God. Christ taught us to think of God as Father, and He
gives us our father to show God to us, how can a poor priest,
years after, make a soul realize that God is a loving Father,

if the idea of Father to him is severity, justice, but no love?"

He stopped and looked at Fernandez's face, but he had not moved, he was sitting with bowed head and his eyes half closed, listening. So Father O'Grady went on:

"God does not just give His children necessities, you have read the Sermon on the Mount, He clothes His children but He is interested in clothing each one beautifully, like the lilies of the field, He feeds them, and *is* their food. But even Himself as food is given in loveliness, the goldenness of wheat, the whiteness of bread. He does not only give our needs, He is extravagant, almost profligate in love. Yes, Fernandez, look at the millions of stars, look at the leaves, at the grass, at the daisies, and look at all the countless millions of seeds, wasted, that one take root to be a tree for us! You see, Fernandez, all creation is only one thing, a Father clothing and feeding, delighting His child, and saying again and again in everything—'I am your Father, I love you!'"

There was a long silence. Father O'Grady sat gripping his old battle hat, and feeling that he had made a failure of his visit, he had said too much, the wrong things, and done no good. He offered up his failure for Fernandez.

When Fernandez spoke again he repeated, "It is very hard to forgive."

"It is not against you that the child has sinned, it is against God, and you too—all of us—have sinned against God."

"Yes—it is hard to forgive."

"It is much easier to forgive, if first we ask to be forgiven."

The door opened, and Teresa Fernandez came in with a tray of tea. They both stopped speaking when she came in, and she too was silent. Father O'Grady watched her arranging the tea things on the table. He noticed the bluntness of her fingers, and that whenever a knife went a tiny bit crooked, she stopped to put it perfectly straight again. She set only two places, and when she had poured out two cups of tea made to take her leave.

"Are you not taking a cup of tea with us?" asked Father O'Grady.

"I do not wish to intrude, Father."

"But, of course, we want your company."

"Stay, Teresa," said Fernandez.

She sat down.

"It is cruel weather," said the priest.

She looked up quietly, almost gratefully. In her mind it was verging on rebellion against the will of God to mention the English weather at all, it was a relief, therefore, to hear a priest complain of it.

"The fogs are very trying, particularly to Spaniards," she said.

"You must long for the sun of Spain."

Teresa answered, in a tone that suggested that to long for anything was faintly indecent. "I do not allow myself to think of it," she said. "Since, after all, it is the will of God that I am here."

"But what makes you so sure that it *is* the will of God?"

"My duty is here."

"You mean your brother?"

"Certainly, and—"

"And?"

"Carmel—my niece."

Her voice was low and hard.

"But Carmel is grown up, she could look after her father now."

Teresa looked amazed and affronted. "But, Father—You know—"

"Yes I know, but I also know the mercy of Almighty God, and the power of prayer, and that she will come back."

"But even so—"

Father O'Grady saw that the conversation was running into a cul de sac, it must be changed quickly if he was not to defeat his own end.

"Have you any other brothers, in Spain?"

"Oh yes, Father, three who are married, and one who is a priest."

"A priest, how very interesting. A great honour too, a priest in the family. Is he in Madrid?"

"No, poor boy. He has a little parish in the country. I ought not to call him a boy though, it is not from motives of irreverence, but he is many years younger than we are, and it is difficult to think of him as no longer a child. His health, too, is weak."

"That is because he has worked too hard," said Fernandez, as if weak health were a fault that required an excuse.

"Yes," Teresa supported her brother. "He works too hard for his frail constitution. Not all Spaniards do so I fear, but he! Ah, poor boy!"

She raised her hands and for the first time smiled, showing a row of large powerful teeth. After all it seemed, there *was* a spark of tenderness left in her, which the memory of this brother and his weak health roused.

Father O'Grady was quick to see his advantage, and Francisco unconsciously prompted him, "He never did know how to look after himself," he said, "and since our mother died, no doubt the case is far worse."

"Well now," said Father O'Grady triumphantly to Teresa. "Has it not entered your head that Almighty God might be asking you, now that your duty here is ended, to go and look after that poor priest brother?"

Teresa set down her cup and folded her hands as if to give her whole attention to this new idea. Her face was quite eager now, it had come to life, and a round pink spot burnt into each sallow cheek.

"Do you really think that, Father?"

"Think it? Why it seems to me as plain as pie crust."

"He has a housekeeper," she said doubtfully.

"Ah, but that is not like a sister."

Father O'Grady glanced at Francisco, and he thought, just for a flash, that he detected an expression of eager supplication in the man's eyes.

"That is so, isn't it, Francisco?" he asked and he added: "And you, you would I am sure, if your daughter looked after you for a time, make the sacrifice of letting your sister go, for the sake of your priest brother's ministry."

Francisco answered, a little too eagerly,

"Yes—it would be a big wrench, but if it is, as you say, God's will—and of course I see what you mean, Father, about our brother's priestly work."

"Well now. That's settled," said Father O'Grady. "And I will make enquiries about the journey tomorrow, for war may be on us any time now, and that will make travelling much more difficult."

"O, but what will Francisco do if war comes here? Perhaps I had better stay with him until it is over. Oh dear, it is a hard thing to decide."

But Father O'Grady had made up his mind, and his resolution was sustained by two considerations. One, that perhaps in Spain, where everything is a stronger colour—even virtue—there might be a kind of Indian Summer for Teresa's soul. The other, that even if the frail younger brother was not so pleased, as one might reasonably hope he would be, with the arrangement that was being made for him, Teresa's presence would certainly give him the opportunity to sanctify *his* soul.

"Hesitation," he said firmly, "is one of the devil's trump cards. I will help you with the arrangements tomorrow."

The round pink spots in Teresa's cheeks had burnt now to a dark wild rose colour, and she was smiling. Father O'Grady knew that he had won. She was thinking of the young priest whom she could not help remembering as a child, who would never kick over the traces, who had poor health, and would always need her. Still smiling, she collected the crockery on to her tray, and left them alone again.

"No," said Father O'Grady to Fernandez, "don't you see the finger of God in the way things happen? Your sister having to go back to Spain, it's really very obvious! Don't shut your door on your happiness, it's ajar, Francisco, open it wide."

He picked up the old hat again and said good-bye.

Alone again, Fernandez sat motionless for a long time—he was trying to recall moments in Carmel's childhood, when he had rejoiced in her, when he had laughed with her, given her little gifts, held her on his knee—and he had no memories. Suddenly he knew that he wanted her to come back, to ask to be forgiven, he wanted to break through the torment of his pride, to forgive, to learn to laugh, to enjoy life, to delight in his child.

Fr. O'Grady's words kept repeating themselves in his mind. "It is much easier to forgive, if first we ask to be forgiven." He got up and went over to the little wax Madonna in the glass case. He lifted the case off and gently set the tiny tin crown straight on the miniature head.

Our Lady looked very young, very gay, in that sombre room, with her full blue skirt, her tin crown, her lace veil and her Child, clothed in a minute chasuble, as stiff as a board with its crusting of glass jewellery, laughing in her arms.

Fernandez opened the parlour door, looked down the passage, and listened. He heard a faint clatter of pots from the kitchen, and knew that Teresa was busy preparing supper. He would not be disturbed.

He closed the door and knelt down before the young Mother and her laughing Child.

CHAPTER 18

DINNER WITH MONSIGNOR FRAYNE

… Let not the first over
his meat, mock at him
who does not eat it, or the
second while he abstains,
pass judgment on him
who eats it.

He had an absurd hope, poor Timothy, that after all this might be the wrong evening, that though he was actually standing outside the wrought iron gates, he still might escape the ordeal.

He fumbled nervously in the pocket of his hired dress suit for the invitation, hoping against hope. But no, there it was, in the Monsignor's own small, ornate writing (a singular honour!) "Dine at my cottage—" and the day and time, unmistakably *this* day, this hour, shortly this minute.

The ghost of a smile moved across Timothy's face, at the

sight of the words "my cottage," for he was at the gateway of a long avenue, stretched like a strip of bleached linen, between grey feathery trees, like trees in an old tapestry, to a large and beautiful country house.

Even now Timothy wrestled with a desperate temptation to run away. Suppose the Monsignor had forgotten that he had asked him? The idea was one that dogged him, whenever he had accepted an invitation, and the embarrassment that would follow such a contingency had assumed ridiculous proportions in his imagination. Tonight, in the presence of Cosma Fether-Preedham, it would be unbearable!

He could still creep away, crouching behind hedges at the roadside, to avoid meeting other approaching guests, feeling and acting like an escaped convict.

He crossed himself as if he were going to the gallows and started up the long avenue, leaving behind him the road to escape, lying between fields under a mist as white and tender as milk, gleaming like pearls.

He would not have accepted the invitation at all, were it not that Cosma was to be among the guests. Now he realized that it was precisely her presence that would make his always painful self-consciousness insufferable.

At the distance of three weeks, when he accepted, it had seemed possible that he might acquit himself in reality as he did in phantasy, contributing brilliantly to the conversation, perfectly at ease, indeed with a certain debonair nonchalance, that would captivate Cosma, and lead to long intimate discussions of her own seeking, through which deep understanding and natural sympathy would begin.

Now that the day had come he knew the vanity of day

dreams. He was more embarrassed than he had ever been in his life. He remembered how a mere glance from Cosma, paradoxically, had power to strip him naked and at the same time make him miserably aware of his clothes, their shabbiness, their cheapness, their unsuitability for the company and the occasion.

This combination of X-ray eye and critical mind which Timothy attributed to Cosma, was the invention of his own hyper-sensitivity. She had in fact a curious absence of the critical faculty, which accounted for many of her enthusiasms. Added to this, hers was the unquenchable almost aggressive good nature that is so often the accompaniment of robust health and a total lack of imagination.

To her, "the Flames," the fashionable youth movement, had become the world, a world of glowing colour, of light and splendour and vision. She had given herself to it with the unhesitating generosity of an ardent happy nature, eager to be moulded into the pattern which it set up, as the ideal apostle, the apostle of to-day. She had by nature all the attributes wanted for the pattern, good looks, good clothes, good health, good humour, and as much magnetism as one so free of any trace of neurosis could ever hope to have. She took it for granted that every young Catholic must wish, as she wished herself, to be moulded, hammered, coaxed into the same shape, the shape of the Flame ideal, which with thoroughness characteristic of the movement was complete in every detail, leaving no flaw anywhere, no chink through which the individual's egoism might project a ray, no possible inlet for any part of his, or rather I should say her (since men were not admitted excepting as useful admirers), previous experience. Wisely great attention was paid to exterior things, which made the least self-conscious people the happiest candidates. The Flames were eager to dedicate to the service and advertisement of the Church, not the drab, the down-at-heel, the dowdy, who have so often discouraged the rich man from the attempt to pass with all his luggage, through the eye of the needle, but the smart, the charming, the attractive, even the visibly opulent, who remind him of the consoling conclusion that to God all things are possible.

Cosma had none of the sadistical satisfaction that many moralists have, who delight in fault-finding, and when they do find a fault, tear off the pitiful covering of pretence or of secrecy, as if they tore a bandage from a wound that it might bleed before the world. No, Cosma brought to all her contacts not so much the destructive spirit of the critic as the constructive desire of the artist to perfect his own work, her single mistake being a failure to realize that all those people in whom, for the sake of the Apostolate, she was interested, were not her work. Perhaps she lacked the quality which distinguishes angels from fools. She had formed a habit of assessing and often re-assessing the apostolic value of everyone with whom she came into contact and had invented a little chart which would measure the surely inevitable increase, that would be evident when a given apostle had for a short time been exposed to the direct influence of the Flames, much as sickly children are exposed to radiant heat. These charts were exactly like those used in hospitals for recording the patient's temperature excepting that the line which in those would measure fever, in Cosma's measured fervour, and that for the double purpose of making the chart pretty and encouraging the apostle, the line varied in colour, being blue at the subnormal, changing through green to daffodil at the normal, and rising in orange, culminating in a splendid vermilion at the fever point, which would in the natural order indicate death.

This chart, besides being a stimulant to zeal, illustrated a joke current among the Flames about "spiritual blues," they being pledged to a perpetual smile.

While Timothy still hesitated outside the wrought-iron gates of Monsignor Frayne's house, Cosma herself put an end to his indecision by arriving suddenly in a streak of silver, or so it seemed to him, as her silver race car took the road at top speed and yet drew up instantly and noiselessly at the gates.

"Get in," she said. "We are just in time, and I'm crazy for a drink. Monsignor Frayne has the best drink in England, did you know that? The best in Europe some people say, which reminds me, the war with Germany is as good as here."

"How perfectly ghastly."

"Not a bit of it. It will do our boys and girls a lot of good. I've just come from a meeting of the Flames now, they are as keen as mustard."

"Are they going to be a First-Aid party?"

"Yes, and all sorts of other things too. The Flames always take on everything you know. You know our motto don't you, 'Act before you think.' Another way, but a *positive* way of saying 'He who hesitates is lost.'—We had a bandage practice and gas-cleansing practice to-day, all done in the Flame way, you know. Not that the Germans will ever bomb London, the defences are too jolly good. My cousin Bimbo, who holds a frightfully high up hush-hush job in the War Office, was telling us all about it. The secret doodas we've got, they are all along the South Coast, no German plane could get through them."

"I'm glad about that—I'm afraid I'll have to join up, though I hate it—in fact I don't think I really believe in war."

"*Of course* you must join up! at least you must get a commission, and you've got to believe in wars whether you do or not, at least you have got to in just ones, and this one is obviously a just one, as we are in it—yes, my boy, a commission for you, we need Catholic officers. Aren't you *thrilled?* It's a huge chance for Catholic Action you know. Do ring the bell, don't stand gaping—I really shall fall down dead if I don't have a drink."

"You know," Timothy answered, "I'm not at all sure about a commission. I can't help thinking that if I have to go at all, if I went into the ranks, I'd be—well a better sort of Apostle, starting at the bottom, not at the top."

The door opened almost as Timothy touched the bell, as if the butler had been standing, his hand on the knob, waiting. He was a grave kind man, with the manner and tact of an undertaker. It seemed inevitable that the Monsignor must become a Bishop, so unmistakably was this man born to be a Bishop's servant. He took Timothy's hat and coat, sensed his shyness, and piloted him into the lounge, where already, with magical speed, Cosma was drinking a cocktail.

It was only at the table that the beautiful confusion of his fellow guests sorted itself out into individuals, and then only rather mistily, for the beauty of the long low room, with its French window opening on to the garden, the soft light of innumerable candles, the enormous splendour of the last of the roses in silver bowls on the polished table, the red shadow of the roses in the glossy wood and the glimmer of softly breathing gold reflected in the red, all this beauty was lapping him gently into itself.

Outside, the garden had the essential qualities for a garden's loveliness, depth and mystery. Timothy looked out on a dusk that was intensely blue against the candlelight, on a wide lawn sweeping slightly downhill to a little copse of silver birch trees, and on pale drifts of autumn crocuses.

The Monsignor's excellent wine flowed softly, warmly, through his blood in waves of rose and gold. It seemed to flood his veins with the beauty around him, to wash the splendour of the roses over his heart, to steep his mind in the warmth of the candle flame.

The self-reproaching asceticism that held his daily life rigid seemed to be melting in his wrists, the agonies of inexpressible charity to be flowing away out of his heels, and Cosma was desirable as never before. Now it seemed that she and the Flames and the Monsignor were right—absurd for Apostles to be dowdy, puritanical, drab. What could be more Apostolic than these beautiful flowing dresses, these sparkling diamonds, these beautiful faces and soft voices?

Yet he struggled, feebly. Under the sweet bliss of his senses, something in him wrestled and struggled and he was angry with himself for his weakness.

To Timothy in the loneliness of his conversion, in the loneliness of his love of beautiful things, the flattering interest of the Monsignor, and the seductive, heady apostolate of the Flames, had been irresistible. But gradually, though meaning only to fashion him to the pattern—which they could not conceive of any man not desiring to be fashioned into, they had troubled his soul. Little by little their ease and *savoir faire* had increased his self-consciousness; he had begun to strive to be just as the other young men in that set, he invited Cosma to lunch where he could not afford to take her, sold his books, pawned his clothes, even borrowed money to take her. He knew how Peter would have despised him and his faith had he known.

He tried to convince himself that the Flames were right, and that he was wrong, that he was a raw convert, who was too hard, too rigid in his own mistaken spirituality. That the standard that he had set for himself was a matter of personal vanity. He tried to smother the inward voice which insisted that, after all *he* had not set the standard.

If he tried to rationalize his doubts, how much more did the Flames try to rationalize them for him, and to convince him that they were not the real scruples of a rightly troubled conscience, but false modesty, mock humility, prompted by the Devil, the Father of Lies, to hinder him from the work of the apostolate, and in particular from the work which he could so obviously do to promote the Flames.

The conflict in Timothy's mind might have gone on indefinitely; to be in conflict with evil people is simple, but to be in conflict with good people is an interminable problem. It might have remained a question in his mind for ever, while his soul gradually softened and compromised, and swung to and fro, from hesitation to hesitation; but this night, with its immediate threat of war, with the strange complacency of Cosma and of her friends who were at table, challenged him to give an answer once for all: to cut Cosma out of his life

and go back to the loneliness of his solitary Catholic life, or
to betray the values of his old, dislocated friends, to be untrue
as it were, to his first love, and to the invisible Communion of
Saints.

Cosma was speaking about him, trying to draw him into
conversation with the huge Portuguese woman in a black
mantilla opposite to them. "Mr. Green has the strange idea,"
she was saying, "that he could be a better Apostle as a common soldier in the ranks than with a commission."

Donna Rosario turned eyes that were almost black, like
onyx, yet intensely alive and penetrating, on Timothy and
smiled: "But why not?" she said. "Haven't I always told you,
Cosma, that though I have no doubt your Flames are the salt
of the earth, the salt of the earth fails of its purpose if it is
always kept in the salt cellar."

Timothy looked gratefully at her. He made up his mind
that if he had an opportunity and was not too shy he would
talk to her, but just now he was less and less inclined for controversy and decisions, he was soothed and lulled into a haze
of irresponsibility, like a child being rocked in a cradle by the
fireside.

Everyone and everything here was beautiful, the girls with
flower-like faces, the long sweet folds of the women's dresses,
the soft, cultured voices; the immaculate young man opposite, with locks of green gold hair, Fr. Perivale with his visible blond youngness, and even the Monsignor himself, whose
voice Timothy became aware of now, that melodious voice,
that seemed to move like waves across the table, weaving all
the material beauty of crystal and silver and flames and flowers into the immaterial beauty of his thoughts.

He was speaking to Dr. Moncrieff now, asking him for his opinions on the psychological aspect of the events in Riverside, the passionate desire for Father Malone's canonization, and the swing over of the crowd emotion—if indeed it was crowd emotion—from the cultus of the old and dead priest, to that of the little living child.

To the other guests he explained, "Dr. Moncrieff does not share our Faith, but he is—though I fear he may not be flattered by my saying so—a great natural Christian and it is he who has looked after the child all through his life—indeed I think I am right, Doctor, in saying that you brought him into the world?"

"I did—and I hope I am not shattering anyone's faith in saying that I expect very soon to see him go out of it."

"In spite of the Novena?"

"Yes, Monsignor. How that will affect the people I don't know, but personally I would have preferred to take the child into hospital, it would have been easier to keep the poor little fellow under observation and comfortable—and it might have done a lot to stop the hysteria of the people."

"Hysteria?—You think then that there is hysteria over him?"

"Oh certainly"—Dr. Moncrieff silently noted the Monsignor's satisfaction—"but there always is over anything of this kind, a percentage you know. However, the people objected to my removing the child from home, they really felt very strongly about it; that was, of course, to be expected from the parents, but the opposition was as fierce from the people who are not related at all. In fact, you would think he belonged to them all."

"And maybe he does."

It was Donna Rosario's voice, a curiously light little voice from such a mountain of a woman.

Monsignor Frayne turned to Father Perivale. "And you, Father, what impressions have you brought back from your recent visit to Riverside?" He explained to the company, "Father Perivale only returned last night, and as I have not yet had any opportunity of discussion with him, we can all learn from his impressions now."

Father Perivale turned a light, bright pink. His heart was pounding, and his mouth as dry as that of a nervous boy, answering the first question in a viva-voce examination.

He knew very well that the Monsignor would not like what he was going to say, and he wished that he had not chosen this occasion to question him.

"I know, Monsignor," he said, "that you think the whole thing likely to give scandal—"

"A view which I have always understood you to share with me, Father."

The young priest swallowed, the sharp Adam's apple in his throat jerked up and down in a way that looked as if it must be painful, and caused everyone who observed it to feel as if his own throat was sore.

"I *did* share it," he said, "but the fact is, since I've been there, and stayed in Father Malone's presbytery, and *seen* Willie Jewel—and the people—well, I suppose it's a kind of little conversion—I just see for myself that it is all part of the mystery of love, and goes much deeper than hysteria, or anything like that. I don't think it *could* give scandal to anyone who really *saw* it. And the Novena, it's—well, it's just something very beautiful. It just is drawing all sorts of very different people, even people of different faith, and people who don't get on in the ordinary way, round the child, in a closer and closer circle of love. It really is quite extraordinary, how praying for that tiny boy has made all those poor people one with one another."

He stopped and looked down at his plate, his hand twisting his glass round and round by the stem, was shaking.

This time it was Donna Rosario who broke the awkward silence.

"And what impression did the little boy himself make on you, Father?" she said.

"I expected to be harrowed—"

"As you would be," broke in Doctor Moncrieff, "if you knew the chemical composition of his bones."

"But I wasn't—I had an impression of joy. I can't describe it, it was something like—something like the morning of First Communion. He was just a white little boy, with golden hair—more the sort of child one expects to find in a Victorian nursery story than in a London slum. But he had none of the morbidity of the Victorian child sufferer, no, he just radiated joy—that's the only impression I had."

"You have told us nothing about the old priest," said Cosma, "there are fantastic rumours of his miracles and stories of his alleged sanctity."

"Oddly enough, it seems as if the old man is just pointing away from himself, to the child, one almost forgets him."

"Ah! I expect that is just what he *is* doing," said Donna Rosario. "Perhaps that is what God is really using him for;

and for my part, I think that the loveliest thing of all is the point that the Doctor brought up about this little child belonging to all the people." She laughed, a light, tender little laugh.

"Do you know," she said, "I have just decided to join in the Novena myself. I shall actually deny myself a second helping of this perfect soufflé, for the intentions of the people of Riverside. After all, every poor little Catholic child does belong to us all."

Then Father Perivale, as pink as a wild rose, made his confession before men.

"I too am making the Novena with them," he said.

There was a painful silence, and again it was Donna Rosario who broke it.

"You were saying, Father," she said, "that it seems as if Father Malone is pointing away from himself to the child—maybe he wants us to look at the child, and see in him—a crucifix—innocence suffering—that is a living crucifix, is it not?"

Timothy broke in, "You mean," he said, "that Willie Jewel is a crucifix for the simple and the poor?"

"Yes—but as much, possibly even more, for the sophisticated and rich. We all need to *see*, we have grown so blind, not only our eyes, but our hearts and our minds are blind. We need surely a new—or maybe, a very old—kind of contemplation, a *looking* at Christ in one another, a contemplation in which our part is the response of love. I can see a likeness, between the crucifix that the contemplative in his cell takes into his hands, and the child who awakens love in everyone who knows him, the crucifix whose feet we kiss."

"A very beautiful idea, Donna Rosario," said Monsignor Frayne, "but we must treat of such matters with the utmost caution."

Doctor Moncrieff laughed. "Since I am outside of the danger of excommunication," he said, "may I presume to support the idea with a quotation from the highest authority. Is there not a passage in your Scriptures which runs something like this. 'For as much as you did it to the least of these little ones, you did it unto me.'"

"It seems a marvellous idea to me," said Timothy, "the contemplating of Christ in a little child—" he would have gone on, but Monsignor Frayne took up the conversation and said:

"Although Christ Himself is undivided, we can, if indeed we have this remarkable faculty for contemplation at all, see but one aspect of His life, in any given individual, at one time; and there is a strong tendency to look for Him in the obvious, the poor, the humiliated, the suffering. There are many other aspects which are overlooked, or nearly always are. We are apt, for example, to overlook the Passion of Christ's mind in Gethsemane, and in the wilderness. Again, Christ, besides being the Man of Sorrows, was the Man of Joy—who ever loved the world as He did, breathing, as it seems to do, the very breath of God? By all means look for our Divine Lord in His suffering members, but look for Him in those who rejoice too, in the grateful and happy members...."

"One rather has the impression," said Timothy, "that Christians must suffer to be happy."

Doctor Moncrieff was swinging' his brandy gently round and round in his glass, like a swinging ball of liquid amber in a crystal. He was listening to the Monsignor with deep respect; if anyone could have converted him, it was this priest.

"What you are saying," he said, "suggests that if the cooling waters of Baptism flow over the pagan's heated brow, he becomes the greatest adorer of all."

They went on talking for a little longer, but now the glow in Timothy's blood was fading, and he was already beginning to feel the remorse and depression that always followed on this kind of dinner. He wondered if he had drunk more than he should have and if that had something to do with his sudden fresh revulsion from the worldliness he was playing with. He felt humiliated and resolved, though he was cynical of his resolution as he made it, that he would give Cosma up, Cosma, and dinner parties, and drink, and smoking: he would give them all up, absolutely and for ever, and while he swore it he unconsciously lit another cigarette to steady his nerves.

He was glad when they went out into the garden. Seen from behind the yellow candle flame, the sky had been intensely blue, the garden full of depths of colour and shadow, but outside it seemed that the colour had been washed away by a flood of silver water. Grass and trees and flowers were softly burning silver, the sky an emptiness of peace.

Cosma was still lively, and the centre of a little laughing group, but Timothy did not join them. He went instead to the far corner of the garden, where Donna Rosario was sitting alone. In the moonlight, her huge bulk cast a deep shadow, and she was sitting so still there that she might have been a carved stone fountain.

"Well," she said, smiling at him, "are you not going to join the young people? You don't want to sit with an old woman, do you?"

"Yes ... that is, if I'm not in the way ... but perhaps you wanted to be alone?"

"Oh no, I'm not so unsociable, but I often sit apart and meditate on the flowers. I am only too happy if someone else wants to join me in that. We are very old friends, the Monsignor and I, and he lets me feel free to humour my whims here. Sit down, and tell me why you were so miserable this evening."

"How did you know I was miserable? Did I show it so much?"

"No, but I'm a bit of a cripple, always sitting still and looking on you know, perhaps my power of observation is a little over-developed."

"I'm afraid I might bore you terribly," said Timothy, but his instinct told him that Donna Rosario would never be bored by a human being, and he longed to unburden his heart to her.

"If you do," she said, "I shall simply walk away, so you will know ... but I don't think that I shall walk away."

So Timothy sat down and told her his whole story, and at the end of it, it seemed very little to tell, very little indeed to account for the burden of unrest and the raging conflict that never left him. When at last he tried to explain his conflict, Donna Rosario herself had to rescue him.

"Briefly," she said, "you feel that Cosma and the Flames and all this little set of people, which probably seems to be very nearly the whole Church to you at the moment, is far less Christian in practice than your Communist friends, and you feel you ought to make a break. But after all, can you not practise your own ideals among them? You are a man, not a chameleon."

"A very weak man ... besides, one side of me says, it is just the very thing I condemn in them that makes me want to get away, a kind of pharisaism ... and you know, it is not too easy to be yourself, they are all the time hammering their ideas into you, it isn't as if they thought of themselves as people all struggling to imitate Christ and helping one another along, they think of themselves as people to set the standard and show the way."

"Possibly ... but hasn't it occurred to you that as all the Flames seem to be leaders, and none of them followers, their influence need not worry you very much?"

"But aren't the poor to be led and what do the Flames know of the ordinary, grinding poverty? If they know anything about poverty at all, it is from reading about the extremes, in books and papers, the sensational things that hardly ever happen. They know nothing of the unfair wear and tear that is so intolerable and so usual. I mean such things as having to let the water come into your shoes day after day because you haven't got two pairs, and dreading cold weather because you have teeth that ache, and no money to go to the dentist, and having to see the people you care for ill without being able to bring them even a bunch of flowers ... what do they know, who know nothing of the drab mediocre misery, of the temptations of it, and the evil, and the hellish things it can do to you?"

"Alas! ..." said Donna Rosario, "there is just as much of the temptation and evil, and of hellish things, among rich people. And in a way it is more frightening, because as a rule, they do not recognize it so soon or so clearly, sometimes they do not recognize it at all, and one trembles, wondering what the result will be."

"To get back to myself," said Timothy, "which is, I'm afraid, what I always do get back to. The worst thing of all is the feeling of discouragement, nearly despair when one sees the pride of life set up and accepted as an example, and realizes that Christ's humility and poverty are more despised in practice among religious people, than they are among openly worldly people or Communists. It is such a hard black bruise to the spirit, and one becomes cynical and feels that one has been a fool to struggle so hard for the ideal of the humiliated Christ."

"Did you ever imagine," said Donna Rosario, softly, "that you could ever willingly practise Christ's humility, and *not* be humiliated?"

Timothy was silent for some minutes and then he said:

"No ... you are right. But what should I do now? It has come to a crisis in my soul. Ought I to go back to the loneliness of my life as a Catholic, as it was before I knew that set? Should I make a real break and be quite alone? Ought I to give Cosma up? Of course she does not care for me and she never will."

"I think," Donna Rosario answered, "that it depends on whether you can be yourself with her, and in her environment. If you can't, then you are in a hopeless position anyway, for how can you really love, or be loved, if you cease to be yourself? To love you must possess yourself; God, who is love, possesses Himself wholly, and gives Himself to all that is. You possess yourself in so far as you are true to His plan of you, which is *your own* likeness to Christ. But I do not think that any drastic decision will be left to you. I am afraid that the war will sweep us all apart."

"But Donna Rosario, do you think that this Flame spirit is wrong or right?"

"That is not really a question for you or me to decide. Our only question is what we are going to do about whatever we come up against in life ourselves. Our answer to all such questions about other people can only be our own lives. The answer is not anger, or judgment, but love. When your own concept of the Christ life causes you to condemn people, even when they seem clearly guilty, something is very wrong with yourself. Love oftens mourns but never condemns. I don't know how worldly or not the group we are discussing are, but I do know that if they, and with them, the whole of society, are ever to see the way to remedy the social evils, it must be through *seeing* the poverty of Christ *as a blessed thing*. They will not be converted by preaching and moralising. It is as useless to tell a greedy-for-gold man that it is wrong to hang on to his treasure in a world where destitution exists and grinding poverty prevails, as it would be to tell a drowning man that it is wrong to hang on to his lifebelt while those who haven't one are sinking. It is useless because those who trust in riches are frightened people, they do not possess their wealth, it possesses them. They will only change and make justice possible in the world, when they *see* that in having nothing they have everything, that peace and freedom are the treasure of the poor. They must see poverty not as a state of virtue, but as a state of joy. Until that happens, there is no hope."

"But how is that possible? It would be difficult to convince a poor person of that, let alone a rich one!"

"Yet that is Christ's teaching; He did not teach in terms

of right and wrong, but of joy and sorrow.... *Blessed* ... joyful, are the poor in spirit, woe, sorrow, to you rich. The only answer to the mechanical masses is the saint, for the saint is the only true *individual,* and in him we see Christ, and see His values, not as something forced on us by school teachers, but as something to envy.

"Take Saint Francis of Assisi, whom the whole world, not Catholics only, thinks of in connection with poverty. He lived in an age as worldly as ours; times change, but human nature never. Saint Francis changed the outlook and the lives of countless people, not by scolding them, but by *showing* them, not by being a reformer, but by being a poor little man in love with all created loveliness. The reason is so simple, he reflected Christ, on whom his eyes were fixed, and when he lifted up his arms in ecstasy to receive his Lord's wounds in his own body, the shadow that he cast on the white roads of Italy was the cruciform shadow of Christ."

Again Donna Rosario paused, and then: "Since Our Lord has ascended in glory, we can only see Him in His shadow cast on the road under our feet, by His saints."

"Now it is getting cold," said Timothy. "How selfish I am, keeping you out so long ... all the others have gone in."

"If I walk away," she answered, "you will think I am bored. So walk with me to the house. I shall need the help of your arm, but if you can stand it, we will go the longest way, because you must see the loveliest flowers."

They were white flowers growing in great clusters on either side of the narrow path, beautiful and unearthly as living light or as a radiance of burning snow. Timothy caught his breath, and they stood still in front of them in wonder.

"Do you not think," said Donna Rosario, "that the secret of their loveliness is that we can never possess it. Flowers can never become possessions, we always receive their beauty and never grasp it. We can never spoil it, as we spoil all our other loves, by possessiveness."

"You mean, because their life is so short, the beauty that we adore is lived out, even as it is given?"

"Yes, and yet is always given again; like everything given by God, the gift of flowers is a gift of life, their loveliness is the loveliness of *life*, just that. And life is never static, it can never be stopped, possessed or hoarded. Its superb wonder is that it is always new. As you say the beauty of flowers is lived out even as it is given, but it is not only lived out, it is a continual renewal. When we receive the loveliness of a flower, the flowering is a little crisis of life-giving; it is a dying, but a dying that is the supreme moment of a living sacrifice. Flowering and dying are one thing. In its dying, the loveliness of the flower is made new to return to us."

"Like every expression of love, Donna Rosario," said Timothy, "even human love, in its consummation, a flowering that is a little death."

"Yes, and like the Host. Just like life in the flower and in the pure expression of human love, Christ's life in the Host is always being renewed in its consummation. It is the flowering of love, in the white Host, lifted up and sacrificed in the Mass." Donna Rosario put out her hand and touched the cool white petals reverently. "Lo," she said gently, "Lo, I make all things new."

CHAPTER 19

THE STATIONS OF
THE CROSS

*If he come to me, I
shall not see him. If he
depart from me, I shall
not understand.*

War came closer and closer, gripping and constricting the
mind with iron fingers of fear. People going about their daily work fell asleep, in tubes or buses, anywhere at all where
they were relaxed for a few minutes. Timothy observed how
sleeping faces reveal what waking faces hide, asleep everyone
had something of a child; sometimes in the unguarded features, sometimes in the open hands or the abandonment of
the body, or perhaps simply because when they were asleep
they were defenceless, all equally defenceless, from the large,
square-faced labourer with his bag of tools, who slumped
over sideways, his head hanging towards his shoulder, to the
little old lady in black kid gloves who sat bolt upright asleep,
looking even a little whiter in the face than when she was

awake, her head nodding under her hat, that resembled a piled-up plate of black vegetables.

They slept because the sorrow, the foreboding that oppressed them exceeded that which human nature can bear. In sheer self-defence they must slip away into a sweet dark oblivion.

Timothy thought of Gethsemane and the Apostles sleeping for sorrow. This too was the eve of Christ's Passion, and men and women were sleeping for sorrow.

He himself wrestled with the dread of what it must mean for him, above all the dread of army life. He was built for solitude, for the long still meditative nights alone. Now to hand himself over, body and soul, like a child going back to school, to army life, seemed an intolerable thought. He put off any decision and found a thousand reasons for complicating and increasing the conflict.

Eric Jacobs behaved like a wild bird in a cage, dashing from one side to the other, bruising himself on both, one day aggressive, violent in his condemnation of Germany, the next day a pacifist, attacking his friends who humiliated him by volunteering to fight.

His desperate fear and need for someone to reassure him caused him to forget that Timothy was a Catholic, and to forget the isolation he had helped to inflict upon him. He was in his room now, as of old, talking, talking, talking.

Then suddenly, quite unexpectedly, he turned up in uniform. He explained, somewhat sheepishly that there seemed no other way for him, the bookshop where he worked was closing down, and the food in the army was abundant. He was leaving the next day, this was good-bye.

Timothy asked him if he had seen Peter and the others. Yes, and there everything was tragic. They were all foreigners and misfits, not one of them knew what would become of him.

Timothy asked if Peter would like to see him. Eric thought not; he was proud, he would not relent because of his own trouble, he would never accept pity.

The nights were sinister. All through the hours of darkness the heavy ominous sound of armoured traffic, lorries, guns, passing through London in an unbroken procession, denying the faint hope the newspapers proclaimed.

On Eric's last night Timothy heard a young man, someone unknown to him, cry out, in a half-strangled voice from a window nearby, "I can't, I can't." It seemed to give a voice to the agony of London, to reveal it, like the tearing off of a bandage from a wound.

It broke through the night, splitting it, and then ceased as suddenly, and until light came, the rattle of the procession of guns went on, with its terrifying official secrecy, under cover of darkness.

The next day, very early in the morning, Timothy's landlady brought him a note from Eric. "Mr. Jacobs has gone," she said, "he seemed properly upset and he told me to warn you there is bad news in his note, he couldn't bring himself to wait and tell you, he went away an hour before he had need to."

"All right—put it down there."

The landlady lingered, waiting with an appetite for disaster.

"You had better go," Timothy said, "whatever it is, I shall have to dress."

"I thought," she said with a little sniff of wounded vanity, "I might help."

"If I want you, I can come to you," said Timothy brutally.

She went out, slamming the door. He heard her indignation in her flouncing retreat, the heels of her bedroom slippers banging out their protest like clappers on the carpetless stairs.

He sat staring at what was written on the piece of paper in his hand, hardly able to take in what it meant.

"Peter is in St. Jude's Hospital. He tried to kill himself."

He did not know if Peter was alive or dead now, if he would want him to come or not, he knew only that he must go to him.

The Hospital seemed quite unreal, so undisturbed, so matterof-fact, so clean and shining and white, so full of air and light. No one questioned him. He went straight in and began to look for Peter in the wards. The patients stared, and a young nurse came up to him.

"Is Peter Lucharski here?"

"Well now, would it be an accident?"

"Yes—no—not exactly"—he stopped because he could not bear it in his own voice, but he must—"He tried to commit suicide."

"Oh yes—I know now who you want, the emergency ward. But are you a relation, were you sent for? This is not a visiting hour."

"I must see him."

"Well, I will ask Sister."

Sister was large and square with immense teeth and a huge bunch of keys at her waist, which caused her to rattle like an oil-less machine, when she moved; a kind but masterful woman who had complete mastery not only over her own feelings, but over other people's. Everything in the mill of her authority was ground and sifted to a kind of milled grain of common sense, life and death even lost their drama in her milling. A patient was "as comfortable as can be expected" unless he was actually at death's door, when he was "not *quite* so comfortable."

She looked kindly at Timothy.

"You are a friend of Mr. Lucharski?"

"Yes."

"Then perhaps you can tell us if he has any relations?"

"Not here—I never heard of any—but tell me for God's sake, will he die ?"

"Oh, no. The Surgeon had to put in a few stitches, but he is fairly comfortable, he is still under the anaesthetic. The danger is that if he has not got the will to live he may try to tear off his bandage—they do that. Later on he will have the help of a psychiatrist, sometimes that does them good."

She spoke as if suicide were as common as measles.

"You may come and have a look at him, and perhaps in a day or two you can have a little chat with him."

"Sister, we had quarrelled, at least he had quarrelled with me. He might not want to see me when he comes round."

"Dear me, what a pity—well, you may go in now for a few minutes."

Peter was behind screens, he was very near waking and was breathing quietly as if he was sleeping naturally. He had a bandage round his throat.

Timothy stood looking down at him. He had never before known such strong composed love for anyone as he knew now for his friend. He lay there before his eyes, the symbol of Youth in a faithless world. Defeated, lost, in his own will, destroyed.

Timothy knew that this love, that flowed through him like a torrent, was the love of the Church, the love of Christ in His Church for the soul that was lost, it was the love for which all the fanfare and splendour of the Hierarchy was maintained, the love that was in the unique loneliness of the Vicar of Rome, in the daily struggle of the parish priests, in the immolation of the contemplatives. The love in a million Masses being offered at that very moment, lifted up in the blood ringed in a million golden cups, proved in the breaking of a million Hosts. It was the love in the sacrifices of multitudes of little children, of legions of holy, unsuitable old nuns; the love in the aching knees of armies of char-women, in the wrestling with sin of legions of the tempted, it was the love of the saints and the sinners throughout the centuries, glowing through his heart like a mighty river.

It was the love of Christ on the Cross, the river of life flowing out of His heart at the moment of His death, the bloodstream of the Life of the World.

All the sermons, all the teaching, all the admonition, all the counsel and tender whispered hope in the Church was meant for Peter, but how would it ever reach him? Timothy looked at his white closed face, he saw how pinched his nose was, how white his mouth and the lobes of his ears, bloodless and white; his ears looked like open wax flowers, but they were deaf to the eloquence, the pleading, the threatening of the multitudinous voice of love—deaf equally to the Dies Irae and to the tender pleadings of the Lamb—and then Timothy remembered, Peter had not been deaf to the misery of human creatures, it was because he had tried to love *alone* that he had despaired. He was the pitiful, logical answer to the absolute statement, "Without me you can do nothing." But, thought Timothy, "If Christ is true to His word, he cannot perish," and he prayed for Peter.

And then he knew, *he* must be the answer to the prayer, he himself. The Love of the Church, of Christ in His Mystical Body could reach even this closed heart, even this voluntary outcast, the loneliness of the Vatican, the labours of the Apostles, the thorny crown of the theologians, the bravery of the children, the sacrifices of the poor could reach him, through his own love.

It could only be through contemplation. Now, very quietly and gently as words and incidents return in dreams, the images evoked by the conversation at Monsignor Frayne's dinner party came back to him, the child who showed Christ's love to the poor as the crucifix showed it to monks in their cells.

He was looking on another crucifix now, on the crucifix that was Peter Lucharski, who had crucified Christ in his own soul.

He thought of the contemplative in his cell, standing not in front of a painted cross, but in front of a white wall, himself cruciform, his arms extended, his hands empty, his naked feet still, his heart broken open for his Lord's sorrows: he has become like the Crucified, on whom he looks always with the dark eye of faith, because he cannot help becoming like one on whom he gazes steadily for ever. Stripped of everything, empty-handed, because the arms stretched out wide enough to embrace the crucified reach out to the width that embraces the world, and hug nothing to self, because the hands open to receive the nails must let go their hold of all else.

Now, Timothy knew that in order to offer himself for Peter, he too must be a contemplative, he too must take on the shape of Christ, he also must look on this living crucifix, and be shaped into the pattern of Christ crucified in this man.

Peter had tried to take his life, Timothy must offer *his* life, give it back to God, that Peter might have life everlasting.

He made his offering, speaking softly to Peter. "Peter, I will offer my life for you, but *my* life is nothing, I will offer Christ in my life, for you, I am going away now to try to imitate Him and to offer Him in my life—and death—for you."

He knew that Peter could not hear, but God heard and a thought came to him that was almost blinding in its tragic glory—Christ, he thought, is man's contemplative. He looked at man and loved him and became like him, and took on the shape and colour of his sins, the shape of the cross, the colour of His stripes and blood.

The Sister came in. "Doing nicely," she said with a shrewd glance at Peter, and speaking of him as if he were the Christmas turkey in the oven. "And now, I think you must leave him for to-day."

Outside the pale primrose of early morning had warmed into a soft blue day of benediction and light. Timothy went to the Lady Chapel of the nearest church. He asked Our Lady to look after the details of Peter's life, and then suddenly very weary knelt for a time silent; the shame of what the human race had done to her and her little Son aching in him, he knelt as if he were a child who buries his crimson face of shame in his mother's wide skirt.

Then he went to a call-box and rang his office. "Will you take a message to the Editor—thank you, I shall not be coming to-day. I am going to enlist—good-bye."

A queue of young men were lined up before him, come out of all manner of lives to the hazard of this new strange life of abnegation: some, wistful city clerks, pale, round-shouldered, escaping from the squirrel's cage; some, countrymen, big and ruddy, wanting perhaps to seize on the world with their large hands, instead of day after day seizing the same worn hollow in the handle of the plough; some, lads hardly out of school, and others who looked like convicts and were taking their biggest chance.

Inside, it seemed to Timothy as if he were taking part in a pathetic pageant of the Stations of the Cross.

One by one the men stood before the officer, who looked them up and down, asked a few questions, condemned them to probable death. One by one they were stripped for the medical examination, and stood, pitifully childlike in their nakedness, immolated men. And then they were given soldiers' clothes, and even on the big men, they seemed to sag and to be a mockery. Perhaps in a few months they would fill them, perhaps then the clothes would have wed themselves to the men and the men would be soldiers. At present they looked incongruous and ludicrous.

His own turn came, and the misery of self-consciousness of an over-sensitive schoolboy came back to him. He felt that his shrinking mind was exposed in his thin body, that it would glare out of his ribs that he preferred poetry to football. He hated the soldier's coat, but it covered his nakedness.

He walked back when it was over to take his place among

the other recruits, and the sound of his heavy army boots on the wooden floor sickened him with its association with school. He sat down in the row waiting for orders, and began to watch the others, to try to see below the masks of their faces, to know them from their hands, the delicate scholars' hands, the broad efficient hands of the craftsmen—"all held out for the nail" he thought, and he thought too "how strange it is, that it is our flesh and blood, these bodies that Christ uses for His purpose of love, as He used common bread for the Sacrament of His Body. Poor bodies of men, broken, twisted, drained, ugly, and Christ present where they are. The Incarnation is everywhere."

He felt peaceful and ready now to wait for orders. He knew that he had only been able to volunteer as a soldier because he recognized no man living as his enemy, because his offering for his friend was equally and inevitably an offering for the whole world, Germans and Englishmen alike. He had laid bare his heart.

CHAPTER 20

THE ARCHBISHOP DOZES

As arrows in the hands of
the mighty, are the children
of those who have been
shaken.

The Archbishop paced slowly to and fro, up and down his room, and at last sank down gratefully into an armchair. He had lately felt more and more conscious that he was now a really old man, a consciousness which came to him rather gently and pleasantly than otherwise, perhaps because the habit of his mind was gracious and his heart grateful.

He was becoming increasingly aware of kindness all about him: people were kind and things too, his armchair was inviting and comfortable, his lamp was shaded and shed a soft radiance, he was conscious of, and grateful for, the countless details of life that daily eased the aching of his mind and body. Perhaps he needed more consideration, more help from his environment than he used to do. It was how God was teaching him in His own way, to be humble and to receive the sweetness of His Love.

He smiled, thinking of how he, as a young man, coveted the life of a monk, and, at that, a contemplative; how he had longed for the narrow cell and the white wall, and the freedom of being no one, and having nothing!

How differently God had chosen, who because the young man's shoulders were said to be too frail for the hair shirt and the scourge, had laid upon them at length the far heavier cross of a bishopric, with its needs and debts, and its ignorance and its slums, with its aspirations and failures and quarrels.

He frowned, nothing distressed him so much as discord, above all discord—however trivial and however permissible the matter—among his clergy: and recently there had been a great deal of it. It was an astonishing thing, he thought, what a lot of trouble that good old Father Malone had always managed to cause him, and even death had not ended it. In his lifetime he was blunt and no respecter of persons, likely therefore to be adored and feared, loved and hated, but he had been, as the Archbishop remembered him, without faults, for in his mind candour was no fault, or single-heartedness, or devotion to his flock. He was said, too, to have had great spiritual insight, and to have told people on more than one occasion some disconcerting truths concerning themselves, which would, of course, have to be very carefully considered should "his cause" be introduced. Monsignor Frayne who, the Archbishop reflected with a sigh, did not cease to worry poor old Fr. Malone's memory, as a dog worries a bone, trium-

phantly cited cases of persons of holy reputation whose holiness had been pricked like a bubble when it was discovered
that they had informed certain pious ladies that they were
stepping rapidly on the downward path and were labelled
for Hell—no matter that anyone with half an eye could have
seen that these good ladies *were* on the way to Hell, no one
could *know* their eternal destiny, and no one who professed to
could qualify for sainthood.

The Archbishop had smiled. There was, of course, no evidence at present that Fr. Malone had committed any ladies,
pious or impious, to Hell, or that he had claimed or revealed
any kind of supernatural power in his candid warnings. These
may have been irritating, not because of any unusual power
in perceiving the particular faults, but because of his unusual
honesty in stating them. Then, said Monsignor Frayne, was
this honesty consistent with charity?

The Archbishop shrugged his thin shoulders. An examination into all the circumstances alone could decide that
point. Some canonized saints had recoiled openly in the presence of certain people, because of the stench of their sins.
There may have been some who would have questioned the
charity of that, before their canonization.

The Archbishop stretched out his hand and opened and
closed his fingers, as if he were a beggar, accepting an alms of
the frozen gold of the pale sunshine. His hand was transparent and very old, like a thin autumn leaf, and his face, too, was
very old and very tired. Ever before his mind's eye now was
a vision of the people of the world arming for war, and his
soul, moved with compassion, cried out for peace. Yet even
here, in his little diocese, men quarrelled, holy men quarrelled

over holiness, men who ate the same Divine Bread and drank of the same Chalice quarrelled over sanctity, men who loved God quarrelled over the love of God.

How petty it seemed; and yet, the Archbishop began to turn the thing over and over in the fine filter of his mind, was it pettiness or simply part of the immense issue being fought out in the whole world? the immense issue which had indeed divided and tortured the world in one form or another since the coming of Christ. The war between the masses, the vast groups of men, and the individual man. Between the armed, organized, unthinking multitudes, with their puppet leaders who were the personifications of the demons that had drawn them together, leaders who were driven by the unrecognized evil in those whom they were said to lead, and tossed along on the storm of their passions like pebbles on a stormracked sea, and the lonely individual men who remained solitary in the crowd.

Nowadays, he thought sadly, there are very few who dare to be alone, very few who do not join the crowd, and he saw in his thoughts the crowds outside the house of Pilate, who shouted out "Crucify Him!"—and the crowds on the *Via Crucis* following the loneliest man in the world with shouts and insults on His way to death.

How many of those men, he asked, would have consented to His death, if they had been alone, if they had not been one of a crowd? And how many to-day are consenting to His death, in Europe, in the whole world, because they are one of a crowd, one of a great group, one of a mechanized group like a machine....

Power, might, the pride of life, those things never stood

alone, never dared to stand alone, and dared not stand against the guilt and misgiving even in themselves. They needed the reassurance of countless others like them, dressing like them, speaking like them, acting like them, convincing them that wrong is right because the great "All and everyone" does wrong. Evil like the devil is named "legion."

And those who stand for humility, thought the Archbishop, are alone, on this earth lonely. Those who hold through the ages to the old conventions of holiness that Mother Church teaches in her Nursery, humility, poverty, the mortification of the senses, lowliness—they are alone, he thought, even among their own kith and kin, among those who share their faith and whom they love; and again, men of goodwill learn only by striving with sanctity, are healed of their own infirmities only by dashing themselves against the rock of holiness.

He thought how the saints have always been alone and lonely on earth, because they held on with aching fingers to the hard simple facts of the Gospel, the uncompromising holiness of Christ. Because they saw the Changeless Vision through unshed tears, and heard the voice of love through the world's din, be it the clash of swords, the humming of machines, or the thunder of guns.

"I have looked for one who would sorrow together with me and I have found no one." Wherever they had been in the world, wherever in time or place or circumstance, they had been alone.

He thought of "dear Saint Elizabeth" in her golden crown, clothed in ermine and crimson over the hair shirt, lonely among the illustrious who loved her; of Bernadette in her patched cotton dress and coarse woollen stockings, isolated from her simple peasant family by her vision; of Joan of Arc, in her armour and her tunic of heavenly blue and silver fleur de lis, lonely on the field of battle among the soldiers who adored her.

The door opened and the Archbishop's secretary came in. He had a bundle of letters in his hand that he put down on the table. "We still have letters about Riverside every day," he said. "The Novena is stirring up an absurd amount of feeling, some implore your Lordship to make an end of it, whilst others have the effrontery to ask you to join in."

The Archbishop smiled. "And perhaps it does not occur to these good people that I cannot give orders to the Holy Ghost?"

"No—I do not think that even Monsignor Frayne has thought of that. His strong line is that the local Communists are encouraging the cult."

"Devotion to a saintly Catholic priest!"

"Yes, on the grounds that Poverty was his strong line, that he was essentially one of the people. They lay great stress on a supposed contrast between his life and that of some of the West End clergy, even of certain Religious Orders, based of course on a misconception of our religion—"

"Of course, Father."

"But—intended as a subtle way of splitting the loyalty of the Faithful—at what is, of course, a most critical point of the world's history."

"It is so fantastic, Father, and so certain to *fade* out, that but for one thing I should give no heed to the matter at all. But that thing is the possibility of even one soul suffering harm by it—but I am afraid no ruling that I could make would in any way influence the Communists."

"In the opinion of Monsignor Frayne," said the secretary, "the remedy is a positive Catholicism, run on the Communist lines, using the sword that the Communists have forged against themselves, Culture, Art, Science, Politics, Organization; above all a strong, enthusiastic Youth. Movement."

"He is right indeed," said the Archbishop, "but all this must come from the heart of the people, it must grow up spontaneously out of the roots of them as the wheat grows up out of the earth, it cannot be imposed upon them from above. We cannot organize the Holy Ghost."

"No, Your Grace, but even the wheat must be sown before it grows!"

"Truly, Father, but by the wind of the Spirit. The seed that we humble priests can plant, or perhaps it is only the fertilizer that we can put upon the seed that the wind has sown, is the preaching of the love of Our Saviour Jesus Christ. When all is said and done, Father, the seed is His blood."

The secretary bowed his head and went out of the room. The Archbishop closed his eyes—he supposed that he would be constrained to give a lead, if this miracle that the people of Riverside were praying for was granted; in one way the miracle would be an answer, in another way, however, it would be the beginning of more controversy.

He closed his eyes and prayed to the Holy Spirit to flood his mind with light. The afternoon sun shone through his thin closed lids and his mind drifted back to an evening when he had sat out after an early dinner in the walled garden of a convent.

In spite of the unrest in the world and the continual hammering of its grief on his mind, he was at peace. Indeed on that evening, one might have supposed it impossible that there could be anything else but peace anywhere.

Silence possessed the garden. The thin green leaves were saturated with gold. Earlier in the daytime, a bee had droned, birds had sung, there had been children's voices in the distance and the faint reassuring sound of crockery being washed up, coming from the open windows of the house; now there was absolute stillness, silence more positive than sound; no droning, no singing of birds, no voices of children, no sounds from the house. The flowers and leaves were motionless, as if they were carved out of jade and ivory, the garden was breathless, listening.

This stillness, this intense silence, was like a pause which in music is the link between a long passage of melody and a sudden dominating discord. It broke in the loud harshness of a sinister voice, hoarse, dominating and grating across the stillness.

First one voice and then a chorus, speaking as mechanically as one, "Krieg!' "Krieg!' "Krieg!"

"War! War! War!"

It was the voice of Adolf Hitler and his Nazi Youth. Someone inside the house had turned on the wireless to listen to Hitler's speech in Germany.

Then the Archbishop tasted the grief of the whole world. He was certain now that nothing could stop war. Far away in Germany from the fanatical heart of exploited youth the cry went up that split the world, and broke the heart of an old man sitting quietly in England in a garden of jade and ivory.

"Krieg—Krieg—Krieg! War—War—War!"

The mental image that had impressed itself on his mind then, came back to him now in dream—for he had fallen asleep. A multitudinous army of robot children, armed children, fierce, mechanical, soulless; a robot army marching from end to end of the earth, marching with loud, metallic, rhythmic sound, unable to stop, unable to slow the pace, unable to turn back.

Power, strength, force, the armed pride of life. What force could oppose it? Could any legion of flesh and blood destroy pride? Even if it could defeat the pitiful army of robot children on the field of battle, could it destroy pride, or would that only have changed hands, to march on and on, gathering its recruits from the whole world, on and on and on to the destruction of humanity?

Another memory entered the Archbishop's dream and was merged into it, a memory of the day on which Monsignor Frayne had come to him with his fair-haired young secretary to warn him of the part that little Willie Jewel would play in the devotion to old Father Malone. In his dream he heard again the sound that he had listened to on that evening, the tramping of the workers in the street, as they went in their multitudes to the lodging-houses and the suburbs, and these footsteps merged into the other, into the sound of the marching, mailed feet of the robot children. Now in this terrible swelling army the Archbishop saw an extension of the child murder that is pursued quietly in England. The murder of the innocents, planned in tender whispers behind flowered curtains, carried out behind white walls and roses. Here, in these legions of children whose souls were murdered, it was extended, it was the same sin, yet still not committed openly, frankly—still camouflaged in organization, hypocrisy, discipline, ideology, even a certain crude Wagnerian sentimentality. The murdered face must not be looked upon, man must not be asked to look at what he has done, because the little dead face against which the whole of civilization is hammering is the blue pinched face of a stillborn child. Therefore war must come. Perhaps when it came, it would fling it out on the screen, even of the wilfully blind world's vision; perhaps men would see it for what it is, only when it scorched their own living flesh with material flame, only when it was smeared across their pavements in their own blood.

And now, in his dream, the Archbishop saw the army of Nazi youth, coming up towards the young Christ on the Cross, facing Him, looking at Him with unseeing, opaque blue eyes, staring unseeing on the face of the Christ.

Lovely children, with slender bodies, with rose-petal cheeks, with small pink mouths, with white bleached hair, silver, gold. The light playing on their helmets, the light glittering on their bayonets, the light flashing on their marching feet. Children swinging along in perfect time, in terrible unison, coming up to the young Christ on the Cross, their metallic tread ringing out the accompaniment to the cry of their coral lips, "Krieg! Krieg! Krieg! War! War! War!"

Christ saw them, with wide open, all-seeing eyes. He saw them advancing, He saw them advancing across two thousand years. He could have come down from the Cross, He could have called the legions of the angels to His standard, but He remained on the Cross, nailed to a plank of wood, and He did not drag back a band to cover His heart.

A cry went out from the Archbishop's soul to the crucified Christ, "Eternal Innocence! Child of the Father, did you see the children advancing when you hung on the Cross? Did the steel tramp of their feet ring in your ears ? Was the drumming in your ears in the hours of death turned to the shout of Krieg! Krieg! Krieg! hammering on your bloodless brain, drowned only in the dark storm of the waters of death, the torrent inside the little skull, trying in vain to burst through the crown of thorns as you bowed your head and died?"

And as if it was in answer to his prayer, another procession of children came into his dream, walking slowly with infinite dignity, one by one, each one alone, each alone walking in the pure majesty of childhood, the holy children of our times. Gentle devoted peasants, grave sweet patricians, children stepping softly on blameless, naked feet. Almond-eyed children brown from caressing suns, Mélanie and Maximin of La Salette, Francisco, Jacinta, and Lucia of Portugal, Bernadette Soubirous, and behind them Anne de Guigné with her wistful face and her deep lace collar, and Guy de Fontgalland in his sailor suit, with his thick, golden fringe and his cry in the teeth of War: "Je veux faire connaître le petit Jésus, dans le monde entier!!!"

With that cry in his ears the Archbishop awoke—and the wonder of the children who loved God remained in his consciousness like a light shining in his breast.

He whispered, "Agnus Dei, qui tollis peccata mundi, dona nobis pacem!"

And then, indulging his habit of talking out loud to himself, he said, "Lord, who knows, perhaps while your old men and your theologians and bishops and politicians and scholars wrestle in vain with the Angel, your battles are fought and won in the nurseries."

And suddenly—with the same surprise that we experience when we first see an open daisy in the field, the expected, the known, the ever with us become sudden, unexpected, new—the Archbishop remembered Willie Jewel.

The whole wearisome problem of Riverside returned, not now in all its adult intricacy, but in the sharp, simple vision of a child dying and a childlike old man watching from Heaven.

The Archbishop got up slowly, and knelt down. After all, he was going to take Father Perivale's advice, he was going to risk St. Peter's view of it and ask Father Malone to hold his hand, not to work the miracle.

He knelt there, an ascetic beautiful old man of silver, clothed in purple, with a ring like a drop of blood on his finger, the shadow of his thick white hair on his forehead was like the shadow of a crown of thorns. "Father Malone," he said softly. "Do you hear your Bishop speaking to you, Father Malone?" and he felt quite sure that he did hear: that the old man was close, leaning out of Heaven. He visualized him, not indeed with theological accuracy, but with childlike simplicity, kneeling at the door of Heaven and removing his battered hat, when he heard his bishop's voice, his umbrella filled up with stars hanging over one arm, the other arm lifted, cupping his ear with his hand as he leaned forward to hear his bishop's request.

"Fr. Malone, it is Archbishop Crecy speaking, you have caused a lot of trouble here, Father, with your holiness; we can't know God's purposes as well as you know them now, Father, but we can't help seeing and thinking and wanting from our own poor simple angle. And it seems to me, Father, that the little child's death is in the world's redemption, and a miracle from you—just now, Father Malone, if you will forgive me for saying so—tending towards imprudence."

Thus the Archbishop made his act of faith in the sanctity of Fr. Malone. It was three o'clock in the afternoon, on the last day of the Novena, the precise day and hour at which Willie Jewel died.

CHAPTER 21

MAGNIFICAT OF MARTHA

And His mercy is from
generation to generation.

The Lamb that was slain
ever since the world was
made.

On the last day of the Novena, Willie Jewel died. The rumour that he was dying swept round the parish like fire in dry grass. People came out and gathered outside the Jewels' house to pray. There was no necessity now for Fr. O'Grady to try to restrain them, for now they were praying simply and solely for the child's life. They were praying not only, or even mostly, to Fr. Malone, but to the Sacred Heart, Our Lady and Saint Joseph and Saint Teresa of Lisieux. For the time being, at all events, the longing to put a halo round the old man's head had given place to the natural emotions that had sustained

and integrated them from generation to generation, mother-
hood, fatherhood, pity for weakness, the cherishing of children, the instinct for life. Willie, always their darling because
of his sickness, had become mysterious to them himself, holy
as their Saint in Heaven was holy, and, what may in the ultimate understanding be known to be more important than
that, their neighbours' grief had become their grief.

Every woman in the parish, married or unmarried, mother or childless, grieved with the grief of Martha Jewel, every
woman was Willie Jewel's mother. In the heart of every man
broke the heart of Willie's father. In the children of the parish Willie Jewel lived and died, the shivering light of his dying sifted their souls with its mystery.

Yet the prayer for the child's life was charged too with all
the ascending intensity of longing for Fr. Malone's miracle
that the Novena had concentrated and gathered to a crescendo; and on this last day the very desperateness of the situation
sharpened their hope, for if the proud, stiff-necked people of
the world were to be made to see, even to look at their saint,
they must see glory, unmistakably vivid as a flash of lightning, striking from Heaven right down into the earth. Only
something as arresting as that could open their eyes to the
beauty of the worn, rusty cassock, the broken shoes, the face
engraved with suffering and love, and the gnarled consecrated
hands, blessing his little flock from Heaven.

If now at the eleventh hour the miracle were granted, it
would not be one miracle of healing but many. It would be
the thawing of frozen hearts, the opening of deaf ears and
of blind eyes. Those deafest of ears that will not hear, those
blindest of eyes that will not see. It would be the answer too

to a multitude of inarticulate hearts beating out the agelong prayers, "Lord that I may see!"—"Lord, I believe, help thou my unbelief!"

At 2 o'clock Clem Hogg called for Father O'Grady. "Mum has gone to young Willie Jewel," he said, "and I was to be sure and tell you that tea won't pass her lips until the Jewels are out of their trouble."

At that the priest knew that Willie was dying. Tea was the consolation of Magdalena's widowhood, with its stimulating sweetness, its companionable warmth and its illusion of fullness. She lived from cup to cup.

But when a neighbour was in trouble and "trouble" had but one meaning to Magdalena, death—she put the teapot from her in heroic charity of compassion, and went to them. Hers was not the utility religion of the modern philanthropist, but the extravagant loveliness that must hunger and thirst when the Beloved hungers and thirsts.

Father O'Grady rose at once and hurried through the narrow streets to the Jewels' house. He saw the people gathered there as he approached. They were close together and though some were standing, and some kneeling on the pavement, they swayed slightly together, moving as one person, in the urgent rhythm of their prayer, as they recited the Rosary aloud.

> Hail Mary, full of grace,
> The Lord is with thee.
> *Blessed* art *thou* amongst women,
> And blessed is the fruit of thy womb, Jesus.
> *Holy* Mary, Mother of God, Pray for us sinners *now*
> *And* at the hour of our *death*. Amen.

"What is the news, Father?"

"How is he?"

Hands reached out to the priest as he approached. Intense imploring faces turned to him. Dark bodies leaned to him. All the passion of their petition tingled through him as if he had the power to heal. But he suddenly felt more aware than ever of his powerlessness, his helplessness. He knew that he could give them no comfort and that he could no more restrain them than he could have restrained the people of Jerusalem from coming out and mobbing Christ as He passed through the streets, calling out to Him to save some sick child of theirs. Crowding, pushing, struggling to come to Him, laying hold of His feet and covering them with kisses in the dust to keep Him.

Father O'Grady lifted his hand to bless them. He felt the sudden hope that shot through them.

"The priest has come," they whispered. "He will bring a blessing to the house."

"God spare the child."

"Lord have mercy on him."

"Jesus, Jesus, Jesus, pity the dying."

An old woman, kneeling on the hard pavement, reached out her hand and touched the priest's cassock. He went into the open door of the house and up the stairs and the murmur of the Rosary began again, following him, surging softly up the stairs behind him.

> "Pray for us sinners *now*
> *And* at the hour of our *death*. Amen."

He went unannounced into the child's room and stood with the others gathered there.

Those who were in his room had accepted Willie's death; they no longer demanded a miracle, there was now no resistance left in their hearts. Where, before, there had been almost unendurable tension and suspense, now there was peace, complete as water or fire. The afternoon was still and shadowless, every detail stood out sharply. Afterwards those who were present at the deathbed, remembered it in connection with some trivial detail, as if some subtlety of mercy allowed some such thing as the recurrent clang of a tram bell, passing below in the street, to act as a partial anaesthetic to the mind, saving it from the full realization of a drama too intense, both in its sorrow and its joy, to be endured.

There was silence in the room that was complete, that seemed to have its own separate existence and was never merged into or mingled with the sounds in the street below. Indeed they did but accentuate it, stressing the fact that two worlds were being lived in, two worlds which by the impact of sacramental love interlock each other, and are yet separate, and known by different kinds of consciousness.

The rhythmic clang of the tram bells went on, the sound of passing cars and occasional footsteps went on, the sound of the ships' hooters down on the river went on, everything in the ordinary world went on, and it was the ordinary world that was extraordinary and fantastic; this afternoon was no different to any other, yet this afternoon a child was dying.

The Jewels' closest friends had gathered to pray as Willie died, standing together, a little way back from the bed, Rose O'Shane, Magdalena Hogg and Carmel Fernandez, and closer to him, quite motionless, hand in hand, Art and Martha Jewel.

They did not come right up to the bed and hold the little child in their arms, but stood back, as if they had laid him on the Altar of immolation and knew that he was already out of their reach. Already independent, with the invincible independence of death.

Carmel Fernandez knelt between Rose O'Shane and Magdalena Hogg. She had gone round to help Martha every day, just as she used to do before she went to Solly Lee, and it seemed that this contact with the child was purifying, especially when she did the humblest personal service to him, helping Martha to give him his bath or his food. It seemed to Carmel that, in Willie, the innocent Christ gave Himself back to her, putting Himself into her hands for a pledge of His unaltered love, as He puts Himself into the priest's hands in the Host, a continual pledge of His unaltered love for the fickle world.

⁀

Fr. O'Grady knelt down at the foot of the bed. Everyone was still. The sound of the people praying outside washed in and out of the room like waves, and neither broke the silence in the room nor became part of the sounds of the world outside.

In the room they were waiting, and in a sense it is difficult to explain what they were waiting for. Had Willie been able to talk, perhaps his parents would have been bending over him, straining their ears to catch his last words, hoping against hope for some word of recognition and love to lay up in their hearts for ever; but Willie had never spoken any coherent words, and he never would.

He was lying so still and he was so white, that it seemed to Magdalena Hogg that they would hardly know when death came, there could be so little outward change or difference; but Rose O'Shane knew that under that stillness something was happening so tremendous, that they could not even dimly apprehend it, and yet she believed they must somehow or other know it, or their souls would perish.

It seemed to Rose O'Shane that Willie was about to do something completely, which no one but a child could do completely. He was going to die, he was going to die Christ's death. He was Innocence and he was going to pay the price of sin. He was going to suffer the passion of Christ.

We who are grown up, she thought, have lost the capacity for any whole experience, either of joy or sorrow, life or death; for us everything is qualified by memory or hope, we remember having suffered something as bitter before, and it passed. We never close our hand upon the moment and know it whole. Die we must, we too, and we must die Christ's death, but we have discovered the way of compromise, even with death, even with the death of Christ. Therefore, it seemed to Rose O'Shane as she knelt there whispering the prayers for the dying mechanically, that if the will of Love is to be accomplished, if humanity is to experience Christ's passion, little children must suffer and die, because they are whole, and possess the eternal now. They have kept the art of dying Christ's death. We have whittled away the Crown of Thorns, but the children are crowned.

A faint ripple of pain crossed the child's face, and it was suddenly covered with beads of sweat like a white rose covered in drops of dew. "It is his agony," she thought, and now

it seemed that they were kneeling in the garden of Gethsemane, but the garden of Gethsemane was no longer a mysterious dark olive grove, but a child's garden plot under snow.

We do not know what people live through in that secret
time before death that we call unconsciousness, we know
only that they have drifted away out of reach. We call them
but they do not hear, they are out in midstream where our
voices do not reach them, we touch their cold hands, but they
are aeons and aeons away, and do not respond.

But from the words we catch as we lean over them, it
seems that most people return to their childhood in those last
hours. It is one more manifestation of eternal pity, that even
the seemingly lost, the worldly-wise, the unregenerate, often
do in the end become as little children, to suffer that last agony with the wholeness of a child's capacity, and so be able,
after all, to enter the Kingdom of Heaven.

But what happens to one who *is* already a child? Through
what woods, through what meadows and cities does the river
Styx carry *him*?

Perhaps he alone keeps his grip on the reality of the *here*
and *now* of the Passion, he remains in the tangible, familiar
room, nailed to the Cross.

Perhaps only for the little child and for the first Christ on
the Cross, there is no wandering away from the hard circum-
scription of the actual material world, his sacramental environment, his body, his pain, his weakness.

The old man dying may go back to suffer his agony in
fairyland, that so he may grow down to the stature that alone
can pass through the low door that the Architect of Love
built into Heaven. He may drift on the dark water of the Styx

in a little coracle among the mists and rosy clouds of early morning. He may find when he comes to the foot of Calvary, that it is the "Green hill far away" of the children's hymn, shining in the dew. But Christ on the Cross was measured to that dreadful limitation that holds a man to the sum total of his capacity for pain, and held there between three nails, and the child on his small deathbed is nailed with Him too, to the actual environment, the tiny span of reality, in which the wholeness of death is contained.

A little before three o'clock, Doctor Moncrieff arrived with a young doctor from the Hospital. He felt abashed by Martha's glance as he came in. It reminded him of that haunting dark fire in her eyes which had scorched him on the day that her son was born.

He looked intently at Willie and noted that the child was suffering, although he was far away, out of the reach of his help, indeed he did not know if this were pain of mind or body. Shadows of pain crossed his face in tiny ripples, his nose was more pinched. Sharp lines that had never been seen on the child's face before became visible, his hands which had always been powerless were gripping the bedclothes now, as if they had been made alive, to die.

"He is holding on to the nails," thought Rose O'Shane. "He is holding on to the blessed nails lovingly." The doctors noted it with interest and exchanged glances with one another.

They have looked and stared upon me.

The words of the prophecy rocked in Rose's mind. As if by so doing she could make reparation to Christ on Calvary, Christ stripped of His garments, Christ naked on the Cross, she forced her eyes that gazed with an intensity of love on the child, to turn away, and hid her face in her hands.

They have looked and stared upon me.

A drift of sad, humiliating distraction passed through her mind. At least they seemed to be distractions at first, but afterwards she knew that they were all part of what was happening. The out-patients in the Hospital, stared at by the circle of young students, the eyes of the passers-by as she returned from the Cat and Fiddle—gimlet points of pain, staring through a haze, and she not knowing what they saw, or did not see.

They have looked and stared upon me.

All the curiosity, all the insensitivity in the world. The criminal trying to hide his face from the press photographer, the intimate letters read out in a court of law, the raddled old worldly woman meeting the lover she renounced when she was beautiful. Grief stared at, pain stared at, nakedness stared at. Human respects a ragged dress with holes, a dress eaten by moths into holes that sores gape through and the shrinking, shrinking, shrinking from the staring eyes.

But there was Willie Jewel accepting. No shrinking, no hiding-place, powerless to withdraw, no rags of human respect, and there was Christ on the Cross, naked with hands nailed back. Given. Wed to humiliation. Wed to the sorrow of the world in the terrible surrender of the secret of self.

Willie moved his head on the pillow. The little movement, just turning his head slightly in the direction of where his mother was standing at the foot of the bed, made the sweat break out and stream across his face. Martha came close now and wiped his face with a large handkerchief of Art's.

Every one held their breath, Willie was moving his mouth as if he was going to speak, it could only be to make an in-coherent sound, but that sound would echo for ever in the memory of the listeners, but no sound came. Perhaps he was too weak, or perhaps it was that he was thirsty. His mouth moved stiffly as if he was thirsty. Art took a little sponge, dipped it in cold water and moistened his lips, the child turned his head away and his face became still again.

At three o'clock Willie died.

In his room there was no longer pain or suffering, but only peace, peace at the flood tide, wordless, breathless, shadowless.

As if some instinct had silenced them, the people ceased to pray aloud.

His dying was not a falling apart, but a gathering togeth-er, a moment of absolute completion, charged with its own beauty and sustained by it.

There was a moment when life was poised like a rose on its stem, when the petals opened to the full reaches of their loveliness, seem to be sustained by the sheer miracle of their own perfection. Life charged by its own loveliness, sustained by the fullness of its own wonder, yet ready to be scattered by a mere breath, balanced to the lightness of a petal.

Willie lay perfectly still, his breathing hardly percepti-ble; sometimes his eyelids fluttered, but at the end his eyes remained closed. Only his shut hands opened slowly, the fingers uncurling, until the hands lay palm upwards on the coverlet.

When the dying came, it came as swiftly, as soundlessly, as irrevocably as the fall of the rose, and just at that moment a drift of wind blown up from the river rang a tiny carillon on the glass chime that Art Jewel had hung in Willie's window six years ago, when they had brought him home as a new-born infant.

There was no way of knowing the precise moment when he died, but no one was in doubt.

The presence that is Life, and that absence that is death are too positive to be mistaken for one another. It is as if a priest could unconsecrate a Host, leaving a white wafer, holy because Christ had used it to be Himself, but which is only a white emptiness now. No Host could really be so changed, but if it could be, that would be a showing of death.

Now the room was empty and the emptiness had its centre, its focus, on the bed, where a moment ago Willie Jewel was lying, but where now there lay only the small and exquisite shell of what once had been Willie Jewel. A dead child, with a feather of frozen gold on a forehead of snow.

All that night and until the afternoon following he lay there at home, and then, towards the evening of the day after he died, they took Willie's body to the church.

It was the first time he had ever been into the church, and he went there now at Martha Jewel's request. She had longed to keep his poor little body at home, to have her baby lying smiling in the bed where he had spent most of his life, until the very last minute. But a great realization had come to her. When she saw her neighbours helping to nurse him, giving all that they had to give, devoting themselves to him, she had taken it almost for granted, for so true is the charity of the poor that it is the only thing in life that can be taken for granted.

But when the child was dead, and she saw their grief and

their homage, how they came in endless procession to pay their tribute to the little body, she realized that her son belonged to them all. Wonderful pride filled her. She was not merely the mother of an invalid child, who had been her life's sweetness for six swift years and had died. She had given a son to all the others. She had brought one into the world, who had so increased the world's love, that he had made all who were childless his mothers; he was the son of all who loved him, he belonged to them all.

Martha tasted the exaltation of Mary the Mother of Christ. She seized that point of bitter glory that centuries of pious meditation does not give, the joy that Mary, the Mother of God knew, in the baffling moment, when Christ had left her to do His Father's work.

Why had he come into this world, this child of hers, this poor man's child, who could not run or play or speak, who was in the hands of people as the Host is in the hands of the priest? Why had he been born from pain and love, and lived in pain and love, and died?

The people passed by the bedside, one after the other, old, broken, shapeless women, thin, flamboyant little factory girls, shy and sometimes weeping sailors, burly dock labourers, mothers of large families holding their living infants in their arms, and Martha stood by, watching them, seeing the meaning of her son's life, and the meaning of his death in the faces of love and grief.

The answer came in the silence, from the child on the bed whom she had washed and dressed, whose hands she had folded, whom she had laid to sleep for the last time.

Did you not know that I must be about my Father's business?

The exaltation of the Mother of Christ! Scholars and theologians can know it in theory, can fumble at it with the mind, but only a very few can know it with the heart. Those few are the mothers of those who die in battle, and the mothers of those who die in innocence.

Did you not know that I must be about my Father's business?

Her son too had gone away and left her for the great work of the business of God. The sweet and terrible work of love. She had given him poverty and pain. He had increased the life of the world.

She could not tell the thing in her heart, even to Art. The glory of it was her sustenance through all the childless years to come.

At her request he was carried out to lie in state, before the Blessed Sacrament in the Sanctuary, to be given to the people of the parish to whom he belonged.

As she followed her son's small coffin to the church, she entered the supreme hour of her sorrow, into the joy of the woman who walked upon the hills two thousand years ago singing:

My soul doth magnify the Lord and my spirit hath rejoiced in
*   God, my Saviour.*
Because He hath regarded the humility of His handmaid; for
*   behold from henceforth all generations shall call me blessed.*
Because He that is mighty hath done great things to me; and Holy
*   is His name*
And His mercy is from generation to generation to them that fear
*   Him.*

He hath shewed might in His arm: He hath scattered the proud
  in the conceit of their heart.
He hath put down the mighty from their seat and hath exalted
  the humble.
He hath filled the hungry with good things and the rich He hath
  sent empty away.
He hath received Israel His servant, being mindful of His mercy.
As He spoke to our fathers, to Abraham and to his seed for ever.

CHAPTER 22

AFAR OFF

And the publican
standing afar off, would
not so much as lift up his
eyes towards Heaven.

For the second time Solly Lee visited the Catholic church, and this time not by chance. All day he had been restless. The whole world seemed to him to be an emptiness, an aching void. Life had become like an empty house, empty only of people, not of things. A house which he had furnished to bring his bride home to, to bring up his family in, but to which no bride had come, and in which no family was born.

In this house, everything was overlaid now with dust and damp, dust sheets like shrouds lay over the furniture and the empty cots.

On the night on which Willie Jewel's body was taken to the church, Solly sat working late. There was no need for him to work, but it was some kind of company. He sat cross-legged on the floor and sewed. His shop was on the route to the church, and his blinds were drawn.

As the light failed, changing gradually from the amber patch through the yellow blind to a sad thick greyness in the room, he stopped working, though from habit he had strained his eyes, holding the cloth up close to his face, until he literally could see no more.

The thick greyness was like veils of cobwebs hanging across the room. Round the empty grate brown mice fluttered in and out of their holes, their swift, noiseless bodies pulsing as if they were filled with water.

Solly never fought against self-pity, he did not now. He was not angry with Carmel, in a way he could understand that she had been compelled to go away. He was not even very angry with the inevitable power of the mysterious system that had taken her away.

In one way, Willie Jewel was the first cause. He should, if he were jealous at all, have been jealous of him, but one cannot be jealous of a dead child, and in any case he was aware that it was the whole vast power which had baffled him again and again, and of which Willie was the core, that had robbed him of Carmel.

Carmel belonged to that power. He supposed he must call it the Catholic Church. But her belonging wasn't simply like his conception of belonging to a church. No, it was like belonging to humanity.

She thought her life with him sinful, and sin meant somehow being outside of human nature, as if it made it impossible to do a kindness to a little sick child, and her link with the whole of human nature was just such a kindness.

And so she had gone, to rejoin her kith and kin, to know the sweet warmth of the family blood flowing in her veins, before it was too late, before the door was shut and she left outside the shut door for ever, haunted by the ghost of a child.

But never had Solly realized his own loneliness so vividly. He belonged to no one, to no system. He could not, or he thought he could not, follow Carmel and say "I too will serve, and will become one with humanity." He felt a desperate need to assert himself, to take some part in this sorrow that all the others shared, to be bereaved as they were bereaved, to have the right to follow the child to the grave.

Loneliness covered his mind like a heavy pall. It was quite dark in the workroom now and there was no sound but the scratching and scuttering of the mice. Solly thought that tonight Art Jewel must also think of life as an empty house; but is not an empty house, from which a child has gone away, less desolate than that in which a child has never been?

He knew that everyone would go to lay their flowers on the coffin, and he wondered, "Couldn't I too?—couldn't I lay flowers on the coffin?"

And then the old vulgarity crept in and he thought: "I could make a wonderful show of flowers—I could buy a much bigger, much more expensive, much more beautiful wreath than all the others."

This idea worked in his mind. The others would all take white flowers, he would take red.

Then he remembered that he was ostracized. Perhaps Martha Jewel would be outraged by his offering. She was, he thought, a hard narrow-minded woman, and she might snub him. She might have his wreath taken away. He wouldn't risk that.

But he would take his wreath, he would take it secretly. After all he would have a part in that little child. He would not take the wreath to impress the others, he would take it to be one with them, even though they would never know it. At least he would have a humble secret part in this child who was dead.

Once he had made up his mind to put his wreath on the coffin he felt better. His thoughts passed as they always did so easily, from abstract ideas to material things. He decided that a spray is nicer than a formal wreath and that a simple bunch of flowers is nicer than a spray. Then he began to wonder about his choice of red for colour. Wouldn't yellow look more glorious, or purple richer? But he always came back to red in the end.

The next day he went far afield for the flowers, and left them to be called for in the evening at the shop. Thus no local shop would know that he had bought them and no one, if he chose his time carefully and was lucky too, would see him with them.

When he reached the church it was already dusk, the workers had gone home, most people were eating their supper or staying quietly indoors thinking about the funeral tomorrow. There was no one about.

As furtively as any thief, Solly pushed open the door. He forgot that he ought to remove his hat, and instead pulled it lower over his eyes as if this could save him from recognition. But there was no one there, no one but God and the dead child.

It was quite still. Silent with the deep soft silence of snow. Willie's coffin draped in a white pall and covered with white flowers, looked like a little mound of snow too.

So absolute was his impression of being in a valley of virgin snow, that Solly hardly dared to look down on the ground, lest he should find that it was not an illusion, but true, and that his dark footsteps had violated the white untrodden path to the sleeping child.

He stood at the back of the church and could not bring himself to go farther in.

For a long time he stood there with his head bowed and would not even look up. He thought, "I am not worthy to give flowers to a dead child." And for the first time in his life there was nothing servile in his humility, no self-pity in his sadness.

He stood there in the silence that was like the pure silence of snow, with his head bowed, and he let the flowers fall from his hands. Slowly the beautiful red flowers fell from his hands, and covered the stone floor at his feet. And Solly beat his breast—"Lord," he whispered, "have mercy on me."

And he went away into the darkness, empty-handed, and with an emptiness in his soul that was the nearest thing to peace that he had ever known.

CHAPTER 23

MASS OF THE HOLY ANGELS

He asked life of thee, and
thou hast given him length
of days for ever and ever.

The people of Riverside are still sufficiently virile to enjoy funerals. They live on familiar terms with death, from the cradle. They do not fear it, most of them have made friends with it long before they come to die. Neither do they banish the dead from their hearts, or hurry their bodies—as so many of their betters do—half shame-facedly away, to be disposed of like rubbish, though of course in stream-lined coffins, sprinkled, not with hyssop, but with such sentimentalities, faintly flavoured with religious feeling, as may soften a little the horror of the occasion, without giving offence to earnest unbelievers: or (which would be in yet more deplorable taste) awakening any doubt of their unbelief in those would-be unbelievers, who in order to avoid thinking of this very thing, death, have almost achieved in themselves the void of not thinking at all.

Progress has not yet wholly worn away man's deepest human instincts. They still prevail in the poor. The pageantry of the dead stretches back through the ages, a funeral cortège, from Riverside to Assyria, Egypt and Babylon, like one of those long frescoes of burial, which are sometimes the only record of a long forgotten people, written across the world in black and sanguine, vermilion and gold, the testament of man's faith in the continuance of life: faith that even the frozen mouth and crumbling heart of the beloved, dead, can never disprove to love.

It was never in the heart of man to send the dead, cold and hungry and alone, into the dark world of spirits, dark, that is, before the Light of the World shone out to illuminate it.

They clothed them in swaddling bands, as they clothed the newly born, and laid them in their shells like cradling coracles to cross the mysterious water, and they sent them with flasks of wine and food for the way, long before Christ came to be Viaticum, the food for the last journey.

This fresco of the pageantry of death still stretches on through Riverside's grey streets; proud black horses, with long thick manes and arching necks, harnessed in plumed and tasselled trappings, pull ornate hearses, hung with long fringes, embossed with ornament of dull and heavy gold and crowned with tufts of ostrich feathers, piled up high with flowers that are no longer flowers but "floral tributes," wreaths, and anchors, broken pillars, cushions, hearts. The cortège moves through time in sombre beauty, not now against the background of the River Styx, but of the River Thames.

The Funeral of Willie Jewel was in shining contrast to all this, a thing of snow and apple blossom, of movement and of song. For the death of a child in innocence is shadowless, pure joy; a swift, brief passage into light; the fledgling's flight from its rifled nest to the sun.

On the day of the funeral the streets and the docks were strangely quiet, almost deserted, for everyone who could, both Protestant and Catholic, came to the church. They came, not to a Requiem, not to pray for a suffering soul in Purgatory, but to celebrate a child's flight to Heaven, by a votive Mass of the Angels.

The quality of snow which had closed upon Solly Lee's mind was evident now too; but it was not now the still silent snow that has fallen and lies thickly in a valley, but dancing, whirling snowflakes, dazzling in the sun, intricate and lovely with the movement and the loveliness of life.

In the sanctuary fifty urchins from the Catholic Poor School were transformed to cherubim, in stiff white pleated cottas, over scarlet cassocks. These cherubim were tough in everyday life, but now the mute mystery of death so close to them shimmered through their hearts, like light shimmering through summer waves, and the knowledge, that there— close enough for them to touch, but for that thin panel of wood between them—was a really dead child, held them in a strange delighted awe.

At the back of the church, Dr. Moncrieff, self-conscious, though no one once turned to look at him, compromised between kneeling and sitting. He shaded his eyes with his hand, and his face wore the mask of accepted anguish, frequently assumed by Englishmen, either dancing or in church.

Last night he had even surprised and shocked himself by his sense of personal loss. He knew that after all, he was not detached. He realized that a perfectly ordinary affection for Willie Jewel had grown unperceived in his heart, and that his death had actually left a gap in his own life.

He would even miss him, he reflected cynically, as a bone of contention. His loss was rather like the soreness and emptiness felt in the socket of an aching tooth that has lately been extracted.

Although he hid his face with his hand, the beauty of the scene in the church was shining on his brain.

In the sanctuary there were three priests. The celebrant, of course, was Father O'Grady, the deacon and sub-deacon, Father Smith from the next parish, and, there by his own earnest pleading, Father Perivale. They wore the white vestments for Christmas, shining with golden grapes and pomegranates, and yet white. White like snow and like blossom, like the fleece of a lamb, and like the white flower on the blackthorn, which is spring.

Everywhere candles shone, burning like stars among the flowers on the altar and like pools of floating stars around the feet of the saints.

The fifty cherubim stirred and twittered in their stalls like flocks of wild birds stirring in the leaves of a great tree. Incense swung from golden censers rose in thick clouds crossed by beams of sunlight high above the altar.

The priest moved like music, with urgent rhythmic movements, his chasuble falling in long sweet folds as he stretched out his arms and lifted them to God.

And the voice of the Mass moved over the doctor's mind like moving water, the tenderness of Latin, intoned in an Irish brogue. But one thought held him and gripped his heart with a new, and to him unknown pain; that all this splendour, this agelong liturgy and beauty, all this passion of love of centuries of Christ, had come into operation for this waif of humanity. It was gathered together and pointed and concentrated on this poor man's child. Not for a Prince or a Pope the glory of this morning's homage, the mystery of the grandeur and the beauty and the love of the Church, its hierarchy, its angels, its saints, its multitudes, were given, but to the child to whom he had grudged life.

But it was only now that he understood what life is, that he had spent all his energies, until now, on something that was only a part, and the least part of life, the part that perishes. Until now, a life from which the possibility of the fullest natural joy was excluded had seemed a blasphemy. Now he knew birth is completed only by death. To-day for the first time he was present at a birth.

The passionless, shrill voices of the choir of cherubim, broke like rushing water on the light, and Dr. Moncrieff's newly wakened heart was drowned like a pebble in the torrent of the "Gloria."

Timothy Green, in his soldier's uniform that fitted him even less than his hired dress suit, was thinking "We are all making the mistake of looking for something new, something like a new wave of conversion or a new sanctity, to revolutionize Christianity, something that is just round the corner and will come tomorrow morning, and we miss what we have here and now, Christ in us, Christ with us, here and now. We have Aaron's rod in our hand and it is in flower. The beauty and the glory of the Church is blossoming to-day and every day in the mean streets, in the dark basements, in factories, and army huts and ships, wherever Christ is in the heart of any man."

And he felt sorry for those who are using all their energies and pinning all their hopes on plans for tomorrow and are blind to the glory of to-day, the here and now.

He bowed his head, cut close now like a convict's, into his hands and prayed to Christ to be in his heart, in the barracks and on the battlefield. And as if it were the answer to his prayer, a passage from the Gospel echoed in his mind: "Art Thou He that art to come, or look we for another? and Jesus making answer said to them: Go and relate to John what you have heard and seen. The blind see, the lame walk, the lepers are cleansed, the deaf hear, the dead rise again, the poor have the Gospel preached to them: and blessed is he that shall not be scandalized in Me." And the torrent of the Gloria flooded his heart too, and swept his mind into prayer.

And Rose O'Shane thought, as an Irishwoman would, of all the blessed dead, how Mother Church does not merely take her sleeping children into her arms, and holds them safely to her heart until the day star rises, but she gathers all her family round them, the living and the dead. She never says: "Now say Good-bye to your little brother," but "Come, gather to him and come closer to one another because you are drawn into a circle round him. Come closer to Eternal Love, because he is in the hands of love. Come closer to Heaven, because he is right at Heaven's door, though the door be thronged with shadows."

For the sake of the dead, the darlings of God, the door between the two worlds is always open. The prayers of the mothers of dead children rock them to their rest: the tears on the cheeks of the bereaved fall into Purgatory, sweet coolness in the flames of love.

Even to be a soul in Purgatory is a wonderful joy, a soul in Purgatory is the pivot of all the love in Heaven and on earth. Even a sparrow that He has made is dear to God, and dearer than many sparrows is a soul that has fallen into the hands of the Eternal Justice. It is in the Father's hands and He smiles on it. Its Guardian Angel fends it with proud wings, maternal as any mothering bird's. All the hierarchy of angels look down upon it, laughing and exulting. Likewise all the saints and the souls of the blessed. But we who are still on earth are as close as they.

Since so it is, for a sinner who is among the dead, what of a little child who is innocent of all sin, whose soul is shining still with the waters of Baptism, as a white rose opening in the dawn shines with dew? Joy, all joy, that we who are left to mourn cannot begin to understand.

And Rose O'Shane too bowed her head, and prayed. The core of her prayer was this, that the tears that flowed down her cheeks were tears both of sorrow and of joy.

When it was time for the sermon, Father O'Grady did not go into the pulpit, but turned round and addressed the people from the altar steps, just as he always did at First Communions. He made a big Sign of the Cross, and said:

"Dear children in Jesus Christ. I am not going to dwell on the deep sorrow I share with you all to-day, in the loss on earth of our little brother Willie Jewel. No one can understand or explain why innocent little children are allowed to suffer and die. Some people, meaning well no doubt, try to comfort the parents by saying 'It is God's will'—that is silly and blasphemous. Suffering and death are never God's will. His will is for us to have life and happiness. 'I have come,' Our Blessed Lord said, 'that they might have life and have it more abundantly.' No, dear brethren, it is not God, it is we, who, by our sins, have brought suffering and death into the world. But God in His mercy uses these things for love. First of all God became man and suffered and died Himself to atone for us. He could have come in glory, and have atoned by one tear, but he chose to come as a little baby, naked, cold, hungry, dependent, and to suffer all that we do. You see He did not only want to be worshipped but to be loved. No one could help loving a poor, needy little child, but that is not enough for Our Lord. He wants not only to be loved in a Child, but in *your* child. He wants the best, and tenderest, and most intimate love we have got. And He wants it from us all, not only from the saints, but from the weak and the sinful. So, brethren, God gives Christ's life to every child in Baptism. I know that you cannot understand that; we all have to take it on faith, as we do the Real Presence in the Blessed Sacrament, on Our Lord's word.

"When I, your priest, pour water on the heads of your little babies and say those wonderful words, 'I baptize you in the name of the Father and of the Son and of the Holy Ghost,' God makes that little one, as we say, 'Alter Christus,' Another Christ, and whatever he suffers has the power of Christ's suffering to atone for sin, to heal the wounds of the world.

"But, brethren, although we all suffer all our life long, we who are grown up have nearly always lost the full power, we have let the Christ life grow feeble in us, the will of Christ in us falters.

"A little child keeps Christ's power to love unspoilt, and before God that little one has the power of Christ's suffering on the Cross.

"Such a child was Willie Jewel, and while he was with us, dearest brethren, we were given a wonderful chance to serve and comfort Christ in him. I know how you took that chance and I can only remind you now of our dear Lord's own words, 'Whatsoever you did to the least of these little ones, you did it to me.'

"We are not gathered here to-day to pray for Willie's soul, we know that he is in Heaven. We are here to celebrate the feast of his birthday in Heaven.

"We must weep, dear brethren, because we are human and frail; but we must also thank God who has allowed us to know and love and serve Him in this little child, we must thank Him because He has taken him home to His heart, and because in the least of His little ones the Word was made flesh, and dwelt among us and we beheld His glory. In the name of the Father and of the Son and of the Holy Ghost. Amen."

All through the sermon, and more and more towards the end of it, the fifty cherubim fidgeted in their stalls; and their teacher, the inexhaustible Sister of Mercy in charge of the boys' school, prayed almost dictatorially to Willie Jewel to "Last them out in every way, to the end. Amen."

Had this been an ordinary occasion, she would have snapped her wooden clapper, an agreed signal between her and the priest, that the tender lambs of his flock had reached the limit of human endurance. But to-day of course, the signal was out of the question. Her relief therefore was measured by theirs, when Father O'Grady turned back to the

altar, and when the whole host of them scrambled untidi-
ly out to the sacristy to fetch candles and fresh incense for
the approaching Consecration. In the sacristy she was waiting for them, proud and angry and loving. She shook half a
dozen, blew a clutch of noses, kissed the smallest one, patted
down tufts of hair, jerked cottas back on to both shoulders,
and hissed encouragement and admonition into protruding
ears. Consequently the procession of cherubim that returned
to the sanctuary, bearing a multitude of stars, appeared more
celestial than ever, and surrounded by them, and by lights and
fragrant incense, and shrill sibilant singing, the Mass moved
forward to its climax.

Now the time had come to carry the coffin out, away from
the intimacy of the sanctuary, from the church with its gentle, plaster saints, its lights and flowers, from the thronging
of the faithful, from the kindness and warmth of their breath
and the smell of their clothes, out to the hard light outside
and through the streets to the London Cemetery, where they
would see the miles of white headstones, crowded together in
expressionless ranks against the background of a leaden sky,
row upon row of them, cheap, identical, making death itself
seem like something to be bought at a sixpenny store.

A momentary chill swept the mourners' hearts, some of
the women began to sob and some of them noticed for the
first time that Art Jewel was white in the face; but he walked
proudly and it was he, who had once leaned upon Martha,
who held out his hand to support her now.

Slowly this time, the cherubim filed down from the sanctuary and surrounded the coffin, the ten toughest were to carry
it, five on each side, bearing it between them like a swung cra-

dle. The rest formed a procession lead by a small cross-bearer, who carried the processional cross—but by a tender ruling of Mother Church, without its long rod, so that it was no taller than a small child's height.

For this child who was dead, love had overcome the world, life had overcome death. He had passed through brief poverty and pain in the dark womb of time, and come to his true birth. Behind him, before ever he came into the world, were generations of greed and power and lust and murder, frustrated. Before him, unimaginable joy, everlasting Life.

The urchins were singing now with the abandon that seizes upon all but the most obstinately pious, at the end of a long church service:

> "O Paradise—
> O Paradise
> Who does not long for light—"

The nun, who had been suffering from cramp, was beating out the time vigorously with a loud, dogmatic foot, and occasional snaps of her clapper, reminiscent of a Spanish dancer—

> "Where loyal hearts and tru-oo
> Stand ever in the light—
> All rapture thru-oo and thru-oo,
> In God's most *holy* sight."

The piercing shrill treble of the urchins' voices, mixed with the voices of celestial spirits, flocking on burning wings to meet the poor man's child, and with them the Holy Innocents, who had mustered to be Art Jewel's strength on the night of Willie's birth, jostling, crowding, tumbling, laughing to welcome him, and bring him home. The Holy Innocents in their scarlet gowns like a blown field of wild poppies, and the Spirits whose very names are melody and song—Angels and Archangels, Dominations, Principalities, Powers, Virtues, Thrones, Cherubim and Seraphim, calling like wild singing birds to welcome the child who was dumb.

So he went forth in a great company of children, urchins and angels, singing and bearing lights, on a river of stars to the everlasting arms.

CHAPTER 24

MASS FOR THE PEOPLE
OF THE PARISH

With Christ I hang upon
the Cross.

Father O'Grady vested himself for his Mass. It was still dark in the sacristy, but through the slit of the window he could see that a sad silvery light was welling up into the sky. It was like the cold, bleak light filling his own mind, showing him his soul as a man might see his face in a mirror.

Had any one of his parishioners come to him as weary as he was now, he would have counselled them with gentleness that he denied to himself: he would have told them not to strive, but to yield themselves to their weariness for a little while, just as a child in his father's arms abandons himself to sleep, trusting to the encircling arms to carry him home.

For himself it was different, he must not relax, he must not cease to be aware for one moment, for he was a priest. He must always carry the whole weight of his flock upon his shoulders. They were his own and he belonged to them. For them he must always make the effort of sorrow, adoration, love, he must always suffer their temptations, bleed with their sins, offer their Sacrifice.

It was a month since Willie's funeral. At first Riverside had been empty.

The presence of a dead child fills a house. It is the presence of a unique and terrible loveliness. It is the presence of a smile of unutterable purity, filling the house with pure and secret majesty.

The loneliness in the house where the dead child lies is beyond words, but it does not begin to compare with the loneliness of the house from which a dead child has been carried away. That is emptiness. It is an empty house, an empty womb, an empty mind, an empty world. With that emptiness, Riverside was empty. At first actually possessed by the stillness, the silence, even the sweetness of the child's passing, with that pause after the funeral, when the air still smells of flowers and vibrates with angels' wings: gradually the emptiness filled, not with stirring and sounds of joy but with the movement and sighing of the old accepted monotony. The light of wonder had gone out. The door into Heaven was shut, there was no blue patch in the grey sky.

In the minds of the people, the hope of Father Malone's canonization ended with the closing of Willie Jewel's grave. Fr. O'Grady knew that it was not ended, that, if God so willed it, He would indeed manifest His servant's glory in His own time. For his own part, he was sure that some day his old friend's holiness would ring out on silver bells in Rome. But the people did not look beyond their own short span, to them it seemed that when the heavy earth fell on the child's little coffin, it fell on their own hearts too, burying their hope.

Depression crept in, like the fogs wreathing up from the river, cold, damp, grey, pervading everywhere.

To Fr. O'Grady, when he made his round of visits, the pavements seemed a little longer, the homes a little dingier, everything a little less alive—even the washing hanging across the street no longer fluttered bright pennons, but hung flapping a wet melancholy sound all day long.

The steps were less white, the canaries less yellow, the geraniums less scarlet. Fewer people greeted the priest as he passed, there were more sad faces, less hope, no expectation. There were more young men out of work, they leaned more disconsolately and longer against the wall. They no longer thought of Fr. Malone as being close enough to them to hear them speaking to him in their natural voices. Hope was too feeble now to stimulate effort.

The people accepted their disappointment. They put on the old resignation, the old boredom, as if after wearing borrowed finery, they put on their old familiar clothes again, hated, and worn to the shape of their monotonous lives.

Fr. O'Grady reflected sadly that Fr. Malone would gradually fade from their memory. As the old people died, one by one, bit by bit the memory of the saint would die with them.

To him, his memory grew more and more vivid. Sometimes, feeling himself guilty for doing so, he took out his "relics" and looked at them, he held them as a connoisseur holds his treasures, caressing them with his hands, turning them over and over. The Breviary with the pages worn soft to the texture of wool, the rosary mended with a string, the disgraceful old hat, the shoes worn down at the heels and the toes stubbed by kneeling, the foul old black pipe.

They brought the old man so close, that it seemed to Fr. O'Grady that if he turned his head suddenly, he would surprise him, sitting in his armchair, just as he used to.

An idea which had haunted Fr. O'Grady was becoming an obsession. Had he, he asked himself, been living behind Fr. Malone's cassock? Ought he himself to be a saint for the people?

Even as a boy, at the age when sanctity, still glowing faintly with the radiance of daydreams, seems attainable to many, perhaps *because* of its unreality, it had seemed out of the question to him. Something quite beyond the reach of his large hard hands, a thing of shimmering light and ecstasy and vision.

Did it, he asked now, make holiness an easier or a harder thing, to learn, as he must from the relics, that it is something real and concrete, to be touched and seen and heard and tasted. That it is not to be apprehended in cessation of the senses in ecstasies and raptures, but to be known in the ache in the bones, in the five senses and the humble persevering mortification of the senses, in putting a little water into the wine, pouring a little beer on the aspidistra, refusing the salt, in the words spoken and not spoken every day, in the slow thinking of the tired mind, in the slow bending of the stiff knees, in the wrestle with sleep in the times for prayer, in the confessional, in the parlour during the recitation of the illimitably indefinite revelations of pious people, in the thousand, thousand miles to God, trudged to and fro in the same few streets. In the long, long patience of the never ending search for the lost Christ Child in the souls of men.

And what, Fr. O'Grady asked, smelling the foul old pipe tenderly, could make such things the substance of sanctity? These things that belong so inevitably to the limitations of human nature?—Surely Christ's presence in men. Surely because God breathed on the dust, and took flesh and blood from a human creature, and worked and ate and slept and loved on earth.

Because the Word is made flesh and we behold His glory, in the least and the lowliest.

Yes, Fr. O'Grady knew it now, that was the secret of Fr. Malone's sanctity, Christ's presence. He was a saint to his people because he was a Christ to his people. In the end he had worn his humanity, worn himself, like an old coat, so threadbare that his bones showed through it almost visibly, but it was not his bones that showed at all, it was the shape of Christ, who had hallowed the name of God in his old bones.

Fr. Malone's sanctity had simply been Christ's "Here am I who have been all this while in your company: hast thou not learnt to recognize Me yet?"

And Riverside had had its moment of transfiguration, the door into Heaven had stood open, Riverside had reflected the light of glory. For a moment the people had laid hold of the feet of snow that shone upon Tabor, and then the glory had faded. Now there was no one there but "Jesus only"—the hard work, the poverty, the sorrow and love, the Word made flesh.

Fr. O'Grady looked at his watch, the server was late. He checked a feeling of irritability, and was shocked by the difficulty he felt in checking it.

Was sanctity within *his* reach after all, he asked; could his great hands lay hold of it after all, he who never knew the sweetness of the complete act of love, the unbroken prayer, the whole hour of meditation, the work accomplished, the sensible sweetness of the sacramental word spoken, even one hour out of the twenty-four, unbroken, for his personal delight!

Could he who never knew that completeness in his soul, that inward closed circle of light, be a saint?

Could his day of fragments be a day in a saint's life?

And the answer came to him paralysing in its beauty, this broken life of his was the breaking of the bread, that in the broken bread, the whole Christ be given to his people. Soon, in a few minutes now, his people would be at the altar rails, opening their mouths like sparrows for their crumb of Life, and in their crumb of Life they would receive all Life, whole.

Father O'Grady paced up and down, rubbing his hands together to keep warm—"Break *me* dear Lord, but in the breaking of the Bread, be whole in Your Body upon earth!"

Lately, he had asked himself as he trudged home from the parish visits, what is the meaning of the lives of these unknown, insignificant people, who yet must somehow fulfil the strange prophecy, "And there are some of whom there is no memorial: who are perished as if they had never been born, and their children with them. But they were men of mercy, whose godly deeds had not failed."

And he answered what the Archbishop answered in his mournful meditations, and what Art Jewel had answered in the passion of his soul on the night of Willie's birth, and Martha in her sweet and terrible triumph on the night of his death.

In these people, who are nothing to the world, the struggle between life and death is fought out. Between love and murder!

And the priest was on the side of life, he had no other work, no other raison d'être but to give life, and the life he gave could not be killed. He was not outside of the world's love because he was a priest and alone, he was the heart of the world's love, its core, because the Life of the World is born every day in his hands at Mass. He looked at his watch again. How late the boy was! He tried to say the acts of Faith, Hope and Charity, to fill his mind with the words of the prayers to dismiss his distractions. But it was no use. This morning, distractions got the better of him, do what he would.

His hands had been so cold, he had hardly been able to tie his girdle, and now everything that he picked up was cold to the touch. He began thinking of a story told to him by a Russian, of a Bishop who was a prisoner for his Faith in Siberia, and this Bishop had a tiny drop of wine in a wooden cup, hidden away until he could say Mass, and when that time came, the wine had frozen in the cup. But the Bishop melted it against the warmth of his breast.

What a picture it brought to Fr. O'Grady's mind, a picture of the Bishop's heart on fire with love, and of the crimson of the wine when it was melted, red as blood against the white snow. But the moving part about the story was, that the thing which humanly speaking made it possible for Mass to be offered, was the warmth of a man's heart, melting the wine for the Consecration.

It was indeed a symbol of the priesthood and of his own humble priesthood, lived not in terms of blood and snow and fire and ice, but in those of the drab, sordid days and nights, failures and hesitating aspirations of Riverside.

Because he was a priest, his human heart must warm and melt the wine in the Chalice, and the water mixed into it, the frozen tears of his people. In him and through him the people must live, his heart must be the crucible in which their experience must be burnt pure. He must give them a mind, a voice, a heart. He must lift up their hands in the sanctuary.

At last a clatter outside proclaimed the arrival of the little server. How often Fr. O'Grady had tried to impress upon this boy that he represented all the Christians in the world before the Altar of God, when he answered Mass, and how well the Christianity of the world should brush its hair and clean its shoes and wash its hands, to enter the Holy of Holies and offer the heart of mankind! To-day he was even more dishevelled than usual, tousled, smeary, his bootlace undone, and it was apparent that the World had overslept and tumbled straight out of bed, and would to-day be even more than usually absentminded and clumsy—yet Fr. O'Grady looked at the urchin tenderly, all his irritability passed. After all the world *is* like that, late, distracted, grimy, but with a good if unstable will to serve; and might not this sudden new tenderness in the priest's heart be a reflection from aeons and aeons away, of the tenderness of the Eternal Father, waiting from Eternity for the scruffy, sniffing, unconcentrated, often unwashed, imperfect, weak and loving Christian world, to come to Him.

"Tie your shoelace," he said, "and damp down your hair— and here flick your face with this wet towel, and hurry now, put on your cotta and light the candles."

And the dishevelled Christian World, transformed, in a smooth white cotta, with a wet golden curl, and nothing of "the old man" left, but the huge boots jabbing out from his cassock, walked out with the expression of a Botticelli angel, to light the candles for Mass.

Even during the few steps that he walked from the sacristy to the sanctuary, the humiliation of being himself left Father O'Grady, the emptiness, the dryness of his soul, ceased to matter at all.

He had only to give himself now, to give himself to the words and the movements of the Mass, to give his body, his hands, his tongue, to give his whole being, easily, unresistingly, to move through the groove trodden out for him, to move in it like water flowing in the deep groove in the rock, worn through the heart of the world by generations of the adoration of men.

At the entrance to the sanctuary, he turned to the congregation and said: "This Mass is offered for the people of the parish."

There were only a few people present, the little server, a handful of old women, an Irish sailor, and a very old man. But since Christ was present in them, the whole Christian world was there.

So all the people of the parish, for whom Mass was offered, were there. The dockers already loading and unloading the big ships; the sailors who had just put out to sea, and the sailors ploughing their way home; the factory girls on their way to work, making the streets gay with their bright skimpy finery; the women scrubbing the steps with their arms up to their elbows in soapy water; the mothers washing up the menfolk's early breakfast before waking the children; the children sleeping the warm, woolly sleep of early morning; the marketers setting up their stalls; the flower women in their shawls, and their gents' straw boaters, carrying their great baskets of bronze and red and yellow flowers; the patients in the hospitals, newly washed and smoothed in cool white wards; the night nurses, pale and craving for strong tea and sleep; the day nurses pinning their starched caps, and wondering if it would be fried bread and bacon, or only fried bread for breakfast; the old folk in the workhouse, sitting quietly on their wooden benches; the prisoners in the gaol, looking up at the slit of silver sky, through the high, narrow windows of their cells: all were there, at the Mass that was being offered for them, the people of the parish.

Father O'Grady made the Sign of the Cross.

"In the name of the Father and of the Son and of the Holy Ghost. Amen," and bowed down under the burden of the sins of the whole world. His own sins were a heavy enough load, and now he bowed under the weight of all sin. But when he straightened himself up from the Confiteor, the burden of the whole world's sin, and his own with it, had fallen from his back, and his shoulders were strong. For it was Christ who rose up and went up to the altar—Christ who had seen evil naked, face to face, Christ who had been brought down to the ground, under the world's sin to sweat His blood into the dust, and Christ who has overcome the world.

The Mass moved forward with beautiful precision.

"Kyrie Eleison."

"Christe Eleison."

Sharp, urgent little knocks at the door of Heaven.

"Gloria in Excelsis Deo ..."

The angels' carillon swung into motion by the beating of a man's heart, and onward, hurrying forward with urgency of a lovers' meeting. The bright, short prayers sparkling over the priest's mind like summer waves over stones, bringing him swiftly to the Offertory.

He lifted the unconsecrated Host, light as a petal on its thin golden paten, and with it lifted the simple bread of humanity, threshed and sifted by poverty and suffering. He offered the broken fragments of their love, made into one loaf.

He lifted the wine and water mixed in the Chalice, and with it offered the blood and the tears of his people to God. The tears of Carmel Fernandez, the thirst of Rose O'Shane, the crimson of Solly Lee's scattered flowers shone in the cup. He offered the long life of old Father Malone, the swift dying of Willie Jewel, the flesh and blood of Art and Martha Jewel in the passion of the child, their only son. He offered the prayers and the humility of the Archbishop, on his knees to the old priest, he offered the wonder of the young Protestant sailor who had seen the power and the glory of God in towering seas and yet knelt in awe before "the weakness of God" in a child. He offered the hearts and the little trinkets of the factory girls, and the toil and charity of the mothers; he offered the realism of Magdalena Hogg, and of all Magdalena Hoggs, with their hot sweet tea and their toil. He offered the friendship and the immolation of Timothy Green, and of all Timothy Greens going out to face death.

And God accepted the offering, the fragments of love were gathered up into the wholeness of Love and nothing was wasted.

The Mass moved swiftly, hurrying forward as if the longing of generations had set its urgent pace towards the climax. But now the pace grew slower, charged with so immense a momentum of Mystery that it could only move forward in larger, fuller, slower gestures. The wonder rising like the rising of a tide to the flood. And as the miracle came closer and closer, time ceased to be at all. Simply, effortlessly, directly the Mass moved, not backward or forward in time, but into the eternal *now* of the Last Supper. Into the stillness of the Upper Room, where the Voice of Christ fell upon the souls of His Apostles, like summer rain falling upon the sown earth.

Slowly, exactly, Father O'Grady repeated the words of Consecration, his hands moved in Christ's hands, his voice spoke in Christ's voice, his words were Christ's words, his heart beat in Christ's heart.

"Who the day before He suffered, took bread in His holy and venerable hands, and lifting His eyes to Heaven towards Thee O God, His all powerful Father, giving thanks to Thee, blessed and broke and gave to His disciples, saying TAKE AND EAT YE ALL OF THIS, FOR THIS IS MY BODY."

Outside the church, Riverside had awoken and was tuning up like a huge orchestra for another day. The gangways were creaking as they swung up and down, from the great ships for unloading. Lorries began to crank their engines, tram bells clanged at regular intervals, and the sound of traffic was gathering to its full strength. Inside the factories the machinery had begun its metallic symphony, all the sound of the rattle and stir of work swinging into action was merging into one vast complex rhythm, that would set the beating of millions of hearts to its pace.

One sound remained single and distinct, the sanctuary bell ringing for the Elevation from the top of Father O'Grady's church, and only one man heard it—a homesick Portuguese seaman on the dock, heard, and stood a moment, bowing in the direction of the church. He had an orange scarf knotted round his throat and he was still golden from the sun he mourned. For a moment he stood still, his dark head bowed, his gentle face rapt, for a moment he was at home. Then with a sweeping gesture of Christ receiving the Cross, he stretched out his arms and held them up to take the great bale, that his mate aloft was lifting down to him.

In his mind's eye the devout Portuguese seaman had seen what was happening inside the church. The handful of people, bowing down low in adoration, the parish priest lifting up the small white Host.

But the Eternal Father looked down from Heaven and saw the nine choirs of angels prostrate in adoration, like a host of flames swept down to the ground by a great wind, and he saw the multitude of the saints bowed down like corn in the wind, and in their midst Christ on the Cross.

Fr. O'Grady lifted up the consecrated Host in his short, chapped hands, the server rang a little bell, the sailor, the handful of old women and the very old man bowed down whispering "My Lord and my God" and the breath of their adoration was warm on their cold fingers.

Father O'Grady was lifting up God.

A cry arose from all over the frightened world, "Come down from the Cross if you are the Son of God!" "Save yourself and us too if you are the Christ."

But Christ remained on the Cross. His fingers closed

on the nails. He would not come down from the Cross: He would not dethrone the children, he would not discrown the poor, he would not scatter the fragments of the bread of love. He would not break faith with sinners or fail the failing. He would not forsake the young men coming up to die his death.

"Come down from the Cross! come down! come down! save yourself and us!"

But Christ remained on the Cross. His fingers closed on the nails. The Crown of Thorns was in flower; the five ribs like the five fingers of the world's pain gripped His heart, and His heart broke open and the river of the world's life flowed out of it. A crimson flood sweeping His heart and brain and flowing out into the tips of His fingers, swept through His Mystical Body. Through the eternal heart of Rome, through the lonely mind of her august Shepherd, out into the least and lowliest of men, and the last little infant howling at the touch of the waters of Baptism, the blood of the world's life flowed into the finger tips, which stretched out on the Cross, measuring the reach and stretch and extremity and ultimate possibility of love.

"Come down from the Cross if you be the Son of God!"

"Save yourself and us too if you are the Christ."

The world strained at the nails, wrenched and dragged, the Cross was shaken in the earth, bent like a tree in the storm, dragged earthward by the weight of man's body, but it was rooted in rock, and the Cross was built to the shape of man, not man to the shape of the Cross. The world's suffering was built and fitted to the size of each man, and the Cross stood.

"Come down, come down, come down!"

But Christ would not come down from the Cross.

The life of Riverside went on, the day's work had begun, a ship was coming in from the sea, another putting out. An old man was dying, and a child was being born.

The little server rang his silver bell. The people bowed down low.

Time stopped.

Fr. O'Grady was lifting up God in his large, chapped hands.

Christ remained on the Cross.

The blood and sweat and tears of the world were on His face. He smiled, the smile of infinite peace, the ineffable bliss of consummated love.

London
Feast of the Holy Innocents
1946

The Dry Wood was designed in Adobe Caslon and Mr. Eaves and composed by Kachergis Book Design of Pittsboro, North Carolina. It was printed on 60-pound Natural Eggshell and bound by McNaughton & Gunn of Saline, Michigan.